Melanie
Nemesis
Catchpole

BY WOL-VRIEY

Other Books By Wol-vriey:

The Bizarro Story of I

Meat Suitcase

Chainsaw Cop Corpse

Vegan Zombie Apocalypse

Boston Posh

Vegan Vampire Vaginas

Vagina Mundi

Novellas and Short Stories By Wol-vriey:

Big Trouble in Little Ass
A novella featured in
Westward Hoes

Forever Ago Sunshine
A short story featured in
The Big Book of Bizarro

Melanie Nemesis Catchpole

BY WOL-VRIEY

Burning Bulb
PUBLISHING

Melanie Nemesis Catchpole
By Wol-vriey

Burning Bulb Publishing
P.O. Box 4721
Bridgeport, WV 26330-4721
United States of America
www.BurningBulbPublishing.com

Cover designed by Kelly R. Martin and Gary Lee Vincent

Author Photo: Lolade Akinsowon © 2014

Second Edition.

Paperback Edition ISBN: 978-0692451564

Printed in the United States of America

Reality has henceforth been abolished – The Fixer

PART 1:
INDIAN ORCHARD,
BOSTON ROAD

CHAPTER 1

111, Parker Street, Springfield, MA.

Bigelow 'Biggs' Jenkins, a fat man in a gray three-piece suit, regarded his female visitor coldly. "Fifty thou."

Melanie Nemesis Catchpole frowned back. "A hundred grand or no deal."

Bigelow looked about to burst the seams of his jacket. His cold little eyes poked at her out of the flab of his face. "It's just downtown, goddammit. You'll be there and back in no frigging time."

Melanie nodded, then rose to her feet. "Look, we're wasting each other's allotment of minutes here. My price for doing it is a hundred grand, and I'm cheap at the price." She smiled coolly at the angry gangster. "I'll be staying at the Howard Johnson Express down the road. If you change your mind, call me there. But please change it before noon tomorrow—I'm quitting this burg of yours then."

Bigelow glared at her. "Sit down; you don't walk out on me!"

Her blue eyes met his evenly. "I'm not walking out on you, darling. Except you're ready to stop being so cheap, we're done here. Besides, I need my beauty sleep. Believe me, it was a long drive over from Indianapolis." She grinned. "Look, just call me in the morning if you have a change of heart, otherwise it's both been nice meeting you, and a farewell to the City of Firsts." She laughed, turned from him to the door, flinging over her shoulder: "Even as a kid, I never really liked Dr. Seuss all that much anyway."

Bigelow frowned at her massive buttocks in their black leather pant sheathing for a long moment. Then, like he'd been deflated by Melanie's backside, his bluster visibly left him. "Okay, okay."

She returned to sit facing him, licked her lips, smiled. "So talk money, honey. My purse is all ears."

He nodded. "I'll pay you to get me the magic teddy bear."

"A hundred grand? No swindles? Man, I'll kill your ass if you double-cross mine."

He scowled. "Don't you ever threaten me, woman; you haven't the balls to take me on. But yeah, you'll get the money without a swindle; just get me the magic teddy." Despite his bluster, Melanie felt he was very worried about something.

Melanie nodded. "I'll take twenty upfront for expenses."

Bigelow rolled his eyes in exasperation. "What expenses? It's less than three miles away."

"Stop saying that. I've got huge expenses. Huger than my ass even."

He pushed two rubber-banded wads of Benjamins at her. "Here. Don't spend it all on lipstick."

She flipped through the wads, then stuffed both away in a jacket pocket, the act wobbling her large breasts. "How ungentlemanly of you to notice I'm not wearing makeup." She regarded her hands. "And my nails look like shit too." Then seeing how Bigelow Jenkins was turning beet-red with anger, she frowned back at him. "Okay, just fooling with you. Your money's good, so playtime's over; give me the facts of the case. What exactly and where exactly is this magic teddy bear?"

Now Bigelow grinned, baring teeth like a wolf placed before raw meat.

Bigelow was very confused by his lady guest. Though coming highly recommended by reliable Techxan friends, she definitely didn't look the part. Melanie Nemesis Catchpole (he'd been thoroughly warned not to attempt a double-cross; her 'Nemesis' nickname was well deserved) was small (about five feet five inches tall in his estimation) and plump. Not fat, no. Just very well padded—huge bosom and behind. Hips he immediately imagined packing full of kids. He controlled himself—one mustn't show a lustful weakness during a business transaction. Melanie was very pretty, with long black hair brushed forward and cut in bangs that hid her eyebrows (the side locks draped in curls over her massive chest), a nice full mouth and nose, and blue eyes that sparkled like the Great Lakes in spring. Definitely not the look of a ruthless killer. *But perhaps I'm outdated*, he thought. *Maybe, big girls do do it better, like they say.*

Oddest of all, she wore glasses, bookish black-framed lenses like she spent all her time reading rather than bounty hunting. Bigelow just couldn't make her out. He'd been expecting some clearly hard-living, hard-drinking slut, and now he'd got this?

She coughed politely. He realized she'd been watching him watch her.

"I'm sorry," he said. "I was just thinking."

She frowned. "Think all you like—you're paying me. I just thought to point out that the longer you keep me here, the longer it takes before your teddy bear's back home again."

Bigelow sighed, his oily gaze turning contemplative. "You're right, of course." He slid a photograph across the desk at her. "That's what you're looking for."

She examined the photo. A little pug teddy bear that seemed to be humping a banana. The pug was light brown with black face and ears.

She frowned at Bigelow. "What's special about this? Is this a bomb?"

He shook his head. "No. I don't know . . . at least I don't think so."

She studied his face. "What *do* you know?"

He scowled at her patronizing tone, but decided to let it ride. "This teddy bear is *alive*."

That took Melanie aback. "Alive? A living toy? Man, you sure you don't want your money back before I leave here?"

"Be serious, lady; *it is* alive. Take my word for it. This teddy eats, shits, talks coherently, and apparently has free will too." He placed his hands flat on the table, glared defiantly at her. "Where it came from? Don't fucking ask: I don't fucking know, okay?"

"Yeah, sure. So, how'd you learn about it?"

He winced; his thick lips pursed like he'd bitten into a lemon. "A friend down in Hartford found the teddy bear and sent it to me. My elder sister Chloe runs a toy factory up in Syracuse, I'm supposed to forward it on to her, do a business deal for him."

Melanie considered his words. She understood how such a toy (if it did exist) would be worth millions. She could just see the smiles on kid's faces . . . and Biggs here grinning all the way to the bank. *Damn, maybe I should have asked for more money. I still can . . .*

Bigelow continued: "The teddy was boxed—its power had run down and my friend had no idea how to power it up again." Bigelow sighed. "Only thing is, the damn courier company put the wrong address on the package." He glared at Melanie. "This is 111 Parker Street, right?"

She nodded.

"Well the idiots—I'll never use UPS again—sent the package to 1111 Parker Street. That location's an old warehouse down in Springfield's oddzone. Lower half of the street is in the old industrial sector of town." He gave a helpless shrug. "Who's actually responsible for the screw-up? I've no idea. The courier was stoned? Possibly. Though to be *that* stoned, he'd been unable to drive in the first place, right? It's more likely my friend accidentally added an extra '1' on the box. Easy oversight to make."

"Are you're *sure* the teddy's *still* there? I'm asking 'cos a hundred grand's my intra-city charge. Intercity, the rate goes up depending on distance. Say for instance your magic teddy's been moved to—"

"It's still there," Bigelow interrupted. "The courier didn't leave town. He couldn't—he was eaten by the gingers."

Bigelow Jenkins looked very pleased at the sudden seriousness that shadowed Melanie's lovely face. Her next question was almost a whisper: "What the hell are gingers?"

CHAPTER 2

When Melanie Nemesis Catchpole left Bigelow, she didn't feel in the least bit flippant or amused. According to him, gingers were cannibal mutants (much like the 'eaters' that plagued the rest of the USA). Gingers looked human, only their skin was white as whitewash and their hair and eyes were orange.

"And their teeth," Bigelow had said, looking about to throw up, "Just imagine a tiger's mouth."

And the gingers' preferred diet was fresh human meat. Melanie winced. *And I'm about driving in amongst them.*

She strode down the sidewalk toward her car, a battered sky-blue Volvo S40. Heck, the prognosis for success wasn't good.

Biggs had leveled with her: he'd already sent three retrieval teams into the oddzone. Only one guy had returned; and he'd been missing an arm and eye. That lone survivor told a horror story—how Biggs's gangland rival, oddzone kingpin James Richards, had sicced a pack of gingers on them. James had mistakenly assumed that Biggs's goons were in *his* part of town as part of a takeover bid. The gingers ripped the men apart—tore them limb from torso and ate them there and then.

(The gory story had an ironic plus: To Biggs's relief, James hadn't believed his men's protests about their being in the oddzone just to locate a magic toy. But then, who would?)

The midsummer day suddenly felt a whole lot hotter. Melanie got into her car. She pulled away from Bigelow's office, headed down Parker Street, towards the oddzone.

***

There were 'oddzones' (the more casual/preferred term was O-Zone or just 'O') in every sizeable American town or city now. The term described that part (or those *parts*) of town where Bizarro had literally fallen to earth, creating a fairytale world, though in some cases (such as here in Springfield), the fairytale was a nightmare.

**

What had instantly stood out for Melanie since her arrival in Springfield was the amount of trees everywhere. Silver and sugar maples, serviceberries dangling ripe purple fruit, buttonwoods and cottonwoods, lots of different horse chestnut trees, massive elms, even huger black and red oaks; redbuds, black gums and hornbeams; loads of flora she didn't recognize . . . Rolling down Parker Street now felt almost like driving through an orchard: red pear trees, cherry trees, and ginkgos lined both sides of the road; besides more of the ever-present oaks . . .

It felt like a diseased orchard, however. Even though healthy and out beneath plain sky, the trees seemed corrupted by Bizarro, like it had once covered the entire city, then shrunk to its current size (which shadowed most of downtown Springfield).

Nah, that's all in my mind, Melanie reasoned. *I'm just super-spooked by Biggs's description of those ginger cannibals.*

Still, it was more than that . . . had to be . . .

She drove past people like ghosts, women and men more shadow than substance. Once, she blinked—a woman up ahead seemed to literally fade into the gray wall beside her. Passing cars appeared even more insubstantial than their drivers, like she could reach through their frames and ruffle the hair of each passenger. The only solid-seeming conveyance she passed was a hearse. The fat hearse driver was laughing boisterously with a similarly substantial female companion. Morbidly, Melanie wondered if the pair ate the corpses they ferried.

Overhead, the sky was cast in a mottled gray-white, spread like milk forming a skin. Pallid as the face of an invalid. The air itself seemed thick with grit. The houses, even the clean shiny ones, had a patina of invisible dirt on them.

Melanie shuddered; this city seemed tainted by the sky. *Or maybe,* she mused, *it's the city infecting the sky with its own rundown depressed feeling.* How anyone could live here was beyond her.

She wrenched her mind from its threatened funk.

Up ahead . . . The location of Springfield's oddzone was easy to make out—the mile-wide clear area of sky between the two flanking fecal-toned floating expanses that dominated the air.

She scowled at the opposing brown masses—Bizarro, the weird come to actual life. (Seeking a theory to explain Bizarro, some scientists had begun calling it R.A.I.N. aka Rapidly Altering Intelligent Nuclei/Nucleotides. Melanie shrugged at their explanations. She just kicked ass; the more cash you paid her, the more ass she kicked, and the harder.)

Overhead, the sun was a mere circular impression in the sky, like it had forgotten its function of lighting the world and was as a result slowly fading from existence.

And yet it was still so fucking hot everywhere. Bizarro's fault, of course.

Here, she was still in the clean half of town. Here, some kind of dogged adherence to the laws of nature still held. Not that much— several houses had dubious outlines, like they weren't actually where they stood.

She slowed the car, stared at the blank space between the juxtaposed floating expanses of weird (which was on her right-hand distantly penetrated by several skyscrapers). Down in the O, all bets were off concerning what awaited her. Just a mile ahead of her, reality had been all but been put out to pasture, the fabric of normalcy warped beyond redemption; the laws of nature spun upside down by alien centrifugal forces that no one understood.

***

While rolling past more colorless cars and people who ignored her, she scraped what Bigelow had told her across the grater of her mind. Shredded his words, filtered the salient facts into a cognitive cauldron. Distilled out the essential truth.

It came down to this: The magic teddy bear could be in any one of five different warehouses now, not just 1111 Parker Street. All five buildings belonged to the same Japanese company, Techzono. In the week since the misdelivery, the magic toy could have been moved to another of them.

Melanie drove past the crumbling Uni First office complex on the right, then sped beneath the overhead Boston & Albany Railroad tracks into the Boston Road neighborhood. Past the Verge and Glenmore Street intersections . . .

She passed Loon Pond on her left, a stagnant mess of reeds in which frolicked families of eight-legged crocs.

She saw no sign of cops anywhere. It figured; since the advent of Bizarro over the USA, medium-sized urban centers like Springfield no longer had police forces. Police stations were a luxury affordable only in major cities like Boston and NYC. Smaller places like Springfield, MA (indeed the entirety of Hampden County, even though a protectorate of Boston) had no mayoral governments, i.e. no one to foot the law enforcement bills. In such cities, the residents either enforced their own law and order, or, like in this case (she was unable to resist a laugh at the oxymoronic concept), the law was maintained by the criminals—robber barons like Bigelow Jenkins who controlled the other residents in a modern day return to feudalism.

Here and now, Boston Road, once a Springfield commercial stronghold, was a mere ghost of itself. Like its people, who seemed almost not there. Like the car and trees, which looked even more faded than their owner/planters. Like the houses. Here, the eastern edge of the city, was considered too unstable, too Bizarro-tainted. Nowadays, most business happened west, in the Liberty Heights and Metro Center neighborhoods, with large amounts of goods being simply shipped up and down the Connecticut River.

She passed a couple kissing under a cherry tree. The woman, a thin brunette with a massively protruding pregnant belly, broke her lip-lock with her lover and regarded Melanie with suspicion.

Melanie sped on. It was late-afternoon. Hot and sticky. Melanie felt a mess. *Oh, I could definitely use a bubble bath right now.* (Some sex too wouldn't hurt; the kissing pair reminded her it had been a while since she'd had a man in her bed.) But there was business to handle; best to get started . . .

She wasn't entering the O-Zone just yet, anyhow. Bigelow had set up a meeting. His nephew Doug Fisher awaited Melanie at the *WTF?*, a bar situated near the start of the O. According to Biggs, Doug had been watching the area since the mix-up occurred. He'd said . . .

Then . . . far off beneath Bizarro, a blue aircraft floated left to right across Melanie's field of vision.

She braked sharply, rubbed her eyes, then peered up ahead again. The blue aircraft now hovered in place over the O-Zone. She considered: *That plane just flew out from under Bizarro. But that's impossible: aircraft can't fly either under or over Bizarro—just like with cellphones, it completely messes up their electronics.*

Equally inexplicably, there was a massive exchange of gunfire going on between the blue aircraft and someone on the ground, likely James's goons. Orange lightning zig-zagged down, while projectiles zipped skyward to explode against the plane's gleaming hull.

After some more shooting both ways and a cascade of explosions that painted the sky orange, the blue airplane flew off beneath the left half of the Bizarro expanse. But not before Melanie made out what looked like a metal tentacle wobbling beneath its tail. She also deduced that it was an experimental craft of some kind—it had neither any windows or engines that she could make out.

Now very bemused, she stepped on the gas again.

Her thoughts as she drove were extremely grim. *I haven't even begun tackling this case yet, and I already dislike it more than anything I've done of recent. Cannibals? Windowless airplanes with tentacles? And what's next? Oh, yeah, I'm headed for the What The Fuck? bar.* She scowled. *How extra-frigging appropriate.*

The die was cast in bronze. It clearly looked like she'd find a lot more questions before getting any answers.

CHAPTER 3

The *WTF?* was a nondescript two-story house at the corner of Parker and Hamilton streets. Filthy windows in a dirty grey-plastered brick frontage. A door that hadn't met a paintbrush in like ten years. A faded wooden sign that might have been hung up way back before Prohibition. Even the pair of sycamores flanking it looked ragged.

Melanie parked the blue Volvo and strode in.

Inside, the bar was mostly empty. The only people aside from the bartender and waitress were a tall man making a phone call in a booth and two blonde women sitting drinking in a corner. The waitress vanished though a back door. It was hot in here, the desolate overhead fan defeated by the temperature.

Melanie returned her attention to the bartender—a thin, stooped, unshaven middle-aged man with bloodshot eyes and dark untidy hair.

He grinned cracked teeth at her. "What's your pleasure, ma'am? Scotch? A beer?" He winked, gestured toward a back door. "Something harder?"

Melanie was unable to help her instinctive dislike of the man. "I'm from Biggs; here to see Doug Fisher."

After sizing her up a bit, the bartender nodded, jerking a thumb across the bar at the man in the phone booth. "That's him; shouldn't be too long 'fore he's done, been talking ten minutes already. Likely to his dimwit sister again." He frowned. "The little fox is mixed up with some no-good—"

"Two Bloody Marys, Joe," a female voice interrupted beside Melanie.

Joe nodded to the speaker. "Sure thing, Lois. Hey, Mary, get your ass back in here!"

"Coming!" the waitress replied from the back room.

Melanie turned to view the woman who'd joined them. It was one of the two blondes from the corner table. Up close, she was about thirty, and beautiful, with long lashes framing cool grey eyes. Large soft-looking pink lips. A trim figure, but with large breasts that pushed braless against the tight white T-shirt she wore over blue denim pants. She wore a large gun in a hip holster. Looked like she knew how to use it.

The blonde smiled. "Hi, I'm Lois. You must be new around here."

"Melanie. Just passing through on my way to Boston." Melanie sensed suspicion behind Lois's smile. There was something else about Lois also: just for a moment, her skin had seemed to switch color slightly, then it was normal again.

Mary the waitress, an anemic-looking brunette, joined them then. She cringed apprehensively on seeing Lois. "What'cha want me for, Dad?"

Joe handed her a massive hypo topped with a thick needle. "The usual. Two portions."

Mary sighed. "Aw, Dad, not a-fucking-gain!" Nonetheless, she took the syringe from Joe, jabbed herself in the left forearm arm with it, and slowly drew blood out of her arm.

Melanie gasped, but otherwise said nothing.

As the syringe filled with her blood, Mary visibly grew paler. Concurrently, her amber eyes widened to the size of eggs. "I don't feel too good," she moaned.

"I really think that's enough," Melanie finally felt obliged to say. She looked at Lois for confirmation. The blonde, however, was waving back at the other woman in the bar, who, Melanie noticed, looked very much like her. Another busty blonde beauty.

Melanie turned back to Joe, pointed to Mary. "She should stop."

The thin bartender shrugged—"She's used to it; more healthy than doing smack,"—then extended a hand to Mary.

Mary extracted the needle from her arm and returned the syringe to him. Then her eyes rolled back up in her head and she collapsed to the floor.

Melanie flinched at the thud she made on impact. Joe looked down once at Mary, then scowled at Melanie and Lois, who'd now returned her attention to them both.

"She's such a bloody drama queen," he said in a bored voice. "Just like her goddamned mother. I'll mix the drinks," he added to Lois. "Would you like horseradish in them?"

Lois nodded eagerly.

Stepping over the prone waitress, Joe got to work. First he prepared two tall glasses with lemon and celery salt, then filled them with ice. Next, he squirted the blood in the syringe into a shaker, squeezed a couple of lemon and lime wedges into it, added vodka over that, added spices. Added more ice, began shaking gently.

Lois smiled at Melanie. She pointed down over the bar. "I know this seems quite crude, but there's really nothing like a *real* Bloody Mary."

Melanie regarded her coolly. She now found Lois's pink-lipstick smile creepy. "You don't say?"

Lois nodded, her tongue tracing her lips wetly. "Oh, I do, honey; you just *have* to try it someday." She giggled. "I'd have suggested right now, only the bottle's unconscious." She rested a hand lightly on Melanie's thigh. I just adore the way you're padded everywhere, honey. Just looking at you has me so . . . oh!" She giggled again. "How 'bout you join my sister and I at our table, let's get to know each other *intimately*?" For emphasis, she squeezed Melanie's leg.

Melanie blushed at the blatant proposal. It was so out of the blue she was lost for a response. She smiled inanely at Lois, the woman's eyes hypnotic crystals compelling her to come . . . and damn, she did need to come . . . She lowered her eyes, then wished she hadn't; she was now staring at Lois's breasts, their super-large nipples taut in their T-shirt confinement like Lois was wet down south.

"Like the view down there?" Lois whispered throatily in her ear. "It's even better without fabric in the way. They're completely natural too. Full of the milk of human wickedness." Her hand on Melanie's thigh had now roved higher, stroking just outside her crotch.

How do I fucking get out of this, Melanie wondered, dropping her gaze further to watch Lois's stroking fingers on her heavy thighs. *The attention is flattering for sure, but—* Her body felt taut; about to snap. She wished it was a man doing this, so she could kick up some drama. Or just kick him in the nuts, period.

She looked up at Lois again. The blonde stared back brazenly; her face an open invitation, leaving no doubt at all that she was putting her soft feminine body on the line for Melanie's use. Her eyes questioned Melanie, who could almost hear both orbs speaking in her head: *Well what'll it be? Your place or ours?*

Then she saw it again. While staring at Melanie, Lois had been running impatient fingers through her own hair. Suddenly, for a brief moment, her hand turned transparent against her hair. No . . . not transparent . . . her fingers *became* the same color as her hair.

Then, just as abruptly, the change was over. Lois fingers were normal pink again, and Melanie was imagining she'd imagined what she'd seen.

Lois giggled, then faked an angry pout. "Do you always take this long to make up your mind, honey?" Her other hand was now massaging Melanie's crotch.

Melanie stared back blankly; her thoughts still on the odd transformation she'd just witnessed. *Once, okay; but twice . . . ? What the . . .?*

"Joe says you're looking for me."

Melanie heaved a sigh of relief on seeing the speaker. It was the man who'd been in the booth phoning.

She smiled coolly at Lois. "Business calls, honey. Looks like I'll have to rain check on that proposal. Nice you asked though."

Lois hissed, collected her drinks from Joe, and walked off in a huff.

"She's pissed-off at me, not you," the man said. He was handsome, with sandy hair. Wore a gray shirt over black trousers and shoes. His dark eyes were those of a killer, merciless as death. He smiled, but it didn't reach his eyes. "We don't get along, and now she thinks I'm about scoring with you." He shook Melanie's hand. "I'm Doug Fisher. Uncle Biggs said you'd be coming over here. Said he's already briefed—" Then he noticed what Lois was setting down on her table, and scowled. "Where's Mary?"

Melanie pointed. Doug peered down over the bar top, then frowned up at Joe. "Man, you can't just leave her lying down there."

The stooped bartender scratched his stubble with dirty fingers. His bloodshot eyes glared with cold indifference. "What the hell do you expect me to do, huh? Read her bedtime stories?" He kicked the prone figure thrice. "Hey, girl, get your slacker butt off my damn floor!"

Slowly, groggily, Mary got back to her feet. A thin clotted blood-line ran from the puncture in her arm to her left fist. Her mouth and chin were covered with puke. She jabbed a finger at Joe, "Dad, you know this shit's gonna kill me one of these days. Then I'll see who'll waitress for your cheapskate ass." Swaying like a breeze was blowing her, she took two steps towards the back door, then collapsed again. She didn't get up again.

Joe stared defiantly at Doug and Melanie. "Like I just said, what am I supposed to do, huh? Don't care what you say—I'm letting her sleep it off down there."

Doug Fisher nodded. "Whatever you say, man—she's your kid." He and Melanie retreated from the bar to a table in the corner opposite the two blondes. Sitting side by side, backs to the wall, they watching the beautiful pair slurp their blood-drinks. The blondes affected not to notice them.

Melanie now saw that the women could be twins. "Who are they?" she asked.

"The Chameleon Sisters. The one in hot pants who hasn't tried to make you yet is Vera."

Melanie laughed uneasily. "Chameleon Sisters?"

Doug gazed reflectively around the bar. "Their real surname is Smith, but they're mutants . . . blend into their surroundings, hence the lizard moniker. Also, they have ridiculously long tongues."

He broke off from speaking, snapped his fingers at Joe. Two beers and some nuts." He resumed: "I'm sure you doubt what I'm saying, right? Okay, look under the sisters' table, at Vera's legs. Don't let her know you're staring or she'll turn it off. Look real close."

Melanie looked, and gasped. Vera appeared not to have any legs under the table. Then, like Doug had instructed, she looked closer . . . Vera did have legs, only, like before with Lois's fingers vanishing against her hair, they'd 'blended' almost perfectly with the brown wood of her chair. Her shoes and feet had matched themselves to the dirty stone floor.

(Vera glanced their way then, smiling demurely. Melanie saw now that the women weren't twins—Vera looked older, also her jaw was more prominent. Her lovely eyes seemed a light brown.)

"Never seen anything like that before," Melanie said. "It even affects their clothes?"

Doug ran a finger across his lips. "It's an uncommon Bizarro effect. The Chameleons make good biz from it, though. They're hunters . . . treasure . . . people . . . whatever's gone missing . . . pay them and they'll find it for you. No questions asked." He repressed a shiver. "Damn, just imagine having those two after you . . ."

Melanie said, "So, do we assume they're also after the magic teddy?" (Despite his coldness, she found Doug very attractive. This pleased her: A little romance and sex would spice things up. This mission was clearly dangerous, it needn't also be boring.)

Doug shook his head. "Nah, the info's still secret. This is just the sisters' usual haunt. He gestured at Mary, who was now staggering groggily across the bar toward them with their drinks on a tray. "I think they mainly like the taste of her."

Mary reached them, dropped their frothy steins and a bowl of mixed beer nuts. She turned to leave.

"Hey wait," Melanie said.

Mary turned back to her. "What is it?" she asked in a scared voice. "You want a Bloody Mary too now?"

Melanie said, low so Joe wouldn't overhear, "That blood-leeching nonsense is sure to kill you soon. You know that."

The girl's eyes widened till Melanie thought she'd have a fit. She giggled nervously. "Y-Y-You just don't understand! I-I-I can't leave my dad!" she sputtered, then dashed off, only barely managing not to topple over before vanishing into the back room.

Joe grinned over at their table. (Melanie winced, his mouth was a total disaster zone.) "That's my little girl. Loyal as a neutered dog. They just don't make daughters like that anymore."

Joe returned to polishing glasses. Melanie turned to Doug. What's that about?"

"Mary?" He raised his beer and took a sip. "Her bloody funeral. She's such a little fool. I've told her over and over again to leave Joe; I'll send her to go live with my sister Kaitlin in Agawam. But no, she doesn't want to behave like her momma who did leave the old coot. She's scared stiff of being thought a worthless tramp, like her ma."

Melanie's eyes narrowed. "So this goes on till she dies?"

"Or until she wises up. Like I said; it's *her* funeral. She's twenty-two; well old enough to make and be responsible for her own bad choices." He crunched on a handful of nuts, then indicated Melanie's beer: "Drink up, we've an expedition to work out. I've been expecting you for the past hour, then my kid sis got on the phone and . . ."

Melanie drank some beer, her gaze fixed on the Chameleon Sisters opposite, their beautiful faces animated as they whispered about something. Vera's legs were still invisible, Lois's feet had also now gone missing. Melanie was glad she didn't have to deal with the pair as enemies.

Lois, her lips red with Mary's blood, noticed her staring and blew her a sloppy kiss. Red drops flew through the air at them.

Doug smirked at the bemused look on Melanie's face. "Don't let their beauty fool you. They'll just as soon kill you as fuck you. Or fuck you *then* kill you; or vice versa. Or even just fuck you to death for fun." His expression turned grim again, his voice hushed. "Alright, down to business: We know for certain that the teddy's still downtown. Problem is, no-one's sure what warehouse it was left in. Courier never said—gingers ate his dumb ass."

"Yeah, your uncle told me that . . . Hey! How'd you know . . . ? I mean, if the gingers ate the courier, how'd you know the package was ever delivered?"

"From the gingers. The pack who ate the courier mentioned it later. And I've also got an informer amongst James's people." He gestured at their bowl of nuts. "These are good; you should try some."

Melanie stirred the nuts with a finger, then shook her head. "Can't eat these, they're mixed. I'm allergic, except it's just peanuts."

"You could just separate them. Here, I'll do it for you."

She shook her head. "Kind of you, but really, don't bother." She grimaced. "Man, you don't want to see what happens if I take the wrong nuts."

Doug regarded her dubiously. "That bad, eh?"

"Worse than—a total Bizarro scene. You really don't want to see it." She took a long pull of her drink. "Okay now, back to where we were. So, your informer told you . . ."

CHAPTER 4

"Stop pouting," Vera Smith told her younger sister. "It makes you look obvious. So she turned you down, so what? It ain't the end of the world." She regarded Melanie and Doug with amusement. "It ain't like she's *that* pretty. Curvy for sure, and I just love her black hair, but . . . those glasses . . . ?"

"I hate the fact that she's going to fuck him, not me," Lois spat.

"I'd be more concerned about the gun she's carrying," Vera said.

Lois sat up straight. "What gun?"

"Shoulder holster. The girl's definitely packing. You'd have noticed it if you hadn't been sniffing her pussy so intently."

Relegating her lust, Lois studied Melanie more carefully. Now she easily made out the woman's gun, nicely concealed by the swell of her left breast. It looked a big one too. She polished off her Bloody Mary, licked her lips clean and stared moodily at her sister. "*This is* odd. She a hunter like us, you think?"

Vera nodded back. "Cutie over there with Dougie, new in town and packing a rod? Yeah—she has to be." She licked her teeth with her mouth shut, then added: "Put that together with the fact that our boy Dougie's been practically living here above the *WTF?* for the past week . . ."

Lois got her drift. "Yep, and also factor in those three teams Biggs sent into the O over the past week, and what do we have?"

"Only one reasonable answer: Biggs is looking for something in the O-Zone."

"Yeah. Think James knows what it is?"

A headshake. "Nah, you know he's too busy balling that ginger nymphomaniac of his." A giggle. "She never lets him out of bed long enough to think deeply about anything."

Lois smiled coldly, her beautiful face a ghoul's in the bar lighting.

She calmly dismissed having sex with Melanie from her mind, then looked longingly at Joe. "Another . . . ?"

The bartender shook his head regretfully. "Mary's finished for the night, I'm afraid." He laughed mockingly, ignoring the disgusted looks from Melanie and Doug. "We don't want to use her all up now, do we? Whatever will the neighborhood drink then?"

Lois laughed. "It's just that she tastes so good with alcohol . . ." She turned back to her sister. "Where were we?"

"Adding two and two and getting twenty two. The clear deal here is that Biggs wants something from the O-Zone. And it has to be something *very* frigging important for him to waste all those guys' lives. Hey, girl—I'm talking to you!"

Lois looked up from peeking under their table. "Your legs are missing."

Vera looked down at herself, made the mental adjustment that showed her legs again, then smiled at Lois. "Yours are too, dear. Okay, now where was I? Yes, Biggs is after something in the O. I suggest we follow these two."

Lois glanced across at Melanie and Doug, the pair now bobbing heads close together like lovers. It looked like they'd shortly begin kissing. She quelled the sudden pang of jealous anger that resurfaced to stab her, her breasts throbbing with frustrated desire. "Sis, you really think just these two are gonna succeed where over twenty guys failed? Why not just tell James? That's safe. He'll pay us for the info."

"Don't be silly. Sure, James'll pay us. But we've no idea what whatever they're after is worth. Could be millions. If that's the case, we'll lose out big time. Best we tail them; once they find what they're after; we knock them off and deliver it to James ourselves, or even to Biggs."

Lois scratched her ear, nodded reflectively. "I love your mind, sis."

"And the other thing," Vera said, with a nod across the room at Melanie. "I think we need to be damn careful about cutie-pie over there. She's a big girl, but trust me, she's got to be deadly—if Bigelow Jenkins thinks highly enough of her to bring her in from out of town and send her alone into the O, we'll need to watch her like—"

Lois laughed. "Now you're worrying too much. Watching *her* is easy." She made her left arm blend indistinguishably with the tabletop. "Rather, she needs to worry about watching us." She stood to her feet. "C'mon, let's go hustle some action, maybe get two hookers from the strip. I need a fuck badly."

CHAPTER 5

"So," Doug was explaining, "he's driving in from out of town, and for some reason—I'm sure he was stoned—neglects the telltale sign that he's entering the O." He raised his hands in a beer-influenced pissed-off gesture. "I mean, how fucking dumb can you get?"

Melanie nodded. "Well, now we know we can't just circle round lower east Springfield and enter Parker Street from its bottom end."

Across from them, the Chameleon Sisters had gotten to their feet and were leaving the bar. Both waved; Lois blew Melanie another kiss.

"You've made a real impression on her," Doug said as the door shut behind the departing blondes.

Melanie rode her fingers along his thigh. "Have I made any on *you?*"

His expression turned a little less cold. "From the first moment I saw you all I've been thinking about is how beautiful you are. Your . . . your eyes look like stagnant pond water—"

She giggled. "How romantic. Is that your dick or the beer speaking?"

The bar door creaked open and a man walked in. Gusts of cold air blew in after him, bringing long-sought cooling to the room. But as the door swung shut again, the chill remained, intensified even, like the new arrival carried a personal winter with him wherever he went.

The three left in the bar stared at the man. He was of average height, and completely dressed in black, including black leather gloves and a cloak that wrapped him like a shroud. The wide brim of his hat draped his face in shadow.

He carried a large black suitcase. A dull obsidian thing.

The man glanced in their direction. Melanie gave a start—he didn't seem to have a face under his hat, just cold gray dimness framed by a mane of hair like melted tar. She also had the strangest of impressions—that the missing face 'smiled' at her.

Then he turned away from her, and, trailing chill like a bridal gown, walked to the bar. He put his suitcase down and addressed Joe:

"Good evening. Does a young woman live here?"

Melanie looked askance at Doug. "Don't tell me he's also thirsty?"

"Never seen this guy before in my life," Doug replied. He frowned at the dark figure by the bar. "At least, now you know why they call this place the *What The Fuck?*"

***

Joe stared worriedly at the black-garbed stranger. Try hard as he might, he couldn't see the man's face (if indeed it was a man)—the entire region below his hat seemed a gray void, like a world being created. And the cold that blew at him from the man, like he'd stepped outside in winter . . .

"You talking about Mary my daughter?" he asked.

"She must be the one," came the creaky reply. "I'd like to see her, if that wouldn't be too much trouble."

"And who the hell are you?" Despite being ill at ease, Joe felt he had to make a stand. Mary was a good kid, and he'd done everything he could to ensure she'd not wind up turning tricks like her mother. Yes, Joe had done his doggone best, brought Mary up good and right the best he knew how to. At least until he'd had this 'blood-drink' idea. But then, a guy couldn't predict what would catch on, could he? He'd had no idea everyone for a mile around would want a genuine 'Bloody Mary,' particularly not with each drink costing five hundred bucks. But they did and so what could he do, but make a good profit? At the moment he and Mary were doing at least four drinks a day, that half a liter of blood equaled a cool two grand. All the kid had to do was take her vitamins and go to bed early, Joe reasoned. And it had worked for two weeks, but now, the little bitch was getting airs, was always too tired to work. Damn, it was worse than when she was on her period. Then Joe reconsidered: *Okay we did have that birthday party come in yesterday, and she had to draw out a liter and a half . . . but the human body's supposed to be full of blood, ain't it, or is that water . . . ?*

A hoarse laugh came from the black figure. "My name?" He tapped the bar top with gloved fingers. "I am The Fixer. Your little girl isn't feeling too good at the moment. I can tell—I sensed it as I was passing by. I'm here to mend her."

Damn, Joe thought, *this guy's just a doctor. But no—he said he 'sensed her' as he was passing by?* That made the guy a charlatan out to get Joe's and Mary's hard earned blood money.

A wall of almost solid cold blew at Joe then, chilling the glass he held so it misted. Joe smirked. *I'm wise to your cheap gimmick, asshole: the freeze controls must be inside that massive suitcase you've got.*

He sneered at the dark man, his unshaven face a caricature of scorn. "Mary's just fine, you goddam quack. We don't need your damn help—"

"But, I—" The Fixer protested.

"Just get the fuck out of my bar, asshole, before I get my shotgun." Joe cast a glance over at Melanie and Doug, who both watched the scene with interest. He winked like to say, 'I got this.'

"Do not be impertinent or impolite with me," the black figure said, his cloak swirling around him like an invisible wind blew it. "I am here to help your daughter." Now there was menace in his voice; an overtone as ominous and foreboding as digging a grave.

"Cool it, Joe," Doug admonished like he sensed danger.

Joe ignored both the cold that seemed to be flowing up his legs to his testicles and Doug's caution. He stared coldly at the man who called himself 'The Fixer.' "I said: Get the fuck out of my here bar, you goddam snake oil salesman. And *stay out*. If you ever show—!"

Joe stopped railing because The Fixer had grabbed him by the throat. It wasn't the tightness of the grip that had paralyzed Joe, but its temperature. The fingers around his neck felt colder than ice.

Also—and Joe could see Melanie and Doug gaping at this—The Fixer's arm had extended across the bar to him, sleeve and all stretching like a black tentacle to four feet in length. He staggered back against the shelves of displayed drinks. The Fixer's arm extended farther also, till it was six feet long. The black fingers holding Joe's throat felt like they were freezing it in liquid nitrogen.

"Now listen," The Fixer said, tipping his hat back so Joe saw that he really had no face, just a mass of shifting angled shadows like mobile cubist geometry. "My services are free to all, and I'll stand for no insults from you." His voice was even, its menace a black sheen like a demon buffed each word he spoke.

"I'm sorry," Joe sputtered, his bloodshot eyes almost leaping from his face from The Fixer's grip, his heart pumping extra fast from the impossibility of the stretched black arm. Fear spread through him like a flock of crows. "I-I-I d-d-d-didn't mean it like that, S-s-sir. Honest. W-w-we get busloads of creeps in here t-t-trying to rip us off; bums without a cent—"

"Shut up!" the dark man brusquely cut him off. "Your daughter is in grave danger and I came to help her. But since you refuse my help—"

Somewhere amidst Joe's horror and dread, it occurred to him to accept The Fixer's help, but he couldn't talk: the preternatural cold had frozen his tongue . . .

"—I'll leave you both as I met you."

With that, The Fixer's gloved fingers loosened their freezing grip from Joe's neck. The extra-long arm retracted back to its dark-cloaked owner, who, after adjusting his hat so it once-again hid his face, retrieved his suitcase from the floor, turned, and walked from the bar without a side glance.

Joe stood staring after the departing figure. The instant the door shut behind him, Joe fainted.

***

Melanie and Doug stared after The Fixer for a long minute, then got up and hurried over to the bar. Doug peered down over the counter at the comatose Joe and winced. "He's lying in Mary's puke."

Melanie peered over the counter too. She wrinkled her nose at a bad smell. "Oops, he's pooped himself."

"Serves him right, the wannabe tough guy. Look, he's breathing okay. Let's just leave him, go get something to eat."

Melanie said, "Hold on a minute." She found a bottle of water on the counter, then, leaning over the division, emptied the bottle over Joe's face.

Joe sputtered awake. "W-w-what . . . ?"

Melanie said, "The badass is gone; go wash your punk-ass."

Joe stared at them, memory creeping into his eyes like a burglar.

Doug said, "You heard the lady. Go wash your ass, you stink like . . ."

"We're stepping out for a bite," Melanie added. She looked at Doug pointedly. "Any good veggie restaurants nearby?"

He thought a moment, then shrugged. "There's a Hindu-owned

place over on Crabtree Street. It's worth checking out." He regarded her curiously. "How can a vegetarian be allergic to nuts?"

She rolled her eyes at the question. "Welcome to the dietary irony of my life." She turned from the bar, strode quickly to the entrance, suddenly desperate to be far from the mingled vomit and excrement smell.

After a last disgusted look down at the revived bartender, Doug headed after Melanie. They stepped out into late evening.

CHAPTER 6

Dinner went like a charm. Chola Biryani with dry Riesling. Afterwards they both drove back to the *WTF?*, stopping on the way so Melanie could buy a box of donuts.

Once up in Doug's room above the *WTF?* Melanie pushed Doug towards the bed; she was aroused as hell, had been through most of their dinner. "Get undressed," she gasped at him, her eyes limpid with lust. "Hurry up!" To underline her urgency she stripped off her own clothes. Black jacket, plaid shirt (the shoulder holster and gun went on a chair), bra, trousers, shoes . . . all were tossed away in different directions like debris spinning off a celestial body.

Doug regarded her back through tipsy eyes. "Okay, gotta pee first though—my bladder feels loaded with lead."

She grinned, tipsy herself; they'd had *a lot* of wine with their dinner.

Cold eyes widening with anticipation, Doug eyed her voluptuous form—the large round breasts, the heavy hips, the thick but shapely legs, the feet and toes—for another few seconds, then disappeared through the bathroom door. She heard the sharp noise of his zipper, then the sound of water striking water.

"Hey, wash it when you're done!" she yelled at his exposed ass. "I plan on eating you!" She ditched her panties; picked up her box of donuts and got into bed. While listening to Doug flush then wash, she ran fingers through the black bush of her mons, finally parting and teasing her sex. She was wet, her sexual liquids dripping from her swollen nether lips. Her bladder too now felt full; but not enough that she needed instant release.

Doug came out of the bathroom; in the interim he'd lost all his clothes except for his socks. She admired his body: He was trim, with nice tight muscles, nice pecs, nice abs. Alethic legs, arms with solid biceps. He was hairy (all men were to some degree), but not too much, just some fuzz over his chest that thinned over his six-pack, then thickened again to fur his groin. He looked nice and hard; just right for love. She was certain his buttocks were nice and hard too—there was nothing like a muscular backside to grab onto when you were being plumbed deep, fucked down to the very depths of your soul. It was a firm, vital pillar of support, one every woman needed at that point—a crutch to her ravaged emotions—at those moments when it felt like you were losing yourself into the other person . . . She grinned: *I'm getting well ahead of myself—we've not reached that part yet.* She resumed her appraisal of Doug Fisher. Yes, she liked him. She liked thin guys like this, ones her arms easily encircled.

Doug clearly liked her too: His circumcised penis pointed proudly ahead of him, stiff as a gun's barrel. It wasn't a particularly handsome organ: it bulged with ugly veins, but which woman cared about that at a time like this? It looked hard as a rock, though, which every woman did care about. The one place no woman accepted disappointment was in bed.

"Damn," she teased. You *are* glad to see me!" Giggling, she got up on hands and knees on the sheets. "Ooh, come to mommy, daddy!"

Doug stood hands on hips, grinding his pelvis at her. "You like it?" he slurred.

She got out of bed, swayed across to him. She grabbed the hard prick, squeezed and stroked it. "Do you really need to ask such an egotistical question?" she muttered throatily up at him, then kissed him on tip toes. "Of course I like *it*. I like you; *it* comes as an addition." She pulled him by the penis after her to the bed, pushed him down on it, straddled his thighs, her large form like a goddess's above him.

She shook a motherly hand at his attempts to stroke her breasts, then jerked hard on his erection. "Just wait; let me eat you first; then we'll fuck. Okay?"

"I like your glasses," he groaned while she stroked him. "I always wanted to fuck Mrs. Moran back in high school. Her glasses were just like yours. She kept giving me extra homework for ogling her fat ass."

Chuckling, Melanie removed her glasses.

"Aw, leave them on, you look so cute . . ." Then: "Hey, what are you doing?"

Melanie had removed a chocolate-glazed donut from the box and was popping the head of his cock through its hole. She did so with clear expertise. Once the glans was through the hole, she slid the donut right down to his curly pubic hair.

He gaped at her; she smiled back. "C'mon, baby—don't tell me a big boy like you hasn't heard of the donut treatment?"

He shook his head, but said nothing. He didn't attempt to stop her either. Melanie hadn't expected him to—everyone loved a new sexual experience, once it didn't look to be painful.

She popped/slipped another donut over Doug's erection, then one more, this top one vanilla frosted with sprinkles. She sat up, licking her lips at her handiwork. About an inch and a half of penis remained uncovered—the glans and a little skin.

She grinned at Doug. "You're wondering what now, right?"

He nodded breathlessly.

"Now I fucking eat you, darling." With that, she bent her lips to his penis and began sucking and licking its exposed head, while her hands slid the three donuts up and down its shaft.

The effect was what she knew it would be. Doug began trembling like he was being exorcised. "Oooooo!" He reached down and grabbed handfuls of Melanie's hair, gripped both jet-black bundles like they were the reins of a horse he was riding.

Melanie slipped his penis as far into her mouth as the stacked donuts would allow, then sucked hard on the member. She swirled her tongue around it, tickled the deep slit in the fat head with its sweet offering of pre-come. As she worked, her own sex dripped and dripped, the juice running down her thighs. Hell, she felt so turned on! Her breasts pressed on his thighs like they sought to compact them.

"Oh my God!" Doug gasped and filled Melanie's mouth with come. She accepted the come like an offering, all the while stroking the donuts up and down, a melting of their glaze acting like lube on his penis, while Doug trembled like he was breaking apart.

She didn't however swallow. Once Doug collapsed back, gasping for breath, Melanie slurped her lips off his manhood. Then, while he watched perplexed, she pulled the three donuts off his softening cock and dribbled his semen over them, afterwards setting the semen-coated friedcakes aside on the light blue bedclothes.

Doug gazed at her in wonder. "That was fantastic," he said. "How did you ever think—?"

She ended his question with a soft but firm finger across his lips, then pulled him up to his knees. "This isn't the time for talk," she reprimanded, "just eat me!" She propped herself back on pillows, parted her thighs wide till her vulva yawned at him—a pink lake flooding velvet banks.

Then, as he knelt between her legs and began lapping her wet sex like a thirsty dog drinking, she ate the three semen-glazed donuts. The smell of the come filled her nostrils as the impregnated dough filled her mouth like his penis recently had. Her body trembled, her breasts felt larger than ever, warm like balls of sweet dough waiting for the fryer, her nerves tingled from her crotch to every part of her body.

Doug ate her; Melanie in turn ate him in effigy. She savored his tongue in her cunt, savored his come on her tongue. A sexual transaction that felt spiritual.

She gasped and moaned out loud when her orgasm arrived, ravaging her like a wolf, tearing her apart like it was a serial killer.

CHAPTER 7

Half a mile away, Lois Smith similarly gasped into orgasm as a hooker gave her head in the shower.

The girl eating Lois was named Gretel. She was tall and athletic, with short black hair, small red lips, and pert little breasts. She currently knelt between Lois's spread legs, licking her clitoris while warm water rained on them both like they were tropical palms.

Everything is wet now, Lois thought. *Wet hair, wet bodies . . . extremely wet pussy.*

Lois moaned as the waves of pleasure took her out of herself. She dropped her long tongue down to lick her nipples, curling it around both stiff brown nubs in turn, slurping at them. Then when the pleasure grew too much for her to control herself, she simply let her tongue dangle from her mouth, so it swung between her breasts, like a wet pink tie.

Between Lois's legs, Gretel's fingers slid in and out of her vagina, till Lois was vibrating from the pleasure, faint from it, feeling like she was dissolving in the wetness cascading over them.

Her orgasmic storm subsided somewhat. She pulled Gretel to her feet, kissed her long and deep, restraining herself from sticking her tongue all the way down the girl's throat into her stomach. Gretel kissed her back equally passionately. Meanwhile Lois worked fingers hard and fast over Gretel's clitoris, quickly bringing her partner to orgasm too. She snaked her tongue down over Gretel's back and her buttocks, licked her anus.

Then, while Gretel moaned and trembled against her, Lois felt another orgasm rising up from her own loins. She ground her crotch hard against Gretel's thigh, riding it like a horse, rubbing the sensation out like she was erasing herself from existence. Indeed, that was what this second orgasm felt like: her breaking apart into nihility, with the universe as witness to her dissolution. Her body blended out for a moment, making it look like Gretel clutched a mass of the bathroom's white tiles, then Lois was back again, solid as ever, while her body and soul exploded with sensation.

The women held each other tight in the warmth of the shower, gasping against one another through the buffeting throes of their passion.

⁎⁎

Through the open bathroom door, Lois watched and heard her sister Vera moaning loudly, as another prostitute, a hard-faced little redhead, serviced her from behind with a strap-on. Braced on elbows and knees, Vera panted hard as she was fucked, her face twisted up like she was in pain. Her blonde hair was tossed everywhere like it was exploding out of her head. Every now and then she lost control of herself; her body disappeared against the bed, and the black dildo could be seen sliding in and out of what seemed empty space.

Sheila, the redhead fucking her, didn't care. She'd had sex with Vera before, and the woman's money was always good.

Vera's tongue, stretched out before her like a snake that had lost its way, didn't bother Sheila either. She found it stimulating, even: both Chameleon Sisters could lick their own clitorises. Weird for sure, but it had to feel great. The only other person Sheila had heard of with a similar ability was Queen Pam of Boston, who (rumor had it) could extend her neck till it was close to fifty feet long.

Tongue dangling sideways out of her mouth, Vera turned to gape at Sheila. She reached back a hand and smacked Sheila's butt, then jerked the soft buttock-cheek forward forcefully several times, indicating she wanted to be fucked harder.

Sheila obliged her, pushing Vera down flat on the mattress and slamming the dildo into her vagina. Beneath her, Vera blended out and in with the colors of orgasm. She stiffened like steel, went limp as a post-coital penis, trembled like a butterfly's wings as she was relentlessly pumped.

Riding Vera like that, Sheila came too. Cold and grim it was, but satisfactory as a long shit after being constipated for a week.

She collapsed on top of Vera, kissed her through her veil of mussed blonde locks as Vera's tongue withdrew back into her mouth.

Lois and Gretel returned into the bedroom, Lois busily toweling her hair dry.

Vera and Sheila grinned satedly at the pair.

Lois pumped her hips at Sheila. "You ain't done yet by a long shot, honey . . . nor are we. Get off her butt—it's *my* turn for some of that strap-on."

She and Gretel climbed onto the bed. While Sheila serviced Lois (Sheila lay on her back, Lois squatted over her in a reverse-cowgirl position), Gretel performed cunnilingus on Vera. Then Lois wore the strap-on and fucked Gretel, who ate Vera, who fingered Sheila, who came to orgasm screaming like she was being murdered.

Vera got out another strap-on. She and Lois sandwiched first Gretel, then Sheila; then the prostitutes strapped on the sex-harnesses themselves and returned the favor.

After that, Vera lay on her back (with Sheila sitting on her face and holding her feet up in the air), while Lois fucked her ass and Gretel licked Lois's anus between thrusts. Then Vera fucked Lois till she squirted jism while fading completely from view so it looked like the glittering liquid arc began somewhere in the air over the bed. (The Chameleon Sisters regularly made love to each other, but generally preferred sex with other partners.)

All in all, it was a hot sweaty night for all four women.

CHAPTER 8

Next Morning

Wow! Melanie thought, eyeing Doug's ass as they left the *WTF?* bar for her car. *Last night was something else.*

The sex had been lovely, great recreation after her previous long abstinence. After finishing off the trio of donuts to a couple of orgasms, she and Doug had made love twice more.

The first time had been oh so hot! Face-to-face, him on top. Digging her nails hard into his ass, she'd creamed almost immediately he'd penetrated her. And, oh no—she'd not been disappointed at all: his butt had been everything she'd hoped for, hard as a pair of basketballs, almost like stone when he'd been pumping his liquid masculine essence inside her.

Their second time had seen Melanie lying on her stomach, a pillow under her pelvis, her legs together, while Doug plowed her from behind like he was tilling a field. Her orgasm had been a tree of carnal pleasure grown from the physical sensation they shared. As he pumped her fiercely, she'd flowered . . .

She recalled how Doug, his eyes well clear of alcohol by then, had panted like he was winning a race, his breath hot on her neck, his body tensing against her hips and buttocks . . . then the spurt of warmth, only a pitiful, exhausted squirt this time, as he ended his quest for pleasure inside her. A cool breeze from the window had bathed their bodies, the air swirling over them both like shower water, dripping down . . . She'd felt wildly empowered as he crumpled on her gasping, damp chest hair wetting her back, his body shivering from the overwhelming pleasure of hers as his rampant male hardness softened inside her . . .

It was a nice sequence of memories. She gave Doug's backside a playful squeeze.

He smiled back, though his eyes remained cold. "You're incredible, baby. I'm sure as hell converted—you big girls do do it better."

She blushed at the compliment; an odd reaction, given their activities of the night. Also, she wasn't a prude, so why did the expression of his pleasure mean so much? Besides, now the lust was out of her system, she sensed a definite danger to herself if she got too emotionally involved with Doug. Yes, they were both journeying into the O-Zone, and yes, she did intend having lots of sex with him before this mission was over, but no!—she wasn't going to fall for him. There was an essential coldness about Doug Fisher, a barely-concealed thread of nastiness that poked through his calm exterior every now and then.

This is a guy who could really hurt me—break my heart big time—if I'm not careful, Melanie realized. *So I'm going to be careful. No emotions here; just 'penis versus pussy' conflict and resolution.*

Might be easier said than done, however. They reached the car. Doug smiled her way. "You ready?"

She nodded, her caution quelling the swell of warmth in her groin his smile had triggered.

"Hey, Doug!" a familiar voice called as Melanie unlocked the blue Volvo.

They looked back to see Joe the bartender waving at them from the *WTF?'s* front door. Joe looked as unkempt as he had yesterday, his eyes seemed twice as bloodshot. He stood outlined in the harsh daylight; a living statue constructed from the grime and decay of the city. "Hey, you guys seen Mary this morning?"

Melanie and Doug shook their heads. "Nah," Doug replied.

Joe glared at them both. "For real?"

Doug scowled at him. "Man, am I her frigging minder? Personally I think she's run away. About damn time too, with the way you treat her."

"It's not that," Joe said in a more conciliatory tone, walking down the bar's front steps towards them. "I'm just scared that that Fixer creep who came here last night might have come back and kidnapped her." His voice pitched up almost to a whine. "You two sure you haven't seen my little girl?"

Melanie was uncertain whether she felt pity or disgust for Joe. Personal opinion aside, however, she recognized the bartender's worry as a valid one. What if The Fixer *had* kidnapped Mary and spirited her off somewhere? That really looked to be worse than Joe bleeding her for profit. Or maybe it wasn't; heck, she didn't know!

"We haven't seen her," she said softly, her concern for the missing girl evident in her voice.

"Mel's right," Doug added. "Look, man, you could be getting all worked up for nothing. Maybe Mary's just taken a walk around the neighborhood to see a friend."

"She never goes to see anyone! She doesn't have any friends."

"That's because you never let her out of your sight, you old fool. It's unnatural for a twenty-two-year old to not have any friends." His expression turned sly. "Or . . . or are you screwing your own kid? That's why you don't want any boys around her?"

Joe's unshaven expression instantly turned defensive, his stance aggressive like he'd charge Doug. "How dare you even suggest that nonsense? No, I'm not sleeping with my daughter. That's sick. Damn you, even suggesting it is sick! I'm just not raising any sluts, that's all. Her mother Carol was—"

"She might have gone to see her mother," Doug said in a mocking voice. "Last thing I heard, Carol was—"

"Okay, okay," Melanie cut him off quickly, realizing this was neither here nor there, and that she and Doug really needed to get a fast move on into the O, "Tell you what: Hopefully we won't be gone long. If Mary still isn't back by the time we are, we'll go looking for her for you. How's that?"

Joe stared at her crestfallen, then nodded. "Thanks; you're a good person, Melanie." Then, after glowering angrily at Doug, he turned away and shuffled back up the *WTF?*'s front steps, muttering piteously: "Oh, where in the world could she be?"

"Damn," Doug said, shaking his head in disbelief. "If one didn't know better, you'd think the creep really loved his daughter."

Melanie shrugged. Joe's odd behavior had her feeling very uncomfortable. "I think the bastard does love Mary," she said, returning her attention to the car door and pulling it open. She looked pointedly at Doug, her blue eyes boring into his from behind her lenses. "He's just like a lot of assholes who don't value what they've got till it's gone."

PART 2:
SIXTEEN ACRES

CHAPTER 9

They drove off. They were taking Melanie's Volvo instead of
Doug's Porsche because she had no idea how reliable Doug's car
was. Besides the Porsche had lower suspension and there'd likely be
potholes to navigate (no one did road maintenance anymore). When
the chips were down, you wanted a sturdy ride, not a pretty one.

Doug was driving, he knew the roads. Riding shotgun, a pump-
action shotgun balanced over her forearm, Melanie scanned the road
ahead. Her black hair was secured behind her in a ponytail. (Suddenly
conscious of her male company, she'd put on blush and lipstick. As a
dead friend had once remarked: "You want your face to be as
attractive as your pussy to the guy you're dating.")

She'd switched her usual pair of glasses for a set on a silver chain,
one which she could, if necessary, lock tight to her face. (She hardly
ever did—her glasses were for distance correction; most trouble
tended to occur up close and personal, where she saw just fine. Still,
one expected the unexpected.)

Doug regarded her admiringly. "You look totally hot. Hot enough
to fry to a crisp any opposition we meet."

"Keep your eyes on the road. Watch where you're going, instead
of who you're going there with." His flattery both delighted and
bothered her. *Or maybe*, she reasoned, *living tough like I do, I'm just not
used to male complements anymore.*

They both had pistols and shotguns. Melanie also had a couple of
time bombs, egg-sized things from Boston that could level a city
block. The time bombs were clipped to the rear of her belt. There
were packs of food and water on the back seat.

They rode the Volvo toward an unwelcoming morning sky. The
trees everywhere (they'd just hit a profusion of dogwoods and elms
that enclosed the road like parents) again reminded Melanie why

Springfield was nicknamed 'A City in the Forest.' Here now, it seemed like the plants were the actual city inhabitants, the sparse housing weird concrete vegetation the trees had planted for their pleasure.

They turned right, off Parker Street onto North Branch Parkway. Crossed the North Branch Mill River. Headed west, parallel to the river, for Bizarro's right edge. On their left—a break in the brown mass shadowing the area—the O yawned like a mouth ready to eat them.

Doug said, "It's damn weird the way Bizarro just hangs up there above the buildings. I keep expecting it to fall, but it never does."

Melanie said, "We're about entering the part that did fall. Once in there, you immediately wish it had remained up in the sky."

"Yeah, and I love your plan of keeping to the edge of the O, where the oddity should be at a minimum. Then we just zoom in—"

"Hey! There's the plane again!"

They were fifty meters from the start of the O-Zone. Just inside its limits, the blue aircraft flew out from beneath Bizarro's eastern half and hung in the air like a silent helicopter.

"Experimental USAF craft for certain," Doug said. "Likely from the Westover Air Reserve Base up in Chicopee."

Melanie didn't reply. The hovering aircraft was again attacking the ground with lightning bolts. The yellow zigzags of electricity it let off at its unseen adversaries all came from a thick black tentacle at its rear, a downward extension of its tail. The tentacle looked about ten feet long and was coal black against the aircraft's blue.

Doug said, "I don't understand how it flies despite Bizarro's disruption of all airborne electronics."

"Maybe that's its entire point," Melanie replied, looking thoughtful. "It could be conducting research. Maybe there's someone—like the Area 51 guys for instance—trying to overcome Bizarro's restrictions on air travel, hence this airplane's odd design. They might even be attempting to reactivate the US's communication satellites." She smiled. "You have to agree that it'll be great to have working cellphones again."

As more lightning flashed ground-ward, Doug parked by an empty post office building. "We'd best wait till it's done fighting." He pointed ahead. "I doubt your analysis of this situation is right. I mean

. . . if it's simply researching to get wireless communications working again, why does it keep attacking the O?"

Melanie considered that while studying the crackling light still pouring from the blue plane's tentacle. Doug's reasoning made sense. "Yeah, I know . . . What the hell is it after down there, right?"

Now, a responsive barrage of rockets zoomed up to explode harmlessly against the gleaming windowless hull.

Doug scowled. "You'd expect the stupid gingers to have learnt by now that they can't harm it, but no . . ."

"That's some heavy artillery they're hitting it with," Melanie remarked.

"RPGs and some anti-aircraft guns. One of James's friends raided Fort Devens," Doug explained in bored tones while they watched the air/sky battle of lightning versus rockets. "Breaking into military bases is easy nowadays. He's also got a supplier down in Techxas; guy by the name of Pablo Rodriguez."

"I've heard of Pablo. Didn't he—"

Up ahead of them the shooting had abruptly ceased, the final surface-to-air salvo terminating in a line of orange/black explosions that traced the plane's hull like ellipses.

"And so the gingers quit the conflict again," Doug said drily. "Dumb cannibal—"

"Wait!" Melanie interrupted, her mouth dry. "Something else is going on."

More disinterest from Doug. "The usual . . . happens everyday."

Since it stopped emitting lightning, the airplane's tentacle had been cracking back and forth like a whip. Now, like a snake striking, it lashed down towards the nearest house.

There was another sequence of explosions, all on the ground this time. Then the black tentacle-snake was pulled aloft again. Now, it bore a desperately kicking and screaming figure wrapped up in its end. The screams—they sounded like a woman's—reached them in a faint cascade of shrill echoes like the end of a fading CD track.

"There goes another one," Doug said.

Melanie sat back in her seat, breathing heavily as she watched the blue airplane depart to their right, under Bizarro's west half, with its thrashing human burden. "You say it does this *every day*?" She asked Doug.

"At least, since I've been here. Two or three times a day. But at intervals. It won't be back again for say like four hours now it's carried someone off . . . meaning, it won't bother us. That's what's important." He put the car in gear and they rolled off.

She frowned at him. "You're not curious as to why it keeps catching people?"

He shook his head. "Curiosity's a dangerous virtue out here. Know what happened to a friend of mine who pulled open the front door of a house in the O two months ago? Fire blew out through the door and burnt him to a cinder." He nodded to himself. "As long as that damn plane stays there under Bizarro, I'm cool with not knowing who owns it and what it wants. Research model or not, let James Richards shovel his own shit."

Melanie didn't comment that she found this very shortsighted. Besides, in a way, Doug was clearly right.

"There's many questions nowadays to which the correct answer is death," Doug said in low voice that held some fear. He swerved the car around some potholes. They bumped past the abandoned Mary M. Lynch Elementary School, its desolate classroom windows crawling with glowing vines, and were in the O-Zone.

CHAPTER 10

Now that they'd entered Sixteen Acres, the bizarreness only hinted at in upper east Springfield was on more obvious display. They passed a row of houses that wobbled like Jell-O. One building was literally a ghost—it was there, but they could see through it. Another house seemed painted over the landscape in watercolors that still dripped. Melanie shuddered, not wanting to know what lay inside it, behind the screen door and the extensive porch with the antique cane rocking chair.

Here, several trees they passed—two dogwoods and clump of Japanese lilacs—had tentacles; in addition, mouth-like orifices gaped in the trunks of two massive oaks. The trees were a definite danger. Bizarro always fucked up vegetation—even the grass looked hairy down here. Oaks, especially gnarled old ones, were particularly susceptible to warping.

A clear sign also that they were now in the O was how they hardly passed any people anymore. The few they saw clung like living shadows to the perimeters of buildings. All ducked into hiding on sighting the blue Volvo. Melanie considered; Maybe the people *were* living shadows—several of those hastily concealing themselves trailed long cords of darkness that connected to the bases of trees.

Bizarro permitted everything, the stranger the better.

(The O sported no actual chunks of fallen Bizarro. The weird brown substance had been absorbed into the area's houses, ground, objects, flora and fauna . . . and its people. Everyone who'd lived there when the chunk of Bizarro had collapsed on them from the sky was certain to have gotten a dose of its weirdness. Some—Melanie's mind fluttered back to the Chameleon Sisters—much more than others. The gingers too, sounded like a textbook example of Bizarro transforming a diverse group of humans with a common mutation.

Strange fluorescent moss glowed on the walls. Several houses were covered with the radiant growths. A pack of two-headed dogs trotted happily along the sidewalk.

In an odd way, all looked normal enough.

But . . . appearances were supremely deceptive here. Stepping through the front door of any of these roadside residences could easily put one on the surface of another planet, or in the center of the sun, or worse still . . . in Hell.)

Once past Mary Lynch Elementary School, the road dipped south. Bizarro floated on their right, its edge almost perfectly tracing the North Branch Mill River. They reached the Moss Road intersection, at which point the concentration of houses increased. Now the buildings no longer seemed concrete astronauts in a universe of plants.

Melanie and Doug rode in silence, scanning each passing window (some of which continually altered shape as if alive) and rooftop for gingers. True, Melanie hadn't seen a ginger yet, but the description of them was bad enough. Few forms of death struck her as more horrid than being eaten alive. Ugh.

She grew bored. "So where the heck *are* the big, bad gingers?" she asked finally, to make conversation. "The bitches all scared of l'il old me?"

Doug said, "Don't joke like that. Pray we don't encounter any of them." He half-turned to look at her. "Which might just happen. This is a smart idea of yours. I mean—I can't understand why Uncle Biggs never though of doing this—entering the O around its perimeter."

She dismissed a glint from a cottage window as merely the sun dancing on glass before replying. "He clearly thought a straight drive down the road, guns blazing like it's the Wild West all over again, would be most effective."

"Bad plan that. For one thing, James lives in Patricia Circle. They had to practically drive past his front door to get to Vincent."

"Vincent?"

"Vincent Street. You remember the map? 1111 Parker Street is right at the intersection corner. Easier to head for that than to start counting house numbers."

(Melanie remembered: The first and third groups of men Bigelow had dispatched for the teddy bear had driven straight down Parker

Street. The second crew had detoured through Woodland Park, which lay east of Parker Street and James's residence. It was an utterly terrible idea; Melanie would have instantly advised against it had she been here then. The park's easternmost half lay directly under Bizarro, and what normally happened in such cases, was, fallen chunks of the brown weirdness mutated the plants into deadly forms. Even if the gingers hadn't eaten the gangsters, traveling through a Bizarro infected/affected woodland was suicidal enough.)

"Oh, yeah," she replied. "But really, their direct approach wasn't a bad plan, not if you're driving at speed, even with five warehouses to check out. You could be in and out like a flash, have come and gone like a premature ejaculation." She pursed her lips as they reached a crossing. "Rather, here in the O is simply a bad location. Anywhere else, your uncle's plan might have worked like a charm." She gestured through the windscreen at the approaching roadway. "But how do you plan for stuff like a herd of elephants suddenly appearing in the middle of the road, for instance, or the road itself becoming a lake? You can't foresee that."

"Yeah," Doug said. "The third team, the one with the sole survivor, were ambushed after wrapping their SUV around a huge statue of blues singer Taj Mahal that suddenly appeared in the middle of the road." He smirked. "The guy was delirious from blood loss. He said the Taj Mahal statue was singing *Willie and the Hand Jive*." Doug gave a humorless laugh and just managed to refrain himself from honking the Volvo's horn. "Yeah, this is a damn safer way to travel. No gingers and shit . . . ooh, yeah, we're just cruisin' through Hoop City, babe!"

They swung left onto Sunrise Terrace, turned right almost immediately onto Creswell Drive, a park/recreation area. Swings and a softball diamond on their left, bleachers and basketball courts on the right. Almost a plague of basketball courts . . .

"Now who's being overconfident?" Melanie asked. "Don't forget we're shortly turning inwards—"

"Yeah, but by then we'll be almost right beside the warehouses." He reached over and stroked her thigh. "Maybe we'll even be back home in time for dinner. I can feed you donuts again."

Despite her sense of urgency and her consciousness of danger just waiting to close its morbid jaws on them, an erotic thrill went through Melanie at his words. She found herself blushing. *Why*, she wondered, *does this coldblooded man affect me so? It's completely uncharacteristic of me to—*

Her train of thought was shattered by a loud banging noise from behind them. Gun held ready, she swiveled round, eyes peeled for the dreaded gingers.

There were none in sight. The space they rode through was as vacant as an airhead's mind.

The banging, however continued. It also seemed to be coming from inside the car, muffled like speakers playing hip-hip with all the treble off. Only thing was, Melanie didn't have subwoofers in her ride.

Could only be one thing then. She looked at Doug, who was regarding her back with a pained expression.

"The trunk," she said.

He winced. "We've got a fucking stowaway."

He parked the Volvo by a set of tree-shaded bleachers. They got out and walked back to open the car's trunk.

CHAPTER 11

Doug trained a riot shotgun on the car trunk while Melanie opened it.

Both stared down at Mary, Joe the bartender's daughter, who lay curled up like a shrimp in the cramped compartment.

Doug lowered his shotgun. "What the heck do you think you're doing?" he growled at the young woman as Melanie helped her out.

If anything, Mary looked worse today than yesterday. She was pale as chalk and covered in gooseflesh, her body trembling. In addition her eyes were as bloodshot as her father's, and she smelt like she'd recently puked over herself. Her dark hair looked like a scattered bird's nest.

"I-I-I . . ." she stuttered. "I-I-I-I . . ."

"Yes?" Doug muttered angrily. "I-I-I . . . what?"

"Leave her alone," Melanie snapped. "It's obvious she took our advice on getting away from her creep of a dad."

"But here? Now? And just look at her!"

"I-I-I-I d-d-don't f-f-feel too w-w-well," Mary stuttered. "F-feel so s-s-sick . . ."

"See what I mean!" Doug grumbled and stalked off.

"Hey—come back!" Melanie growled after him.

Doug stalked back to them. His face quivered with suppressed rage, his lips a thin taut line. He stood, shotgun butt resting on his foot, glaring at Mary, who now shivered pitifully, her body shaking like she had a fever, her arms needle-tracked like a junkie's.

Then, looking at Melanie, Doug sighed heavily. "I know I advised her to leave, but *this?*"

"She's already here," Melanie said flatly. "It's already happened—let it go. We now fix the current mess." She spared a glance for Mary, who now leaned on the Volvo's trunk, gasping at the floor.

"She's in no condition to accompany us," Doug pointed out. "If we meet trouble, she'll just be a hindrance to our escaping it." Frowning, he scanned the buildings around them, his grim gaze finally settling on a duplex behind the nearest basketball court. "Best we lock her in a room upstairs there; come back for her after we're—"

"N-no no no!" Mary interrupted fiercely, her bloodshot eyes bulging. "D-d-don't desert m-me! I'm . . . I-I'm leaving t-t-town with y-y-you!"

To Melanie, the girl looked like a drenched dog, misery personified. A feeling of intense compassion overcoming her, she walked over to Mary and hugged her close, stroking her pimply arms to calm her. While at the back of her mind she realized how dangerous this was, them being exposed out here in the open with unseen unreality all around, the girl's immense horror and her bravery to attempt an escape from her dire circumstances appealed to Melanie. But no, like it or not, they couldn't take her with them now. Doug's suggestion was the correct one; they'd best shut Mary away somewhere safe, collect her again on their return trip. While sure she'd later reprimand herself for doing so, with the way Mary currently looked, Melanie felt they had no other choice but to take her back home to her father. At least there was no way Joe would bleed her now. The man wasn't completely heartless, just very stupid.

"We're not leaving town yet," she said soothingly to the girl. "We'll be back for you. We'll take—"

"What the hell is wrong with her now?" Doug interrupted in a pissed-off tone.

Melanie shot him an angry look, before understanding what he meant. Mary had begun shaking violently, so much so that Melanie was forced to let go of her. She stepped back and regarded the girl, who now jerked back and began vibrating along the car's side like the metal vehicle was electrocuting her . . .

"Guys-s-s . . . I-I-I really d-d-don't feel good!" Her eyes stared wide and her teeth were chattering. Sweat dotted her forehead. She'd also developed a nosebleed, two dark red lines that painted her lips.

Then her ears began bleeding too.

Even Doug's cold face now showed grave concern. "What the . . . ?"

Melanie got over her surprise. "We'd better get her back home right now! I just hope we're not too late to save her."

Doug nodded. They hurried to grab Mary, then stopped, as, Mary, her mouth gaping open, her legs flexed like she was about leaping at them, her hands hooked into claws, froze like a statue. She held the pose for a moment, then went limp, slumping like she'd been whacked over the head with a ball-peen hammer.

"Fuck," Melanie hissed, quickly bending over the fallen girl to search for her pulse. "She's dead," she informed Doug a moment later.

Doug squatted beside Mary. He too examined her for vital signs. "Now what the hell do you make of this?" His mood wasn't flippant; he was disturbed, feeling her passing ominous.

They stood up, looked at each other. "No point taking her home again now," Doug said finally. "Let's just stick her back in the trunk; Joe's fault, not ours."

Melanie bit off a retort, choked back a sob, brushed away a forming tear. The girl's death hurt her a lot. "She looks like she's in Hell being tormented," she remarked of Mary's twisted face, with its expression of intense suffering.

Then they both became aware that the temperature had dropped.

"Why's it suddenly freezing?" Doug asked.

Struck by memory, Melanie looked quickly around the recreation area. "The Fixer's here," she whispered, pointing out to Doug the black-garbed figure approaching them from between two houses west of Creswell Drive.

Shivering in a chill that seemed directed right at them, their breath misting before their faces, they waited patiently for the Fixer to reach them.

The Fixer walked with measured steps. So seemingly calculated were they, Melanie imagined each pace he took to be exactly the same length. Now in daylight, he seemed a condensation of night, his form and cloak—even his suitcase—comprised of those hours when the moon ruled the Earth.

And the cold . . . was everywhere around the dark figure. (*Man, are you from frigging Alaska?* Doug wondered.) He walked toward them through a dim tunnel amidst the bright of day, the dimming otherwise extending several meters in all directions around his body.

He reached them, tipped his wide black hat at Melanie, nodded to Doug, then pointed down at Mary. "I was just passing by and sensed her distress. She's the same one from last night, isn't she?"

"You're too late," Melanie said glumly. "She's dead." Being this close to The Fixer disconcerted her. The man—she assumed The Fixer's gender from his creaking voice—had no face that she could see, just a mass of intersecting/bisecting gray planes that defied logical conception. Like a mass of blurred mirrors floating on an ocean surface.

Doug added: "We were about taking her home when she just upped and croaked on us. Never seen anything like it."

"It is not yet too late," The Fixer said, his cloak swirling around him. "Though it would have been much better if she'd not yet died, her spirit hasn't departed for Hades yet. It still hovers near." He put down his suitcase, lengthening his arm downward to do so.

Melanie and Doug now saw that the black case lacked both latches and a seam showing where it opened. It looked (and indented the ground) like it was carved from solid stone.

The Fixer knelt beside Mary, placing his gloved fingers on her forehead for a few seconds. He looked up at his two companions. "Move back out of the dimness. It's about to get even colder."

The pair backed away from him—about six meters—till they felt warmer, then instantly felt the temperature around them drop yet again. Simultaneously, the space around The Fixer dimmed further. In curiosity, Melanie stuck fingers into the dim air. It felt like putting her hand in a freezer.

"Who are you?" she asked the black figure as he began unbuttoning Mary's top.

"Not now; there'll be time enough for answers later." With Mary's top open, revealing her bare white torso, The Fixer pointed his right index finger down at her body. Melanie and Doug stiffened when the finger elongated and flattened into a shiny silver blade.

The Fixer dipped the blade down into Mary's skin and began cutting. Like he was autopsying her, he cut a y-section into her flesh. Then he yanked apart Mary's ribs and began pulling out her lungs. There was no spillage of blood, the cold having seemingly frozen it inside her.

"This is fucked-up," Doug whispered to Melanie.

She nodded back and kept looking.

The Fixer cut Mary's lungs out of her and dropped them into his suitcase. He didn't open it up—he just placed them on top of it and they sunk down out of sight into its black substance.

"Now, I've seen fucking everything," Doug said.

Melanie said, "Somehow I don't think that's true yet." A horror at what she was witnessing gripped her and she in turn gripped Doug's hand tight, relieved that he didn't shrug her off. They both stood there, breath misting before them, and watched. Around The Fixer, the ground was now caked hard with white ice.

Next, The Fixer cut out Mary's heart and similarly disposed of it into the ebon suitcase. Then he excavated her body of her stomach, liver, kidneys and guts. Shortly, Mary's entire torso was empty as a canoe. Her horrible death grimace seemed pathetically ironic now, almost like she'd died of being excavated, rather than from blood-loss fever or from an unsterilized-needle infection.

Now, Melanie felt impelled to question him. "What are you going to fill her with?"

The dark mortician said nothing. Almost as response, however, he stuck his hand 'into' the black suitcase (as if the solid mass was in fact a black hole) and pulled something out of it.

"What . . . the hell is that?" Melanie whispered.

"You were right, babe," Doug whispered back. "I hadn't seen everything yet."

What The Fixer gripped in his hand looked like two black footballs placed end-to-end. Or a black barbell with oblong weights. It had the same dull glint as his suitcase.

Doug squinted to see better. "That's some kind of machine. It's a mass of gears and cogs . . ."

"Wires too . . ."

Before they could fully make out the workings of the strange machine, The Fixer stuffed it inside Mary's body. Then he began smoothing it out inside her like it was a paste or black cake icing. They watched strange mechanical components flow like water and take up arrangements inside the dead girl.

Braving the Arctic freeze surrounding The Fixer, Melanie and Doug crossed the ice to peer inside Mary. Both just had to view the end of this up close. Once beside the dark figure, the cold felt like knives stabbing their lungs.

"It's like clockwork," Melanie said of the gears now whirring inside Mary, the interior of whose torso now looked like someone had spilled black paint over the guts of a grandfather clock. "You've making a clockwork woman of her?"

Doug said nothing, just stared bemused at the refilled corpse.

The Fixer paused in his work, spared Melanie a fractal gaze. "No one will be able to tell the difference. Not even she."

After a last stirring of the clockwork wheels in Mary's innards, he shut her ribcage again, then ran cold fingers down the front of her body, seamlessly sealing flesh and skin back together. "Like I said, no one will be able to tell the difference."

He rose to his feet, black boots noisily crunching the ice. The temperature around them all instantly dropped from cold-hellish to merely winter. Suddenly it was easier to breathe. Standing there freezing beneath the midday sun, Melanie swallowed several gulps of air.

Doug said, "Man, she's still dead."

The Fixer reached inside his black cloak and produced a black key. "You need to wind her up."

Melanie's eyes widened. She looked down at Mary, the corpse bare-breasted since The Fixer hadn't seen fit to do up her top again. "Did you say: *Wind* her up?"

The barest dipping of The Fixer's expansive hat signified a nod. "There are currently sockets in both her ears. Now remember these instructions: She needs twenty-four turns a day—one for each hour. You can also wind her up in advance to a three-day limit, seventy-two turns is the maximum her springs will stand. Remember that—never screw her more than seventy-two times at once."

"Thrice at once is well enough for me," Doug said.

Melanie almost smiled at that. She accepted the black key from The Fixer, regarded it carefully. Its metal seemed cold as The Fixer himself.

"You had some questions for me?" the creaking voice asked.

"Who are you?" Doug asked in return.

A dark laugh. The Fixer pointed out across the flanking basketball courts, past the houses on Bellwood and Bellamy Roads, up over the stone buildings of West New England University, at Bizarro's brown mass. "I am one of the creatures Bizarro foisted on your world." His voice held a sardonic, somewhat sad note.

"But you came into town last night," Doug protested. "O-Zone creatures can't leave—"

"Not the O," Melanie corrected. "He said Bizarro." She looked at The Fixer's impossibly faceted 'face.' You're saying that you're like the eaters and vavs, right?"

"No. I arrived here via a breach in your realm's structural integrity. I am initially from—"

Then, with a start, he looked up into the western sky and made the sound of taking a deep breath (this was their interpretation of the noise—his non-face made accuracy impossible). Next he growled: "Blast—it is back again!"

Melanie and Doug followed The Fixer's gray gaze. Like a toy suspended from a ceiling, the experimental blue aircraft hung beneath Bizarro about three hundred meters from them.

"The plane?" Melanie said. "What's it to you?"

The Fixer turned from regarding the blue aircraft. "I must catch that plane," he said in a hurried voice, picking up his suitcase. He reset his hat so it again shadowed his face. "Excuse me; I must go now. It does not seem to have noticed me. Maybe this time I'll be successful—"

"Are you responsible for it abducting people?" Doug asked.

"What do want with it?" Melanie insisted.

The Fixer sighed, sounding like fracturing ice. "I have a situation to fix aboard it," he replied them. "Something dire." (As he spoke, Melanie imagined she heard a deep longing for something—it felt like homesickness—in his voice.) He pointed a gloved finger at Mary. "Take good care of her . . ."

"Hey, wait! Don't you need to be around to explain to her?"

But the black-cloaked figure was already striding away from them across one of the basketball courts, pulling his zone of freezing air behind him like a train drew its carriages. Words floated back to them: "It doesn't matter. She won't notice anything."

"Not even when we stick a key in her ear?"

"It doesn't matter . . ."

The Fixer had suddenly picked up great speed, like each step he took covered ten meters though he remained exactly the same size. While seeming to move even faster, he disappeared between two houses.

Doug looked up. "Is it my imagination, or does the plane actually seem to be fleeing from him?"

Melanie looked up also. "Yeah, it is flying away." She shrugged. "None of our business. She pointed down at Mary. "Let's just get her up and running again."

CHAPTER 12

They looked at the bartender's dead daughter, whose mouth still gaped open. Her brown nipples looked like buttons sewn onto her small breasts.

Melanie bent and stuck the key in the girl's left ear. It clicked into place and held firm. She turned it once. It rolled easily, silently, so she spun it several times more.

"She's started breathing again," Doug said in a nervous voice.

Melanie spun the key five more times. She straightened up, leaving the key in Mary's ear. "That should do it."

Mary's face lost its tortured expression, then the brunette opened her eyes. "W-w-what am I d-d-doing on the ground?" With a gasp, she realized her top was unbuttoned and hastily pulled it closed over her breasts. "W-w-what have you been d-doing to m-m-me?"

"Take it easy," Melanie said. "You fainted."

Mary quickly did up her buttons and stood up. "I-I-I d-d-don't un-un-understand . . ." Her voice stabilized. "Okay, so I fainted. Why'd you strip me?"

Doug sighed, stared west after the departed Fixer. Like he'd been correct in his suspicion that it had been fleeing the dark-garbed man, the blue airplane was now gone.

Melanie said gently, "It's okay—we didn't molest you or anything." She now wished they'd had the foresight to do up the girl's top first. *But . . . but surely she should sense a difference in herself; can't she even feel the key—cold metal—in her ear?* "Girl, thank God you're okay; we thought you were dead."

"I felt dead. Only . . ." eyes dreamy, she stared through them, "only . . . it wasn't like you'd imagine. I was in this very cold place and this man . . . no it wasn't a man—he had no face, just . . . anyway, he told me I couldn't go yet, that I had to return to my dad . . ."

Mary's face broke down into its usual harried expression. She began trembling. "Shit! Dad! I ran away from home; I'm a slut like mom! Oh, no!"

Melanie gaped.

"I'm a total airhead!" Mary yelped. "Shit, how could I be so dumb!"

Melanie rolled her eyes.

Then Mary began weeping. "Oh, no, I'm a slut. Oh, daddy . . . daddy . . . I'm so sorry." She glowered at Melanie. "This is what my dad meant! Already I feel corrupted." She inspected her pallid arms, then began scratching them. "Oh, shit! I'm dirty, dirty . . . can't you see?"

Melanie nodded in disbelief, then quickly dragged Doug away from the car for a conference.

"Maybe we should have left her dead," she whispered. "I've never seen such a horrible case of Posttraumatic Stress Disorder before in my life."

"She's incurable," Doug whispered back. "Can I just blow her brains out?"

Melanie looked at him coldly. "Don't you dare."

His replying gaze was equally grim. "The Fixer fixed everything but her mind. She's fucking cuckoo." He jerked a thumb at Mary. "Just *look* at her. She's miles worse than before."

Melanie could hardly disagree. The reanimated girl was yanking at her hair and moaning: "Oh, daddy—I'm sorry I left!" She shrugged at Joe. "Cut her some slack—you'd be that screwed-up too if Joe was your dad."

"Okay, okay—you make a good point. But that doesn't alter the fact that her revival currently looks to be even more of a problem for us than her death was. I mean, what the heck do we do now? The longer we're out here in the open the more likely it is we get discovered by the damn gingers or something even hungrier. And all the noise she's making isn't helping one bit." He winced at a burst of Mary's sobbing. "Okay, I'll just knock her out; we'll stuff her in the trunk and carry on."

He made to move back towards the car. Melanie held him back with firm fingers on his bicep. "Don't be so violent; she's likely had enough of that shit already in her life. Also, try to remember all those clockwork bits inside her. She's half machine now—hit her on the head and she might blow up on us. And The Fixer's nowhere in sight to put her back together again." She wondered how Mary still hadn't yet noticed that there was a metal key sticking out of her left ear. *Girl, don't you feel even the slightest oddity about yourself?* It was uncanny, but The Fixer had been right—Mary *was* behaving exactly the same as before.

"So what *do* we do with her?" Doug was speaking between grit teeth, his face strained. "If she continues like this, I'll—"

"We'll take her back home," Melanie said sweetly.

"What?"

Melanie shrugged. "We've no other choice. She's too fucked in the head to take along with us, and too fucked-up to leave here, either. We lock her in anywhere, she'll be out in a minute and heading back home anyway."

"We're wasting time."

"We'll come back tomorrow."

"If you'd just let me knock her out . . ."

"No. That's final."

"But the way she keeps gibbering like an ape . . . It's getting on my fucking nerves!"

"Mine too. She'll calm down once we inform her she's going home; you'll see. Come on."

They walked back to Mary, who was staring intently at several strands of brown hair pulled from her head and mumbling incoherently. She looked up at their approach, her eyes wild like she was high on drugs. The key poking from her ear glittered like jewelry. "So this is what a slut's hair looks like? Dirty matted locks like a rat's ass—"

"That's your normal hair, you little fool," Doug spat.

Mary nodded at him. "Of course it is. That's because I left home and now I'm a piece of shit!"

"Hell! I don't believe this!"

Melanie hid her irritation with both of them. "Get in the car," she told Mary. "We're taking you home."

The girl regarded them both with deep suspicion. "For real? You're not going to kidnap me? Steal me out of town?"

"For real," Doug said with deadly restraint. "Just plump your ass in the back seat."

After one last look to ensure they weren't lying to her, Mary got in the Volvo.

Heaving joint sighs of relief, Doug and Melanie got in too.

CHAPTER 13

While Doug drove them back up through the O, Melanie, turning in her seat to look back, attempted talking to Mary. The girl's fragile nervous state nauseated Melanie; Mary was quivering like a junkie on cold turkey and her eyes were manic.

"I just want to be back home," she said. "I was wrong to ever leave. Dad was so right; I was so wrong. You run away and look what happens. I've been a bad girl, a very bad girl. I deserve to be punished, beaten, whipped."

At that moment, Melanie, hearing the girl's plaintive words, spoken with all the pathetic conviction of an asylum inmate, would have murdered Joe on the spot if he'd been there. She hoped she'd be able to restrain herself when she actually saw the man face-to-face again.

"Does Joe beat you?" she asked Mary.

"Nah, he doesn't," Doug retorted, driving past the North Brook Road intersection, "she's just screwy." Then seeing the cold glare Melanie gave him: "Okay, you don't believe me?"

"Dad doesn't beat me," Mary confirmed sadly from the back seat. "He just tells me I deserve to be beaten. I never agreed before, but I do now. I mean, if he'd beaten me I'd never have become a slut."

"Now, now," Melanie said compassionately as Doug drove on. "Your dad's simply old-fashioned, not to mention cruel, to say that to you. Besides, being a slut's no longer a big deal. We reclaimed the S-word in the nineties. Now, liberated women all over the world—"

"Since running away from home I feel like a piece of garbage. Like the only use I can be now is to put myself at the disposal of male pigs who root through such garbage." She drew in a long breath. Melanie thought she heard gears whirring in the girl's chest at the action. "Since running away," Mary continued, "I—"

"That's another thing," Melanie fumed, praying they reach the *WTF?* soon so she could wring Joe's neck. This was uber-pathetic. "You didn't run away. You're twenty-two, old enough to make your own decisions about where you want to live. You left home of your own free will."

"You're old enough to go—you did so," Doug added. "I really wish you'd get that through your head."

Mary stared defiantly at Melanie. "You two just don't understand. It's not like that at all . . ." then her eyes widened at something ahead and she screamed.

Melanie instantly spun around to stare out the windscreen. The car jolted as something white and orange crashed down on its hood, then another similar something.

Melanie realized the things hitting the car were people.

"Shit! Gingers!" Doug yelled. "Now we're really in for it! Hold on!"

More of the dropping people landed on the Volvo, both on its hood and roof, which dented inwards from the force of their impact. The gingers first seemed to be jumping down from the roof of the apartment building Doug was driving past, then from the row of sycamores that flanked it.

"I can't see the fucking road!" Doug yelled as the concentration of white bodies on the hood increased.

"We're gonna be fucking eaten!" Mary screamed maniacally from the back seat. "I should never have left home! I'm being punished for my sins!"

"Shut the fuck up!" Doug yelled back at her.

"We're all gonna fucking die!"

"Fucking shut up before I fucking shoot you!" There was no chance of him carrying out his threat: all his attention was fixed on trying to see through the many legs and faces (of gingers looking hungrily in at them) barring his vision before he totaled the Volvo.

"Oh, my God! They're gonna eat me!" Mary screamed and began sobbing.

The only partially calm person in the blue Volvo as it caromed left-to-right across the road was Melanie, who'd instantly dropped her shotgun and pulled her pistol when the crisis began.

(Melanie's first view of the gingers [as they pressed against the windshield despite Doug's best attempts to dislodge them] was a harrowing one. [She was also surprised by their incredible sense of balance—like that of cats.] Bigelow *had* mentioned the gingers' bleached-white skin, and their orange hair and eyes. He'd left out mention of the fact that their hands and feet ended in claws, and . . . of the size of their jaws. The gingers' jaws were massive, seemingly too large for their heads. Open as they were now, slobbering at the three in the car and licking the windshield with their tongues, some of their mouths hung open to below their necks, their chins resting on their chests. And their teeth . . . huge yellow fangs like those of sabertooth cats . . .)

Other gingers had landed on the trunk and were peering in the back window. Those gingers on the roof were grabbing inside at the three humans.

"Oh, God, please help us!" Mary screamed, then began blabbering incoherently.

"Roll up your goddamn window!" Melanie shouted back at her. "Stop being such a wimpette crybaby!" She wasn't judging the girl; she felt cold with fear herself, like she'd piss herself in a jiffy. She realized she needed to clear away the gingers thronging the hood; at the moment it was only by some sort of miracle that they'd not crashed into a fire hydrant or streetlight as Doug rode up and down curbs, using shadows as markers. (She'd not even realized when he'd spun off North Branch Parkway; had no idea where the hell they currently were.)

The gingers had ceased dropping on the Volvo, but it was heavy with them now, its roof practically caving in on its occupants. Doug drove with one hand; with the other he beat off attempts to yank him out of the car.

Mel pointed her gun at a ginger man licking the windshield and pulled the trigger. A cobweb crack appeared in the glass and his head exploded. The mutant slumped forward, coating the windshield with gore, some of which dripped through the bullet hole into the car.

The other gingers trampled the dead man, inadvertently smearing the windshield with his blood and obscuring vision further.

The car hit a bump and lifted off the ground. Mary shrieked loudly.

The car crashed down again. Mary shrieked louder. "Oh, God, I'm so, so sorry for becoming a slut! I promise I'll never masturbate with a carrot again!"

"Keep your mouth as shut as your pussy!" Melanie snapped at her.

"Damn!" Doug yelled as their ride grew steadily bumpier. "I can't fucking see where were going anymore!"

"Keep driving anyway!" Melanie shouted back. She swung her pistol at the gingers in front of the driver's seat and fired twice. This time the results were better. The shots blew both gingers off the hood and into the road, clearing the windshield for Doug.

A hastily snatched glance revealed them to be streaking past 15 Sparrow Drive.

She aimed again, pulled the trigger. The ginger she hit had been holding on to another nearer her for support. As he dropped off the Volvo, he dragged that man sideways across the hood. To check his own fall, this second man desperately grabbed at the legs of two gingers on the car roof, dislodging them so they fell forward over the windshield.

For a moment, the world ahead vanished. Then . . .

The car went up over the curb again. Then down again. Then . . .

The mutant pileup cleared slightly. Doug swerved just in time to avoid a huge pine tree standing in the middle of the road, then they went up an unseen incline and found themselves upside-down in the middle of the air.

Melanie had a surreal moment of watching the cannibal mutants fall off the upside-down Volvo's hood like white/orange raindrops, then the car was the right way up again (though with its two left wheels off the ground), completely out of control, and skidding toward a parked yellow school bus.

Too fucking late for seatbelts now, Melanie thought. *I just hope Mary's not really pissed-off the Almighty with all her moaning at him and he's decided to cash in our chips early.*

The Volvo's left-side tires gained purchase with the road seconds before they hit. Doug twisted the wheel hard right, preventing a head-on collision, but that was all he could do. The car's left side smashed hard into the bus.

CHAPTER 14

Melanie sat stunned for a moment, fighting to get her breath back. The beat of her heart pounding in her ears like a quartet of African drummers. All around her was silence, like the world had ended. The impact had first thrown her left against Doug (and the side airbags), then back across the car, so that she was now pressed against the front passenger door, with Doug half lying on her. She was aware of him breathing heavily beside her, their gasps for air almost in sync. Mary, for once, was quiet behind them.

Melanie checked herself for torn flesh and broken bones, wheezing in relief on finding none. Other than for a bump on her forehead, she was fine. She began wondering if the others were also okay.

Then she heard loud yelling and screaming coming towards them. She roused herself, looked out of the window. Her vision was fuzzy; she realized why: the crash had knocked her glasses off her nose onto her breasts. She found and replaced them. Looked again. Almost wished she'd left her glasses off.

"Shit, the cannibals!"

At her voice, Doug roused himself from pressing on her and sat up. Together, both peered out at the horde of gingers charging them from about three hundred meters away.

"We need to get out of here extremely fast," Melanie said.

"Can you get your door open?" Doug asked grimly. "Or are we climbing out the window?" Doug's face was white with fear. Melanie was sure she looked just as scared. She was relieved that he seemed unharmed.

She tried the door; it opened easily. Her shotgun was stuck between the front seats. She forgot it, grabbed her pistol off the floor where it had fallen, and leapt out. While Doug scrambled across the seats after her, she opened the rear door to let Mary out also.

Melanie frowned. Mary was out cold. She lay limp on the seat, her amber eyes glassy. The black key in her ear stood up like a flagstaff.

The gingers were about a hundred meters off now and closing fast. They'd slowed their charge to a jog, however; possibly because their quarry was armed. Signaling quickly to Doug to help her get Mary out of the car, Melanie wondered where so many gingers had come from so fast. The road was packed full of them now.

She and Doug desperately tried to pull Mary off the back seat. It was useless; the collision had warped the seat forward over her leg. The limb wasn't broken, just locked in place. Without Mary conscious and helping them maneuver her body, there was no way to free her.

Melanie cast a frightened glance at Doug. "We'll have to leave her behind."

"Shit. And to think she's the reason we were going back . . ."

"I don't like this any more than you do. It's a good thing she's unconscious, else she'd be screaming Heaven down on Earth."

"They're almost here, let's friggin' go!"

They fled just as the gingers reached the Volvo, charging down the road. Kathleen Street, a sign read.

Melanie looked back once. Through the mob of orange-haired people pursuing them, she glimpsed several at the car door, yanking at Mary. Closer to home in the foreground, their pursuers had wide saber-toothed grins on their faces.

Her fear redoubled, she raced after Doug as hard as she could.

Then, cold calculation broke through Melanie's instinctive terror. She found hope in a memory from past experience. *Hey, this is the fucking O-Zone, ain't it?* Suddenly inspired, she began examining each house they approached.

Not this one, not this one, not . . . where the hell is this damn thing? There has to be one around here somewhere!

A hand clutched at her, she shrugged it off, felt claws rip open the back of her jacket. Behind her the gingers laughed as they pursued. Ahead of her, Doug was a fleeing mass of male terror. She herself was terrified, praying she'd find what she sought.

Then, just when she thought her chest would burst from the exertion of keeping ahead of the pursuing cannibals, she found the symbol she sought—a blue upright human palm between upright parallel lines. The image flickered briefly against the wall of an abandoned grocery store up ahead, then was gone. To Melanie's relief, the store door was open.

"Quick—in here!" she yelled at Doug, dashing past him and into the store. He followed her, slammed the door shut, bolted it fast. The first gingers arrived at the door and began banging on it.

Hell, if I survive this, I really need to get more exercise, Melanie thought while wheezing painfully.

"This wasn't as smart as it first seemed," Doug panted, his eyes wide with fear. "They'll find a way in soon . . ." He pointed to the metal grill protecting the display window, where two topless female gingers, long orange hair draped over their naked breasts, stared hungrily in at them. "Or just melt through it with a torch."

"There's a way out inside here," Melanie said. "We need to search for a symbol—a hand between two upright lines."

"What does it do?"

"Just look for it. Trust me—once we find it I won't need to explain."

Doug looked instead out the display window again. It now thronged with gingers. Fat, thin, tall, small, female and male, kids and the aged, every variation of the corrupted human form. The single unifying factor? The unrelenting hunger in their fiery eyes.

One of the two topless ginger women—tall and with a good figure—hiked up her denim skirt, stuck fingers into her bared vagina, and masturbated at Doug, rolling her eyes and moaning while her tongue licked the window through the grill. With her free hand she brushed her orange hair off her right breast and pinched its nipple hard so it visibly stiffened. Doug gaped in horrified fascination.

The other gingers, realizing what was happening, laughed at Doug and pointed. "We're coming to eat you, asshole," a fat man in a well-cut suit mouthed at him. The masturbating lady fingered herself faster and harder, glistening sexual juice dripping down her bone-white thighs.

Angry, Melanie pulled the entranced Doug away from the erotic display. "What is it with you guys and pussy, anyway? We're about being eaten alive and you're watching a stripper? And . . . it's a distraction anyway." She pointed beyond/above the front row of mutants. Two gingers were climbing on the shoulders of the others up to the first floor balcony. "If they find a way inside upstairs before we find our way out—"

Two gunshots rang out. The bullets thudded into a Bon Jovi poster by the condom rack to Doug's right, eliminating Richie Sambora's head. Plaster rained back on them.

Doug swung his pistol at the gingers. Melanie knocked his hand down. "Don't—we haven't enough ammo. Save it for when we need it. Let's just get away from here." She leapt back as another burst of gunfire exploded the cash register. "Fucking go! I'll take left, you go right—keep your eyes peeled for the symbol. It could be anywhere."

Ducking gunfire that blew cans off the aisle shelves while they searched, the pair looked everywhere for the symbol.

Doug finally found it inside the toilet. Two flickering blue lines and a blue hand between them on the wall over the toilet paper dispenser.

"We're safe now," Melanie said. "From those freaks at least."

"What does it do?"

"Watch." She placed her right hand flat on the symbol hand. For a moment, her hand glowed blue, then a door opened inwards into the wall. Beyond the door extended a wide plain dotted with sheep.

Doug stared speechless into the impossible space.

Melanie nudged him. "Come with me back into the store. If the gingers haven't broken in yet, let's get some food."

A minute later, they were back in the toilet with a shopping bag containing canned peaches and bottled water. Outside the store, worryingly, the gingers now had an oxyacetylene torch set up and were melting away the grill.

The door in the wall had since shut. Melanie opened it again. They stepped through.

Once inside on the plain, Melanie closed the door (which now floated in midair). This side of it also possessed the same symbol as the other. Here, however, she pushed firmly on the symbol till she heard a soft click. On removing her hand from the door, the hand-between-lines glowed red instead of blue. That meant it was locked— no one could follow them in here—the symbol on the entrance's other side would be missing till they exited.

She turned to face Doug. "Welcome to the parallands," she said; adding before he could ask: "Parallel universes that exist at right angles to ours, in at least one of which anything is possible."

He nodded. A pitch-black sheep was walking past them. It had 'Vote For Bill Clinton' painted on its side in white.

CHAPTER 15

They walked awhile, their entrance point dwindling behind them to a glowing white rectangle.

Aside from a distant flesh-toned monument that they decided to avoid, the primary oddity about this place was the sheep. All of which were painted with political slogans from the 1992 US presidential elections. A good number of the sheep had colored photographs of the candidates somehow printed into their fur. Several of the animals even had loudspeaker grills in their rumps from which blared pop versions of *The Star-Spangled Banner*.

The adrenalin rush of their flight over, Melanie was now filled with immense relief. She was however exhausted. Her heavy hips felt leaden, her large breasts like weights she was lugging around. *Yes, I damn do need to put in more time at the gym! I feel like I've just run the Boston Marathon!*

Her thoughts turned melancholy. *And we didn't . . . couldn't . . . save Mary.* With an effort, she shook off her grief over the girl's certain violent death—Mary had been unconscious, no way was she escaping the gingers.

Doug seemed to read her glum thoughts. "Mary's really just a machine now, anyway," he said. "It's unlikely she'll feel any pain when they kill her."

Melanie looked at him. His handsome face was again impassive. His comment, however, lifted her mood somewhat. "Even so, it's a hell of a way to die."

Doug grunted. "Yeah, really horrible. But . . . she's already died once today; how many times can you mourn the same person?"

Melanie had no answer to that question. Callous as it sounded, it made sense. Still, possibly because of the girl's miserable life with Joe, she felt a deep sense of loss at Mary's passing.

She gestured around them at the plain, changed the topic. "We'll look for another door around here to exit through," she said. "For all their apparent extent—and some seem to be the size of countries— the parallands are localized, locked to each O-Zone. There could be anything up to a hundred of them connected to this one, but they all open into the same general area, unlike the ODs, which can put you on the surface of a planet in Alpha Centauri, or even back in the Stone Age, if you aren't careful."

Doug nodded grimly, carefully digesting Melanie's lecture on how they'd just stepped through a space-time door into a part of Bizarro. "I thought Bizarro was just the mass floating over the city? Are we now *inside* it?"

"I honestly don't know," she replied, her pretty face serious. "From my understanding, Bizarro is many absurd places in many insane times, as well as being the illogic of their existence." Behind her glasses, her blue eyes scanned the distance.

They shooed away two sheep sporting grinning pictures of George W. Bush Sr. from beneath a hackberry tree and sat. Opened their cans of Del Monte Sliced Peaches with a knife and ate; drank their Poland Spring water.

They watched bemused, as a heavily wooled sheep whose ass-speakers blared out Jimi Hendrix's 1969 Woodstock interpretation of *The Star-Spangled Banner* pilfered then ate the plastic bag they'd carried their food and drink in. Still chewing the bag, the sheep strode off, virtuoso guitar notes pumping from its backside like it was farting.

A short distance in front of them, a ram with a 'Perot for President' banner was humping an ewe emblazoned with Dan Quayle's photograph. Watching the animals copulate, Melanie grew aroused herself.

She dipped her hand into Doug's lap, fondled his penis through his pants. She felt a vague twitch of response from his penile meat.

She winked at him. "How about one for the road?"

Doug groaned. "Not if we're leaving here soon. I'm so bushed from running that I could—"

A black sheep roughly brushed past Doug. Instead of a political slogan, this one bore the symbol of two blue parallel lines and a hand imprinted in its ebon wool.

Melanie instinctively leaned forward and placed her hand on the symbol in the sheep's flank, pressing down on the softness.

The black sheep instantly froze. A moment later, it transformed into an upright metal door. Behind the door, the two copulating sheep humped disinterestedly.

"Imagine that," Melanie said. "A mobile one."

She and Doug peered through the door into an unfamiliar room now lit up by the paralland's light. It was small, with cream walls, a shuttered window, two office chairs and a computer on a dusty desk.

Doug asked, "Any idea where it leads?"

"It isn't where we entered," Melanie replied. "Meaning the gingers won't be waiting for us." She winked saucily at him—suddenly she felt *really* horny. "Do we have time before we go?"

Doug shook his head regretfully. "You should just have left the damn sheep alone. Now business calls—we rain check the fuck."

Melanie recalled her similar comment to the Chameleon woman, Lois Smith. "Seems like there's a lot of that going around lately," she wryly remarked.

After a cursory glance at their discarded food and drink containers, and a further peek out across the sheep-dotted grassland, she staggered to her feet.

She pulled Doug up after her. Pushed him through the door in the air. Followed.

It closed behind them; they stood in darkness. Together, they watched the blue paralland symbol float left across the wall, bounce off the corner angle, then float back right to the opposite corner, where it repeated the process.

"Come on," Melanie said, crossing to where she'd noticed a light switch. "Let's find out where we are now."

CHAPTER 16

Thankfully, the lights worked.

They were in the Webster Bank on Nassau Drive. Desk stationary confirmed this.

They'd emerged in a secretary's office. The adjoining office was much larger, with thick brown carpets, a red sofa, and French windows flanking its massive pinewood desk. Behind the desk hung a large map of the USA.

Pulling back the drapes from the French windows confirmed two things: Firstly, that they were on the building's fifth floor, and secondly, that it was now nighttime.

"Damn!" Doug exclaimed, walking out onto the balcony. "We weren't in that paralland place for more than thirty minutes. It was just after two when we—"

"I hate space-time transitions too," Melanie said. "Don't stress out over it."

Leaning on the balcony railings, she looked round at the nighttime O-Zone. Half the houses were darker than The Fixer's suitcase. She had no idea if people lived in the lit buildings or if their departed residents had simply neglected to turn the power off when moving uptown. Whichever it was, she and Doug's suddenly turning on the bank's lights shouldn't call unwanted attention.

She peered up. The moon hung to their left—a celestial chandelier. It looked more healthy that the sun had. Across from them, over shadowlike rooftops, Bizarro's brown mass hovered like an immense bird of prey.

Despite the broody night, she felt confident, thrilled by the danger now it was past. The need to feel alive, to feel her blood pumping hard through her arteries was part of the reason she did these kind of jobs. Sometimes, the adventure that accompanied a job was a sweeter reward than the money it earned her.

Well, we survived today. Tomorrow? We'll see.

Doug had left her musing at the railing and reentered the office. Now he returned. "There's a working clock on the table," he said. "It's now a quarter past ten."

Melanie took a moment to reset her watch. "This address is 256 Nassau Drive. Where are we relative to where we need to be?"

He drew close to her, put a strong arm around her waist. "We're on the other side of Parker Street now, same side as the bar . . . and a bit further north, so rather than heading back up, we need to head down."

"How far down?"

His hand moved down to stroke her heavy buttocks, making her shiver. "A half-mile south. Barring us running into more gingers, about thirty minutes walk in the morning."

His hand kept stroking her ass, kneading her cheeks like dough. Her sex, already tingly warm from her previous arousal, quickly grew wet. The belated thrills of the day's terrors mingled with erotic sensation. Her knees felt weak; her body, though tired, clamored for the satiation of penetration—him deep inside her.

"You're distracting me, Doug," she said as her heart began beating faster. "Not now, please. We really need to plan our—"

He spun her to face him, whispered throatily in her ear: "I think it's time we cashed our bedroom rain check."

She nodded in the dark, her face flushed, the passion suddenly strong as a lioness in her. She shed her pretense of disinterest. "Yes. Let's do that. We'll plan tomorrow."

She pushed him ahead of her into the office and drew shut the drapes.

Both of them were hot and in the mood. They stripped off quickly.

Stepping out of his underpants while Melanie, already nude, removed her glasses, Doug asked, "Is it true what they say about veggie girls?"

She paused, looked at him curiously. "What do they say?"

He grinned. "That you always have a cucumber available."

"Wha . . . ?" Without warning, she hurled her glasses at him. Laughing, he ducked.

The eyewear smashed against the wall.

Doug looked at her in shock.

"It's okay," she giggled. "The lens are plastic—they won't break." Not bothering to retrieve the fallen glasses, she heaved herself up onto the massive desk and crooked a finger at him. "Come on and lick me, and if you dare make any more cucumber jokes, I'll bite your dick off." She positioned herself comfortably, jerking her heels up onto the edge of the desk. Doug now noticed an octopus-shaped birthmark on her right foot.

Staring him dead in the eye, Melanie stroked her vagina amidst its sleek black fur. "Don't waste time—you know you *need* this pussy, baby."

He walked across to her slowly, stroking his erection while savoring the sight of her. The milk-white legs, now spread before him in invitation, between them the large-lipped vagina; the clitoral hood hanging down almost like a cowl over the vaginal vault; beneath it, the tight brown anus; and her thighs themselves, massive expanses lined with the faintest of veining. He looked up at her huge breasts, their nipples hard, inviting him to suck on them; then further up to her lovely face, now flushed with her intense desire for him, her lips parted with her tongue playing over her teeth; her eyes—those wondrous blue depths—calling on him to give her pleasure, to flood her body with delicious sensation.

He bent between her legs, and like a supplicant worshipping a goddess, proceeded to lick her vagina, the instant trembling of her thighs and copious flooding of her sex with moisture the sign that his offering of love was acceptable to her.

He laved the swollen vulva, sucked each labial lip, licked the clitoral hood softly and delicately. He stroked her creamy thighs, loving the silky feel of her taut white flesh against his palm.

"Oooh, suck me," she groaned.

He obliged, pushing the extensive hood back with fingers to uncover the sweet bud of pleasure; over this he wrapped his lips and sucked hard.

"Harder," she encouraged him. "Finger me."

He slid his middle and ring fingers deep into the juicy cunt and stroked her insides while licking, licking, licking out her delicious female nectar . . . pollinating his tongue, throat and belly with it . . . he bathed in her sweet sexuality like it was bubble bath.

Melanie shivered as he licked her. The feel of his tongue . . . of his fingers inside her sex, stroking her smoothly . . . In a mental attic she remembered Doug Fisher was a very dangerous man, but at the moment that didn't matter one bit . . . This, the pleasure of him eating her just right, was what did . . .

Her worries blanked out. She came, her body stiffening, her thighs clamping against his head and fingers. She wasn't squirting but it felt like she was—like her whole body was becoming liquid and ejaculating out of her vagina. She grabbed his head and held on tight like she'd fall into an abyss if she let go.

Her legs swung apart again, freeing his head. Doug licked and fingered her on. He didn't dare touch himself now. He knew that if he did, he'd instantly ejaculate. The day's stress twitched in his muscles, his come boiled like stew in his testicles, straining to vacate him in violent spurts of fecund semen.

He tasted Melanie's cunt, sucking up her juices, teasing the large lips, loving the fierce tang of her womanhood. His fingers delved deep, rolling and twisting, feeling and pressing, probing like he mined gold out of her . . .

Melanie shuddered into a second orgasm, then fell back limp on the desk, panting. She felt wonderful. "That was fantastic," she gasped.

She felt Doug lifting her legs and rolling her over on her side so her buttocks faced him over the edge of the desk. She felt him insert himself into her sex from behind. She felt . . . she relaxed on an afterglow plateau of pleasure . . .

Doug groaned as he penetrated her. Melanie's sex felt heavenly around his penis. It felt like the vagina was sucking him up, vacuuming him into her body.

Her massive round buttocks delighted him, and also frightened him with their immensity. He thrust energetically between them, like her milky ass was an obstacle he had to overcome. Already, he sensed within himself his massive looming defeat: Melanie's ass was too much for him to master, for any man, he supposed. He thrust deeper, bumping against the soft blockage of her cervix, seeking to reach the depths of her, desperate to understand her strange power over him. Her buttocks simply mocked him—the smooth rounded expanses bounced like balls with his strokes, bobbed like white buoys on a stormy sea. Just watching them wiggle filled his penis with fire, hardened his balls into stones.

In the rush of his passion, he stroked her arms, grabbed her heavy, sweat-specked breasts, teased her brown nipples. All the while, his penis slid in and out of her tight dripping sex. Each stroke between her nether lips felt heavenly; pushed him closer, teased him with defeat. Vagina was unknowable, he concluded as her cunt's stretched textures blurred into terrible indistinguishable pleasure. All the penis could do was fuck it and hope for the best.

He stroked Melanie's face; she looked back at him dreamily, happily fucked-out and half asleep. "Come for me, baby," she whispered. "Fill me up with your love-juice."

There was no way Doug could last long and he didn't. His orgasm hit him hard. The sperm cells burst up from his testicles like rats fleeing a sinking ship. Doug felt like he was drowning in Melanie's ass. Her buttock hemispheres were half moons pulling him violently apart in their tides.

He was helpless, draining from himself. Helpless.

As his semen surged from his loins and pumped into hers, he held on for dear life to Melanie's huge backside. It seemed then a universe of its own, one he was disintegrating into to be reborn as his own offspring.

Finally, he collapsed against her ass, too overcome by it to even stagger over to the sofa.

"You're incredible," he gasped as he draped himself over her, sweat dripping off his sated body.

Dozily, she reached back and stroked his sweaty face. "You're no slouch yourself, you know."

When he'd recovered enough, he helped her down off the desk. She fell stone asleep almost immediately he got her onto the brown sofa. Doug covered her over with her jacket.

***

Once he'd determined that Melanie was sound asleep, Doug got dressed. Though tired as hell, he had a meeting with his younger sister Sylvia, who was also his informer in James's camp. He checked his watch; the rendezvous was for midnight, and half-a-mile away. He'd be on time for sure.

After scribbling out a note for Melanie explaining where he'd gone, Doug checked that his gun was loaded and left.

CHAPTER 17

Upstairs in No. 75 Patricia Circle, the expansive white duplex that served as James Richards's gang headquarters, Sylvia Fisher recoiled in disgust as she peeked into the house's lush master bedroom. James—nominally her man—was making love with the ginger Queen again.

The pair lay entwined in bed, the woman's bone-white skin starkly contrasted against his darker body. Her long orange hair spread like fire over the pillow. James's hairy buttocks rose and fell with his thrusts. He grunted, she moaned. Together they gasped.

Sylvia could see them clearly though the slit door. Anger burnt in her chest as though her breasts were on fire. She watched James's penis dip again and again into the wet pink recess between the Queen's legs, each time reemerging glistening wet. The slurping sounds the erection made on its travels incensed her. The couple's shared pleasure assaulted her—each of James's endless penetrations into the Queen felt to Sylvia like a knife stabbing her in the heart. She felt like charging into the room and killing them both.

Which would of course be committing suicide. James would be furious for sure, might even slap Sylvia around; but the cannibal Queen? *She* would simply tear Sylvia to shreds. Then eat her. (Gingers could rip people's limbs off with their bare hands. Not hearsay—Sylvia had seen it done. Then she'd puked herself sick.)

The Queen twisted her face towards the door. Sylvia winced with jealousy. Even with her face warped by the grotesque grimaces of passion, the woman was beautiful beyond belief. High cheekbones, a perfect nose, full lips . . . The Queen gasped, baring her doglike yellow teeth; in this light, they seemed almost natural. Her body too was exquisite, slim and toned, the breasts small but perfectly-formed, the ass compact, just fleshy enough to not be overwhelming. She looked like a redhead European supermodel with canine dentition. (Most female gingers looked that good—sexy as hell, like human flesh was the ultimate miracle diet.)

Sylvia almost wept with rage at the ginger Queen's perfection. It was one thing to have a romantic rival, another for her to clearly be much better-looking than oneself. Sylvia Fisher was no slouch in the looks department herself, but in this case she was hands-down beat. And she knew it. And it stung like a swarm of angry hornets.

But . . . despite her gorgeousness, the ginger Queen was an inhuman horror. The bed she and James made love on was speckled with blood. Human blood, likely fallen fresh from a ripped-up body. And on the floor by the bed—Sylvia forced her eyes to look at it— lay a severed human leg, most of the meat clearly ripped off the thighbone by the 'woman' her man was lustily servicing.

Her disgust at the horrid sight threatened to make her puke. *It's unbelievable—James ignores me for this flame-haired monster?*

There was, of course, more to it than that, as Sylvia well knew. James was no fool. He was romancing the ginger Queen to ensure his control over the O-Zone. Being the Queen's paramour ensured the cannibal mutants' loyalty and servility. The Queen loved with her vagina; whoever controlled it controlled her and her tribe, it was that simple.

On the bed, the pale orange-haired woman yelped as her orgasm hit her. She dug her claws into James's back, drawing blood—his back was decorated with many similar wounds and scars from their previous lovemaking. She violently kicked the air. She bucked and thrashed and shrieked and then went slack, hardly moving at all as James groaned loudly and flooded her with his seed.

James kissed the Queen; she fondly licked his face. Slowly, as James softened, his come dribbled out of her to stain the bed.

Sylvia suddenly felt intensely pathetic, peeking like a thief into a bedroom that was rightfully hers. Her face hot, she turned and hurried away from the door.

***

The ginger Queen laughed to herself. She'd noticed Sylvia peeping through the crack of the door. The scared, puny thing, angry as an old maid. The Queen sensed Sylvia's emotions—how she *hated* having her man taken from her, hated even more being too weak to do anything about it. The Queen found her contemptuous—she despised weaklings.

The Queen saw Sylvia leave and promptly forgot her. Scratching an itch on her right hip, she snuggled closer to James. She stroked his balding head, was delighted when his handsome middle-aged face creased in a smile.

"Again," she said. "Love me again."

"Hold on a few minutes more till I get my sixth wind back," James pleaded.

The cannibal woman pouted prettily. "You're always saying that."

James said, "What do you think about Bigelow's new boldness, trying to expand into our territory?"

The Queen stroked James's hairy chest. "His men tasted delicious—I really hope he'll send more of them . . ." Then, realizing her lover was simply trying to distract her from more sweet sex, she reached between James's leg and cupped his scrotum in her palm. She gently squeezed the hairy sack. "Enough talk," she moaned. "You've rested enough. Love me again."

***

Sylvia Fisher hurried downstairs.

In the living room, several ginger couples lay on the green carpet. Most were kissing or having sex, their lily-white bodies entwined like ropes. Two couples conversed and giggled animatedly over a bowl of wet human remains, their lips bloody.

The gingers paid Sylvia no attention as she swept angrily past. *They're like animals*, she raged. *No sense of modesty whatever. And what about me? Am I any better? What the heck am I doing here amidst this insanity?*

It was with relief that she reached the front door. *I really need to be away from this madhouse for a bit.*

***

Outside the protection of the house, Sylvia skulked in the shadows, studying the street for danger. All the Patricia Circle residences looked normal enough, but that meant nothing. Sylvia's concern wasn't the gingers (most knew her by sight and would leave her alone), but other Bizarro-created predators who'd consider her a tasty morsel. At this time of night, with all sensible people behind barred doors, there'd be no help if she got attacked.

She nervously tapped her purse. Her small .22 handgun might stop a rapist, but . . . *But what if I encounter something larger? Not to mention a creature hungrier for more than just my vagina?*

Her best bet was to keep unseen, move carefully in the shadows. Which held its own dangers. Sylvia shuddered; there were much worse things than monsters or rapists here in the O. *Even the fucking plants have teeth.* (Several creepy-looking oaks lining the road were a definite danger.)

Shit, Doug, she thought, *couldn't we just meet up in the afternoon?* But no way was that on the cards. There was too much likelihood of being noticed by a pack of prowling gingers who'd then report her movements back to James. James knew Doug. He knew too that Doug worked for Bigelow Jenkins, but didn't know either that Bigelow was Sylvia's uncle, or that Doug was her brother. (It helped at lot that brother and sister didn't look alike: Sylvia had corn blonde hair to Doug's sandy brown, and her eyes were leaf-green compared to his dark, almost black, ones. She also had their mother's stature, was petite and curvy; he, taking after their father, was tall and thin.) If James ever found that out . . . Sylvia knew she'd be in the ginger Queen's belly five minutes later. And she was certain to be tortured both for the truth and for fun first. She cringed at the thought. The Queen had a particularly nasty habit of ripping people's tongues out of their mouths.

Another, lesser, worry was their Uncle Biggs finding out. Bigelow Jenkins had no idea that Sylvia was currently James's mistress. Sleeping with the enemy? Sylvia shrugged it off—If Uncle Biggs found out, they'd simply lie that she was working undercover for *him* on Doug's orders.

Sylvia smirked in the darkness. *Doug and I have big plans. Big plans come with big risks. We're both prepared to take those risks.*

A large chunk of which involves my not getting eaten out here tonight, and returning alive to James's mansion, she mused.

Now out of James's headquarters, she felt much calmer, as if the cool night breezes were extinguishing the flames of her anger. Out here, there was no gorgeous ginger Queen to contend with, no murderous bloodshed to witness, no coupling cannibals. No, outside here, in the silent near-midnight, it was pseudo-perfect.

I really should get out more often, she joked to herself and even managed a soft laugh.

Convinced that it was safe to cross the road, Sylvia Fisher did so. There, she blended again into the shadows again and hurried cautiously to the meeting point.

CHAPTER 18

Doug was relieved to find Sylvia waiting in the Rainbow, a disused womenswear store on Sunrise Terrace. The front lock was long busted; the glass front door swung freely, but creaked a little. Once inside, the streetlight out front provided illumination to see by.

After a hug, brother and sister sat in the rear beside some underwear mannequins and talked.

"How's life with James?" Doug asked.

Sylvia winced. "Utterly horrible, I can't wait till this is all over and I can leave." She looked concernedly at him. "How's your end of things?"

"We're good. She's asleep now." He scowled. "We almost got killed today. Your damn crew. We had to stop and the gingers swarmed us. It was just thanks to Mel that we escaped, and even then just by the skin of our teeth." He shivered.

Sylvia pouted. "What's Melanie Catchpole like?"

"Nothing like what either I or Uncle Biggs expected. She's really cute—pretty and well rounded; and I mean full-figured: even her curves have curves. Her black hair is cut in bangs; she's got full lips, big breasts, and her ass is just—"

"Hold on a moment! Don't you start falling in love with her!"

"I'm not. I like her though. You would too. She wears glasses, for heaven's sake."

"Glasses?"

"Yeah, they look real cool on her. She's like a badass librarian."

Sylvia rolled her eyes. "You've been screwing her, haven't you?"

Doug grinned, though his eyes remained icy. "She does this donut trick which—"

"Stop it. Stop it. Stop it." Sylvia got to her feet and paced. "Okay, so she's fun in bed. So what? I'm screwing James too. Or I was . . ."

Her expression turned ugly. "You won't believe this—at the moment, I only see James once a week, and then he's too used-up for anything other than cunnilingus. Oh, the ginger Queen sees to that—"

"You need to calm down, Syl. Hey! I thought you *hated* sleeping with James."

She walked to him. Poked him hard in the chest. "He's shit in bed, hardly ever waits for me to come first. I always have to bring myself off afterwards."

"Then what . . . ?"

"What I *hate* is the fact that he *prefers* her to me. I'm human for heaven's sake—she's a goddam mutant cannibal monster!"

"Sshhh, lower your damn voice."

"Don't tell me—"

They were alerted by the sudden sound of the store door creaking open. Both siblings froze and looked at each other in fear.

Sylvia winced. "Shit, Doug! Didn't you lock it after you?"

"It doesn't lock, Syl. You fucking know that."

"I'm just jumpy. Go see if anyone's there. Hurry up! If it's just one or two gingers we'll take care of them."

Doug left and returned. "Stop eating your hat. It was just the wind, and some dumb rat's gotten into some display cartons."

They moved out towards the storefront to keep watch on the door, just in case. Sylvia sat on a grimy pay counter, Doug leaned against it. The street outside the womenswear store was deserted; despite which the O-Zone's very nature made it impossible for them to feel safe. At any moment something totally inexplicable could happen; usually something bad.

Doug said, "You're certain James knows nothing about the magic teddy bear?"

She shook her head emphatically. "He doesn't suspect a thing. I told you, he's too busy screwing that cannibal nympho. Morning, afternoon, night . . . all his brainpower is tied up in that pussy."

"Good for us. In the morning, Mel and I will locate the right warehouse—we're round the corner from them now—then I'll meet you here again, and you can tell James what we've got; see if he's interested. Then we'll do a deal."

"You're leaving out something important."

"What?"

Sylvia winced. "What do you intend doing to the new love of your life? She's dangerous. You can't just steal the teddy; she's sure to come after you—without it, she doesn't get paid, does she?"

Doug grimaced. "Don't worry about that. Mel won't be a problem."

"You'll kill her if you have to?"

He nodded. "Yeah, sure."

Sylvia wasn't convinced. "Listen, Doug, this was your fucking idea to stick it to Uncle Biggs and steal the teddy bear, not mine. We both know that damn teddy is worth millions. Uncle Biggs just wants it as a nest egg—he's running scared now James has the ginger Queen on his side and is desperate to leave town before James begins expanding."

Doug smirked. "Yeah. Our Uncle Biggs is as yellow as they come. As a gang boss, he's a total disgrace." He laughed mirthlessly. "It's okay, Syl; I'll kill Melanie as planned once we've found the magic teddy." He gripped Sylvia's shoulders, peered intently into her green eyes. "This is about *us*. Nothing disrupts the plan. Besides, Melanie's middle name is 'Nemesis,' apparently gotten 'cos she never forgets or forgives a wrong suffered. We don't leave her alive, no matter what."

"That makes me feel so much better," Sylvia said. "There's nothing worse than a guy taking business advice from his penis." She winked at her brother. "You know, we could just knock off James, and you take over running the O-Zone—"

Doug let go of her shoulders, ran fingers through his hair; his brow creased with contemplation. "Tempting . . . but how?"

"Poison," Sylvia said without hesitation. "He won't be expecting that at all. Get me something to slip in his food; preferably something that'll simulate a heart attack—no one will suspect shit, he's a middle-aged fuck."

"Damn, Syl, is your vagina that angry with him?"

Her answer was a dark brooding glare. Outside the store display window a multicolored dog chased its tail beneath the streetlight.

Doug considered getting rid of James. "Hmm . . . yeah, poison might work . . ." Then his eyes widened in horror.

His alarm in turn alarmed his sister, who reflexly looked behind her, to see if someone was hiding in the shadows. She imagined she saw a flicker of something moving, then realized it was just suggestion.

She turned angrily back to Doug. "What the heck is wrong with you? Pull yourself together!"

"I didn't see anything," he growled back.

"Huh? So what's the matter?"

"If we do poison James and I take over the O-Zone, don't I also inherit the ginger Queen as well?"

Now Sylvia's eyes widened. She giggled. "I'd totally forgotten that." She calmed. "She's beautiful though, disgustingly so even— imagine a more sexy version of Anastasia Ivanova. You'll like her—"

"Like her? Her tribe almost ate me this morning . . ."

Sylvia went on like he'd not interrupted her: "—Only thing is, she doesn't do breakups."

"What d'you mean?"

"The ginger Queen mates for life. She's loyal to the death—you can never leave her; there are simply no divorces on her romantic horizon. You decide to quit her halfway, she'll kill and eat you. Same goes for any mistresses you acquire—they'll be lunch. She'll likely insist you two fuck after she's eaten her. Or *while* she's eating her"

Doug barely hid his revulsion. "But *you're* still alive."

"She tolerates me because I was with James before she arrived on the scene. I can read it in her eyes that she'd love to make food of me, but for the moment at least James won't allow it." Sylvia shivered. "Doug, we need to get this shit done and dusted before I end up being gutted like a pig."

Doug nodded. "Okay, but forget killing James. No way am I marrying some clingy nympho monster chick for the rest of my life."

"Sure you won't reconsider? She loves sex. You'll love her ass."

"Hell no."

Sylvia checked her watch. "I'd best be getting back." She stroked Doug's face affectionately. "So we meet here tomorrow then? Same time?"

He nodded. "Yeah. Barring any unforeseen shit, I should have the magic teddy by then." He read the concern on her face. "Don't worry; I won't screw this up—by this time tomorrow, Melanie Nemesis Catchpole will be history. I'll slit her throat—less noise that way—"

"What was that?"

Doug was about telling Sylvia to calm down when he saw the horror in her eyes.

"No . . . no!" she gasped.

Sylvia was staring to his right. Pulling his gun, Doug spun toward whatever had her spooked, ready to squeeze off a shot once he had the monster in focus.

Then a horrible jolt went through his right wrist, followed by a terrible pain, and the next moment he was staring down at his right hand, still gripping his gun, on the floor. Then blood began spurting from the severed limb.

"What . . . ?" he gasped in horror as the shock set in. Then he quickly grabbed and squeezed his wrist stump with his left hand to keep from bleeding to death.

The shadows facing them thickened into Lois and Vera Smith, the Chameleon Sisters. Vera gripped a machete, which she now tossed aside, plucking Doug's gun from his severed hand instead.

Both beautiful blondes beamed at Doug.

Horrified as both women materialized seemingly from thin air, Sylvia fumbled for her gun. Lois flicked her tongue at her, wrapping the chameleon-like organ about Sylvia's wrist. Utterly terrified, Sylvia dropped her handbag, beat on Lois's tongue till it slurped off her arm, then fled screaming from the store without looking back.

Lois reeled her tongue back up into her mouth. "Keep watch on lover boy here," she told Vera, pointing to Doug, who stood stupefied by the loss of his hand, "I'll fetch back green-eyes."

Vera nodded. Lois dashed off after Sylvia.

The door swung shut behind Lois. Vera pushed a chair at Doug, then waved his gun at him. "Sit down, we've some talking to do.

Doug stared listlessly at his severed hand, then at his gun in Vera's hand. (Her own gun was holstered at her waist; so why'd she chopped his hand off other than sheer sadism?) He sat on the proffered chair, realizing everything had just taken a turn for the worse. A deadly turn. (Doug knew he had no chance of getting away. He couldn't fight—he either maintained pressure on his arm stump or bled to death.) Oddly, he was more worried for Sylvia than for himself. He prayed desperately that his sister would escape Lois Smith.

Vera pulled up a chair and sat opposite Doug. Her eyes glistened with pleasure. Her beautiful face was as calm as if she was watching TV. She was clearly aroused by his pain—her nipples were stiff beneath her blouse.

"Now, Dougie," she began, "what's this deal you two were discussing about a teddy bear worth millions of bucks?"

"I-I don't get it," Doug sputtered. "How'd you find us?"

Vera giggled. "Dumb luck, that's all. We were rooming for the night in the same bank as you and your fat-assed girlfriend—we followed you when you left." She sneered nastily at him. "Now start talking before I retrieve that machete and chop your feet off."

CHAPTER 19

Melanie Nemesis Catchpole imagined that she dreamt.

In her dream, she saw The Fixer.

"Come with me," The Fixer said to her, "I've something to show you; something you must see."

Melanie accompanied the dark figure, uncertain how they could walk through walls out of the bank. The cold zone surrounding The Fixer wrapped her naked body, paradoxically warming instead of chilling her—she felt like an Eskimo, comfy in an igloo.

"Where are we going?" she asked.

"Into the past," came the creaky reply.

"The past?" (She was unaware of any alteration to the world as they walked through other walls and crossed moonlit streets. She had the odd sense, however, that the air was growing progressively less stale.)

"The recent past, just a few hours ago."

Now she began to notice the change. The sky grew lighter; suddenly there were people on the streets again. Only . . . the people, gingers and humans alike, were all walking backwards. The cars were rolling backwards.

It hurt her head. "Speed it up, please."

The reversal of time sped up around her. They now proceeded through the chaos of a backward-moving world.

They passed a car crash un-happening—mangled bodies unpacking from twisted metal wreckage into healthy passengers again—then a wino with puke streaming back up into his mouth.

That sight did it for Melanie.

"I was wrong to suggest that. This is a lot worse."

"It will shortly be over; we're almost there."

He slowed the reversal slightly.

They walked through one more house, through a nightmare being reversed—chunks of human flesh streaming from the bloody mouths of three gingers, then reforming into the body of a toddler.

"Oh I see—you've kindly saved me the worst for last," Melanie said drily, as the little boy came alive again in a backward scream.

In a corner of the living room, bloodstains coating the wall over the kid's headless mother spurted down into her neck, while her head bounced up from the floor to rejoin her body.

The woman—a tired-looking young redhead—came to startled life. In reverse—the slack-eyed look of death became the pain and disbelief of being beheaded, then open-mouthed fear, then reversed pleas. Melanie instinctively knew she was screaming, 'Don't hurt my baby!'

Then thankfully, after walking through a kitchen where a spider patiently unspun its web, they were outside again in a street.

Melanie instantly recognized their location. The mob of gingers ranked around her crashed Volvo made it impossible not to.

***

"We've arrived," The Fixer said. He set down his black suitcase by the yellow school bus the Volvo had crashed into. "I've timed it to shortly after you and your friend vanished inside the shop. Unable to find you two in there, the gingers have come back to the car."

"You know I'm naked, right?"

"They are unable to see you, and *I* am not interested in your body—it still works fine. Just watch and listen."

Melanie watched and listened. Her dark companion's odd powers meant she was able to see through the gingers' bodies.

The orange-haired mutants had pulled Mary out of the car. None too gently—her left foot had been ripped off; jagged flesh flared at the torn ankle.

"She should be bleeding," said a fat ginger. "Why isn't she?" (Melanie remembered him: When they'd been trapped in the store, he'd been pressed against the shop display beside the masturbating woman, mouthing how she and Doug would shortly be lunch.)

"Don't sweat it, Cody," a woman said, emerging from the car with Mary's severed foot in her mouth. "She tastes fine anyway." She licked her lips. "Just dainty."

Mary was propped up against the Volvo. When Melanie and The Fixer had first arrived at the scene, she'd looked half-comatose; now some color had returned to her face. She stared at the woman eating her foot and began shaking in horror. "Help, me! Somebody please help me!"

Another ginger woman slapped her. "Shut the fuck up, you l'il slut! Ain't no help comin' your damn way."

Wobbling on her single remaining foot, Mary looked at the woman who'd struck her. "You called me a slut! Oh my God, it's true! Running away from home has corrupted me! Dad, I'm sorry! I'm so, so sorry!" Then she gaped around at the male gingers. "I honestly didn't mean to do it!"

"Oh fuck, she's nuts," the fat ginger named Cody chortled. "Ladies and gents, we've found us a cuckoo!"

"Cuckoo makes good stew too!"

"Nuts or not, eat the bitch!" another man growled. He took firm hold of Mary's left arm and wrenched it off her shoulder. Mary screamed and almost fell over.

The ginger took a good bite of meat from the severed arm, then handed it to the woman beside him.

Melanie scowled at The Fixer. "For God's sake, help her."

"I can't. She died for good twelve hours ago."

"But we're back then now! You—"

"Just watch."

Lips pressed tight together, Melanie watched.

Once again, there was no blood. While hopping like a bunny on one spot, Mary gaped stupefied at her torn-apart shoulder. "Oh God, no! Stop it! Please!"

A ginger woman ripped Mary's top off, exposing the girl's pale body. Next, she dug her claws deep into the soft belly skin above the pubis and raked her hand upwards to the ribcage. "Time for some steaming tripe and liver!" she cackled gleefully as she ripped Mary open.

Then she stared confused at the mess she'd made of Mary's abdomen. "What the hell is this shite inside her?"

The other cannibals also stared at the black liquid clockwork that filled Mary's belly. "Aw shucks!" Cody moaned. "She's gone bad!"

Mary, who'd been screaming from the horrendous pain, now also looked down into her rent-open body. She gasped at her strange filling. "Oh my God! I really am a fucking slut—I've caught an STD." Next thing, she fainted.

Melanie winced as Mary collapsed senseless to the ground. "That young woman has to be the dumbest person currently walking the face of this planet."

"You judge her too harshly," came The Fixer's croaky reply. (Melanie had now decided that if a bullfrog learnt to speak English, it would sound like him.) "Mary is the product of a stupendous parenting screw-up, one of colossal magnitude. If things still worked, Child Services would have taken her away ages ago."

"I just hate the way she carries on about her sexual impurity. Nowadays, even straight-laced religious folk laud the virtues of sodomy . . ." She trailed off. The gingers were now pulling Mary to bits and eating her. Her remaining arm and both legs were torqued off her torso and chunks of meat and skin handed around.

Mary screamed awake again, eyes bulging, her terror an endless "Nooooooo!"

"For fuck's sake—shut her up, somebody!"

Her head was instantly ripped off her shoulders and passed around, the skull bitten into, the brains greedily slurped out. Her wide-staring eyes were plucked out and eaten like olives, her nose and lips bitten of her face . . .

"Hey!" a ginger squealed, holding up Mary' windup key. His mouth was bloody. "This was in her ear! I broke a fucking tooth on it—the damn bitch!"

The orange-haired man angrily flung the key away. It landed by Melanie's feet.

"Go ahead and pick it up," The Fixer said.

Melanie did so, without questioning how it was possible. The key was cold. She looked up into The Fixer's impossible face, that expanse like a constantly fracturing mirror in shades of gray. "What do I do with it?" she asked.

"Hold onto it as proof."

"Proof of what?"

"That you're not dreaming."

"I'm not? I'm actually in the past watching a girl get butchered?"

"Thankfully, that part of this is over." The Fixer pointed; Melanie winced. All that remained of Mary now was the strange black engine that The Fixer had put inside her. It lay on the ground beside the blue Volvo. Around it, gingers stood chewing on Mary's ribs and picking their long yellow teeth.

"Now the problem begins," The Fixer said.

The ginger woman who'd ripped Mary open pointed at the dull black machine. "What do we do with it?" she asked. "Take it back to James and the Queen?"

"Queen'll be pissed-off if we bring that to her, Sheree," a squat man said worriedly. "Not after we've eaten all the meat off it."

"Not our fault that the other two got away," Sheree said. She was clearly worried, like she'd not previously considered the Queen's anger. "And this 'un here? Barely enough meat on her to go round."

"Let's just blow it up, guys," the squat man said. "Destroy the frigging evidence."

Cody, Sheree, and the others pondered that for a while. "Might be a good idea to take it back to James though," Sheree said, "You know how much he likes technology and shit." She raked a claw through her hair. "The way the gears are turning inside it, it might be a power source of some kind."

"Power source my ass," Cody said. "You heard the girl herself say it was an STD. Most likely the bitch was a runaway hooker—the little slut." He assumed a defiant pose between the black barbell-like mass and the other gingers, thick legs akimbo, hands on hips. Glaring orange eyes—like LEDs in his plump face—dared them all to contradict him. "If we take it back and it infects everyone with her STD, *we'll* be to blame, O.K.?"

The other gingers backed down. "Okay, Cody, cool. We'll blow it up."

"Leslie's got a few grenades. Hey, Leslie, we need you over here!"

With fat Cody watching closely to ensure his plan was carried out, a tall bony ginger stuck four grenades into the black mass, two in each oblong. The grenades sunk into it till just their safety pins were visible.

(Melanie watched without understanding. Without knowing why, she felt she was witnessing the birth of a major catastrophe.)

Leslie looked up and bared his fangs in a yellow grin. "Okay, get well back, everyone. Say like two hundred meters clearance. I've no idea what's going to happen once I pull the pins."

The gingers all got well away, down the street.

Melanie made to follow them.

"Don't worry," The Fixer said. "You're safe with me."

Melanie didn't feel comforted by his protection. Her sense of impending disaster—like standing inside the crater of an about-to-erupt volcano—was almost overwhelming.

Leslie pulled all four grenade's safety pins in sequence and set off running down the street. They could see him counting as he dashed past them. Ten paces later, he flung himself to the ground.

"Here it goes," The Fixer said grimly.

The black engine blew up. It was a spectacular explosion. The noise was stupendous, as was the effect of the grenades. Suddenly the air was filled with seemingly a million black dots, motes that swirled violently around like they were caught up in the grip of a twister.

"What the hell is that?" Melanie asked.

Her companion groaned. "That which should not be. Total chaos, in other words."

Melanie, heedless of the now-returning gingers, stared at the swirling mass. "The dots are getting bigger."

The swelling dots were also assuming a recognizable shape. The air around Melanie and The Fixer—all along the street—soon milled with a million . . . no, it now seemed a billion . . . birds. Fist-sized birds that were blacker than crows, and all totally eyeless. Even more eerie, other than for the rustle of their beating wings, the birds were completely silent.

"What are these things?" Melanie was chilled by the sight of them. She felt like the protection from cold The Fixer had cloaked her nude body with had been stripped away.

"Morph birds—dark wings of transformation."

Melanie said, "You don't *need* to tell me this is bad; but . . . just *how bad* is it?"

"Very." He turned to point behind them, at the gingers who were now hastily retreating again as the plague of birds spread farther outwards. (As previously with the gingers, Melanie could see clearly through the dark flock.) Several of the orange-haired cannibals were outright running away. "It is of course human nature to meddle, even when the consequences will be—"

"Forget *them*," Melanie interrupted him, her eyes riveted on the swirling black avian tumult. "What do *these* things do?" To her, the gingers were no longer important. True they'd facilitated this oddity occurring, but what was *the nature* of the oddity? Besides, she was relieved to see the last of the cannibals, with their hungry pallid faces and immense yellow teeth.

The Fixer stroked the broad black brim of his hat. "They alter things." He reached out a hand and plucked one of the black birds from the air. It squirmed in his grasp, but made no move to peck or scratch him. Melanie saw that the bird's body was liquid, despite which it had a multitude of spinning little clockwork gears inside it, wheels that flowed from one part of its interior to another. "Worst thing is—they reproduce like swine." The Fixer squashed the bird in his black glove. It squirted as jelly between his fingers, then each black dollop became a fresh bird.

"Could you please explain better?" Melanie growled. Standing in the middle of the dark airborne swarm, which had now blanked out daylight around she and The Fixer, she found it impossible to let the enquiry die.

The Fixer sighed. "Whatever isn't either natural to the O-Zone, or already corrupted by Bizarro, will be now. Additionally, the morph birds aren't restricted to just the O, they'll fly out into the rest of the city, altering everything."

"Shit. You mean the entire city of Springfield's going to be transformed?"

"Yes, that is correct. Consider these morph birds a mobile means of dispensing Bizarro everywhere."

"And you . . . can't you do anything to stop it? After all, you're the one who stuck that machine inside Mary."

"There's nothing I can do. You're overlooking the fact that we're currently viewing the past. 'Viewing' is the important word here. What we are watching has already occurred. At this point in time— twelve hours ago—I was pursuing that plane. Too far away to prevent this happening."

"Plane? Ah, yes—the blue one that keeps abducting people." She frowned. "Well, did you catch it?"

"No, I didn't. And please, let's remained focused on what we're here for."

"Sorry—the plane interests me, I'd really like to understand what it's up to with all the kidnapping it does." She gestured around at the birds. "Are you sure these things are really a danger? I mean, they're not going anywhere—just flying up and down and turning circles."

The Fixer nodded. "An astute observation. No, they won't leave this forming point yet. Not yet. They need several hours for their power to peak—imagine the morph birds as charging batteries of bizarreness—and then . . ."

Melanie eyed the swirling birds dubiously. Their beating wings created a wind she could feel. "Is there any protection against them?"

The Fixer produced something green from within his dark cloak and handed it to her. She saw it was a ten ounce plastic canister of Emerald Deluxe Mixed Nuts. "What do I do with these?"

"Eat them—they're the only protection available."

She scowled at the glossy green cylinder. "I can't. I'm allergic to any except peanuts. You don't want to see what'll happen if—"

"That is temporary. What the birds will do to you will be permanent."

Melanie dubiously regarded the nut canister. "Are you certain of this?"

"Yes."

"Okay then, thanks. I'll use them."

"It is of the utmost urgency that you do. And now, my work is done. It's time for me to depart and try to catch that plane again." He sighed. "Unfortunately, my arms won't extend up that far."

"Wait a minute."

"Yes, what's the matter?"

She gestured around them both. "Why? Why'd you bring me here, back in time, to show me all this?"

The Fixer laughed grimly. "I figured someone has to know what's responsible for the changes to this city that are shortly to come. Don't you feel better knowing?"

Standing beside him like a voluptuous nude marble goddess, Melanie mused a moment. "I'm not sure. Sometimes, ignorance really is bliss; other times it'll cost you your orgasm 'cos the guy doesn't know how you like your clitoris licked. Hell, I haven't seen the extent of the changes yet."

The Fixer laughed again, a horrible hacking sound like he had TB. "Trust me; they'll be more wide-ranging than anything you've ever imagined possible. Have you ever been up on Bizarro?"

"Once. Fairytale land. Hated it."

"Now, imagine that come to Earth."

"You're describing the O-Zones."

An emphatic shake of the dark head, hair flowing like oil, refuted her. "No, the O-Zones are a mingling of Bizarro and normalcy, with normality holding a weak upper hand. What the morph birds bring is a total unlocking of the walls between . . ."

"What walls?" Melanie asked as his voice tailed off, realizing he was about keeping something from her.

"Oh, it's not really important."

"*It is* fucking important—tell me! What goddam walls?"

The Fixer nodded, waved his hands at the birds. "Releasing the morph birds will unlock all the parallands—"

Melanie breathed a sigh of relief. "That's all? I thought you were going to say—"

"—and merge them permanently with Earth . . . here," he finished.

Her face instantly fell. "Oh? Yeah, that's really bad." She looked from The Fixer's mirror gaze to the canister of nuts she cradled against her breasts along with Mary's windup key. The nuts' assured protection was little solace against the promised horror to come.

The Fixer picked up his suitcase. "Now I must be leaving. I can sense that the plane is near." Black cloak swishing behind him, he strode briskly off through the mass of birds. In a moment, he was gone. It was almost like he'd dissolved into a flock of morph birds himself.

Melanie realized that he'd abandoned her. "Hey, what about me!?" she yelled after him. "How do I get back to the future!?"

"Your future is right now." His voice came from all around her, cawing out from the black birds' beaks.

First she was scared, scared of being abandoned here by him to be swallowed up in this impenetrable darkness. Then she realized that she was just dreaming, and all she need do was somehow wake up. But then . . . the world transitioned into a blur around her, with her stuck like glue in the same place . . .

CHAPTER 20

Sylvia Fisher ran and ran, fleeing mindlessly in her terror. She ran like a horde of gingers were after her. Seeing Doug's hand fall to the floor like that, his wrist jetting blood . . . all the fears Sylvia had so far managed to repress about death and cannibalism had leapt to the forefront of her mind . . .

Two transparent women . . . the other blonde's impossibly long tongue, how it had felt around her arm, all slimy like . . .

She paused beneath a dull streetlight. Hacking out frightened breaths, she slowly regained some control over herself, while her eyes scanned the street for signs the blondes had followed her.

Sighting a flicker of motion at the top of the road, she ran on, ducking through a sequence of unfamiliar alleys to lose her pursuer(s).

Now she knew what it meant to be afraid. Every shadow, every fluttering shred of paper, every cloud, seemed to watch her.

She finally ducked into a short cul de sac, one side of which was a series of haberdasheries. Both its other side and farther end were high stone walls.

Sylvia leaned back against cold upright stone, expelling her relief in a long breath. *I've lost them for sure. But I'm lost now myself—I'm completely unfamiliar with this part of the O.* It was a terrifying thing to lose your way in the O-Zone. Her fear of a transparent pursuer was replaced by another: *Oh my God! Where the hell am I? How do I get back home?*

She peeked out of the alley, searching for the street name on the houses across the road. Then suddenly she remembered Doug. "Oh, shit!" she groaned out loud. "I abandoned Doug with those two women. Oh God, oh God, oh God . . ."

"He's clearly not answering your prayers tonight," a soft voice said.

Sylvia froze. She couldn't move—her body felt like water—as the alley wall opposite her seeming disgorged one of the blondes.

Sylvia took in the woman's figure—utterly hot body in an AC/DC *Back in Black* T-shirt and short denim skirt. Her heavy breasts were rising and falling violently as she too got her breath back.

The blonde was pointing a gun at Sylvia. "Hi," she gasped. "Remember me? I'm Lois Smith by the way."

Sylvia slumped down to sit on the cold ground. "Please, please, please . . . don't hurt me!"

Lois laughed down at her. "Who's gonna hurt you?"

"Y-y-you cut off Doug's hand!"

"Oh . . . that? That was just fun; besides he might have shot us." She walked over to Sylvia and grabbed her hair. "Alright, get your ass up. My sister and I wish to talk business with you and your brother."

Sylvia rose slowly to her feet. It took all her energy—she was so damn tired from running. "Please, let me go! Doug too!"

Laughing, Lois leaned towards Sylvia and kissed her full on the lips. "You know you're real pretty," she said after breaking the contact. "How about giving me some head?"

"What?" Sylvia couldn't believe what she was hearing. "What did you just say? Oh, no—I've never done it before!"

"Don't be a goddamn prude," Lois retorted. "With a lovely mouth like yours, you must have sucked lots of dick in your time—guys must be lining up around the block to sample your oral talent." She laughed. "This is easier, and much more hygienic—no smegma for one, and unlike a penis, it's self-cleansing." Holding the gun on Sylvia, she rolled down her panties and stepped out of them, then lifted her denim skirt. "Come on, get started. If you do it good, we won't kill you and Dougie."

The thought of saving their lives impelled Sylvia to action. She was willing to suck every clitoris under Heaven if it'd get herself and Doug off the hook. She'd abandoned thoughts of fleeing again—resisting Lois seemed useless. Not while she could clearly see the woman's hand had blended itself to match her gun's gray metal color. How did you escape someone you couldn't even see?

So she prepared to give Lois all the cunnilingus she wanted. She didn't even consider this sexual abuse—this was simply bartering for her life.

Then, as she was dropping to her knees, Lois jerked her up again.

"What now?" Sylvia asked dully. "You don't want head anymore? You prefer killing us instead?"

"Let's move farther into the alley," came the husky lust-tinged reply. "Just in case some of those white-orange cannibals are around."

They moved in farther, Lois dragging a protesting Sylvia after her by her hair.

Lois leaned back against a shop front, spread her legs and bent her knees. She angled her hips forward, pushed Sylvia down between her thighs. "Okay, get to work, honey."

Sylvia got to work, spreading Lois's vulva open and teasing out her clitoris, tonguing the stiff bud. Lois was completely wet— immediately Sylvia poked her tongue into the vagina, juices flooded her mouth. The blonde's musky scent filled her nostrils. Pubic hair tickled her nose and cheeks. She braced herself with hands on Lois's incredibly toned thighs, admiring their perfection despite herself. *Lois is right*, she decided: *sucking clitoris is like sucking a tiny dick.*

She licked and sucked, ever conscious of the gun Lois carried. She no longer felt fear, however, nor even a sense of violation. Her emotions were as numb as her knees were becoming from kneeling on the ground.

She wet a finger with spit, slipped it up inside the vagina and stroked gently in and out.

Lois groaned with the penetration, running slim fingers through Sylvia's corn-colored locks. "I thought you said you hadn't done this before," she gasped with pleasure. "Honey, you're either a frigging liar or a frigging natural."

Lois's body began fading in and out of view, blending against the tailor-shop's wall. Sylvia simply tongued and fingered her on, doing her damn best to make the blonde orgasm, so they hurry back to *her* brother and Lois's sister.

***

Almost swooning from the waves of pleasure pulsating up from her sex, Lois idly noticed that someone had drawn a human-shaped figure on the stone wall opposite them. *That's some damn great graffiti; it's at least ten feet tall. They'd have needed a ladder . . .*

There also appeared to be several little black birds fluttering beside the wall. Then the birds dissolved into the stone—splattered on it, dripped down it, and were gone—and Lois decided she was just making shapes from shadows.

She gave herself up again to the sweet sensations of sex: *Oh boy! . . . this chick gives some mind-blowing head! Wow, I feel like I'm gonna explode!* She tapped Sylvia's head with the gun. "Holy shit, girl! Keep doing it like that! Ooh yeah, honey—stick another finger up my—"

She stiffened, jerked out of her pre-orgasmic daze. *Hell!* she realized in shock, gaping at the wall opposite. *That's no damn drawing! That fucking thing is alive!*

What happened next happened incredibly fast. The huge outlined figure pulled outward from the stone wall, towards Lois and Sylvia. The rest of the wall collapsed inward toward the resulting ten-feet-tall creature, the freed stones wrapping themselves around it, resolving themselves into parts of its body.

Lois found herself staring at a ten-feet-high stone-skinned 'man.' The creature had thick bumpy arms and legs, and a broad jagged torso like a mass of compacted rubble. This body was topped off by a massive misshapen head from which two boulders peered as eyes. It opened a cavernous mouth; Lois cringed on sighting its huge sharp-looking rock teeth.

Then the monster stepped towards them, reached a hand down at them.

***

Sylvia Fisher, too mentally numbed to recognize the sounds behind her as anything other than echoes of her own depression, finally jerked out of her emotional apathy when Lois began urinating in her mouth. It took her a moment to work out what the warm flow trickling over her tongue was, then her depression turned to rage and she yanked her mouth off Lois's vagina and glowered angrily up at her.

"Hey! Quit that pervert nonsense, even if you are holding a gun to my head! What the fuck is wrong with you, you stupid—!?"

She stopped speaking because at that moment she'd noticed two things: Firstly, that Lois (who was still urinating all over Sylvia) was staring blankly upward, over her head; and secondly, that a dark shadow loomed over them both, like someone had blocked out the moon.

She rose to her feet in a rush, turning at the same time. She saw what had Lois speechless at the same moment as it grabbed her up into the air in massive stone hands.

Sylvia was already screaming her lungs off as the stone monster lifted her to its mouth.

***

Lois's inertia broke the moment the stone monster placed Sylvia's head between its jaws and crunched. It was only then she realized that she'd been peeing herself from fright. The piss hadn't stopped either—it was still pulsing warmly from her urethra, trickling down her legs into her boots.

Blood gushing out in torrents over its gray-brown lips, the stone monster pushed Sylvia's body farther inside its mouth and took another bite. Sylvia's left forearm dropped onto the stone cobbles.

Gibbering in horror, still furiously pissing herself from fear, Lois Smith dashed out of the alley. She didn't stop running till she was a mile away from there.

CHAPTER 21

Melanie Nemesis Catchpole jerked awake. She sat bolt upright, eyes staring straight ahead, out through the opened French windows.

Whew! I was dreaming! she thought, gulping air deep into her lungs.

She was cold. The whole room was cold, freezing. And Doug was nowhere in sight. Had he gone out to pee?

Slowly, her terror at being abandoned amidst the black flock subsided. The chill remained, however.

She was just about getting up to shut the French windows when a blast of warm air blew into the room.

That's odd, she thought. *The night's hot. If I was dreaming, where'd the chill come from?*

Something shifted in her lap. She looked down. Her eyes widened. A green canister of Emerald Deluxe Mixed Nuts lay on her thighs. And something else besides.

She lifted the nut canister to one side, picked up the black rune-engraved key it had been covering. No doubt about it—this was the same windup key she'd personally stuck into Mary's ear barely twelve hours ago.

"Oh crap—I wasn't dreaming," she gasped, staring at it in horror. "I really did go back in time with The Fixer."

She had little time to reflect on her discovery, however. A dark cloud suddenly floated past the French windows, the moon casting the moving shadow across the wall to her right. Startled, Melanie looked outside.

"Shit! It's the morph birds!" She leapt up, grabbed her glasses off the floor (where they'd fallen when she'd earlier flung them at Doug), and rushed out to stare after the passing flock of darkness. The birds moved like bats—silent, their wings whispering like lovers. The main flock had passed her; behind it bled a long line of stragglers. She had the impression that the eyeless birds flew at random. The way they darted left and right like they sought direction. Or were they impelled onward by some instinct she didn't understand?

Momentarily, her mind flashed again to Doug's odd absence. *Okay, now where the heck is he? Even if he went out to pee, he should be back by—*

From up the road to her right came a sudden piercing scream. Startled yet again, she looked in that direction. A moment later, she glimpsed—about a hundred yards off—a woman (a blonde it seemed) dashing out from an alley and fleeing into the distance like the hounds of hell were at her heels. Odd thing was, no one was after her.

Melanie sighed. Another crazy. Warm air caressed her nude body. She regarded the passing morph birds with relief. *Maybe The Fixer exaggerated things. They're not doing any damage yet.*

Like they'd been waiting on her thoughts, a portion of the flying stragglers broke from their fellows and flew towards the house opposite Melanie.

They hit it and faded. Melanie first stared to see what would happen, then gaped when it did. "What . . . ?"

The house opposite had suddenly altered. Now it seemed covered with skin, skin that twitched like it was alive, a pale surface marbled with throbbing dark veins. A thatch of brown hair topped it.

Oddest of all were the gleaming motorcycles sticking out of the transformed building.

Melanie knew she was gaping. She only stopped when a morph bird broke away from the others and flew right at her.

Shit! In a flash she'd darted back inside and slid the glass partition shut.

The bird kept coming. Without breaking the glass, it flew through the shut window at her.

In near panic *(Hell no! I don't want fucking motorbikes growing out of me!)*, she flung herself flat on the sofa, bruising her breasts with the hard impact.

Ignoring the pain, she instantly rolled off the sofa onto the floor. Looking up, she saw the bird's liquid tail vanishing through the wall into the next room.

She snapped up the canister of mixed nuts The Fixer had given her, twisted off its top, and spilled a heap of its roast contents into her cupped palm.

She hastily began eating the nuts, not bothering to chew them properly, just swallowing, bolting them down—anything to get them into her stomach. *He was fucking right!* her thoughts shrilled as two more morph birds flew in through the closed French windows. *Yes! This time I really don't care about my allergy!*

The two new black birds ignored her, also flying through the wall opposite the French windows into the adjoining secretary's office.

The second after they vanished, a muffled explosion came from the next room. Melanie, her belly and mouth full of nuts, winced at the oddly subdued vibrations that shook the floor. *What did The Fixer say? That the morph birds are going to open up all the parallands? And . . . oh shit! There's a space-time portal in the next room!*

She could already feel her nut allergy starting up; her body felt odd, alien as fuck. But she *had* to see what was going on in the next room.

She leapt to her feet and cautiously opened the door.

The office next door no longer existed. What *did* exist was bright sunshine over the plain where the sheep that bore political slogans lived.

More interesting, the wide plain was at Melanie's floor level. To make certain she wasn't experiencing a mirage, she bent down and plucked up a few blades of grass, raised them to her nose, and sniffed them. *Oh, it's here alright.*

She looked behind her, it was night; looked forward again, it was daytime. She shrugged. *'Bizarro comes to Earth,' he said. Hey weird! You're fucking welcome!*

(Melanie Nemesis Catchpole was very used to living and dealing with Bizarro, indeed she did most of her best work in the weird zones. It was just that . . . normally there were partitions; one didn't just open a door and find oneself in the midst of stupendous oddity. Actually, one did, but *that* was different—there were rules as to how Bizarro played its game with humanity. But now those rules [for better or worse, and at the moment seemingly for worse]—at least here in Springfield, MA—looked, like Elvis, to have left the building . . . for good.)

She peered out over the plain awhile, the midday sun radiant above it. The sun was hot on her face.

All wasn't sunshine, however. Over in the distance, morph birds filled the sky, their mass so dense they formed a literal black cloud. And that cloud was breaking apart into smaller black clouds . . . that were themselves growing bigger by the moment. And below the far-off clouds (she couldn't see this clearly), there seemed to be a massive tumult going on, like machines were demolishing and building several skyscrapers at once.

Then a gigantic orb bounced up into the distant air . . . *Hell no, that's not an eye, is it? . . . It is?*

A bemused expression on her face, Melanie shut the door again and locked it. She crossed the room and pulled the drapes shut over the French windows.

She began picking her clothes off the floor. It was then she saw Doug's note.

She read it hastily and winced.

You went for a meeting with your informer? And I've no idea where you are. Oh hell, man! This is one night when you don't want to be outside—she looked down at the green plastic container in her hand—*without a pack of nuts!*

CHAPTER 22

Doug Fisher knew for certain that he was fucked. It was so obvious, 'Fucked' could have been his middle name, like was the case with a girl he'd once dated. Sitting across from Vera Smith (who watched him with eagle eyes while training two guns on him and wondering why her sister wasn't back yet), squeezing hard his severed wrist (which dribbled blood and burnt with agony), he saw only one chance of surviving the night.

With his hand gone (Doug kept darting disbelieving glances at it), a fight was out of the question. Vera wouldn't miss if she shot him. Nor would she hesitate to if he rushed at her.

So Doug was doing the only thing that he figured would keep him alive. Keeping mum.

A cold smile danced over Vera's luscious lips. "Playing the tough guy's a waste of time, Dougie. You'll save yourself two lifetimes of grief if you just cooperate with us."

"I've nothing to say to you, Vera. I don't know anything."

Her mouth laughed. Her eyes didn't. She was as coldblooded as he; she just hid it better. "I'll ask you again, Dougie. The magic teddy bear—tell me about it."

"I don't know—"

Her eyes caught the motion of a flock of passing black birds out in the street. The birds flowed past like water, a turbulent dark swirling like corrupted vernal emotions. For a moment the street was thick with them, like they were the essence of night fallen to Earth.

Vera sensed that the birds were up to no good.

Doug said, "I've never seen that many birds flying at night before."

"Neither have I. I've a feeling . . . No, don't change the topic, Dougie. You were telling me about the magic teddy bear."

"I was telling you I know nothing about it."

Vera lost patience. Rising to her feet like water bursting from a spring, she smashed Doug across the face with the grip of her pistol.

He reeled back stunned, the cold metal ripping open his forehead. Then he smirked. "You do that one more time, you'll break my head—"

"Might be the best thing; your noggin seems a hard nut to crack. Now, tell me about the damn teddy."

"I already told you—"

The store's front door burst open and Lois ran in. She dashed over to Vera and Doug and stood panting and trembling.

"What the hell happened to you?" her sister demanded. "Why'd you take so damn long? And where's his sister?"

"She's d-d-d-dead!" Lois sputtered. "A m-m-monster ate h-her! It c-c-came out of the s-s-stone wall and-and-and ate her up!"

Doug sat bolt upright at the news. *Oh, fucking no.* "Sylvia's dead?"

More black birds whizzed past outside. One flew through the store display, circled twice and flew out again.

Not taking her eyes off Doug, Vera hugged Lois, who snuggled into her shoulder and wept, her body fading to match Vera's clothes.

Vera considered. Her sister clearly wasn't faking this behavior. Something real bad had happened back where she was coming from. *I mean, the front of her skirt is all wet and it smells like piss. Damn! Lois hasn't wet the bed since she was sixteen.*

"Ask her what really fucking happened," Doug said savagely. "I think the bitch killed Sylvia!"

His words galvanized Lois to get control of herself. Detaching herself from Vera, she dried her eyes then strode purposefully over to Doug. She planted a wet boot on his left thigh, grimaced frostily at him. "I'm not lying, douchebag. A section of a fucking wall wrapped itself into human shape and ate green-eyes." She moved her foot till it was trampling his crotch. She pressed down on his penis, her boot changing color to match his jeans, then dangled her tongue down to lick his face. He grimaced as the long wet lingua slobbered down over his bleeding forehead.

Lois drew in her tongue momentarily.

"He tastes almost as good as Mary," she said. "All that's missing is the vodka."

Opposite them, Vera sniggered and grabbed her crotch, fondling herself through her pants. "You don't say, darling."

Lois dropped the long hot wet lingua onto Doug's face again, first slobbering over his wound some more, then tracing lower, down over his eyes and nose, then pressing it at his lips like a penis seeking entry.

Doug reeled back at the thick stench of fear and urine that poured from Lois. Her bare vagina gaped at him with outwardly-curled wet lips—it looked like the underside of a snail just picked up off the floor. Her boot on his manhood had begun to hurt badly. And did she have to keep licking his face with that massive tongue of hers? The stream of saliva spilling from her mouth onto his head felt like someone dumping hair gel on him.

He gasped for breath. "Okay, okay—I believe you. Back off—you fucking stink."

Lois scowled at him but removed her boot from his penis. She drew in her tongue again, leaving Doug drenched in spittle. She bent, picked his bloody hand off the floor, waved it in his face. "If you dare imply I'm lying again, you're going to be fisting your own ass, dig?"

Doug said nothing. His thoughts were black and scrambled. *She's really telling the truth? Sylvia's dead? Dead? Eaten?*

Lois dropped the hand and booted it out of view. Now calm, clearly in control of herself again, she turned back to Vera. "Has he said anything yet?"

"Nah, the bastard's still giving me the old runaround."

"I've always said you're too soft. A little torture never hurt an interrogation." She glanced over the rows of mannequins behind them. "I'll look around for something to tie him up with."

Lois flicked on a penlight and vanished into the rear of the store.

"Look," Doug said, "be reasonable. Just let me go, and—"

"Dougie honey," Vera interrupted, a sudden look of pleasure on her face, "please shut the fuck up."

***

Five minutes later, the Chameleon Sisters had Doug all duct-taped up like a package. Both his arms and legs were taped to the side of his chair; several loops around its back restrained his body. Lois had also found some twine with which she'd tourniqued Doug's severed wrist.

The women weren't taking any chances of him bleeding to death on them.

Lois had also returned with a clear plastic bag. Doug couldn't figure out what she needed it for.

Lois walked over and whispered to Vera. Vera's eyes first widened with shock, then she nodded and giggled. Then she kissed her sister. Both women stood there for a minute, breasts squashed together, tongues entwined. Vera dropped her hand to Lois's bare crotch and began stroking her clitoris, then slipped a finger up through her vulva. Lois stiffened, sagged against her, and began trembling and moaning: "Oh fuck, yes!"

"Hey!" Doug spat at the two blondes. "Fucking quit fucking yourselves and let me go!"

The sisters reluctantly separated. Both glared at Doug. "You could have at least let me come first," Lois said coldly. "Are you in that much of a hurry to take what's coming to you?"

Vera sighed. "Alright, we're fair players, Dougie—you know that. So, we'll ask you one last time: Tell us what's the deal with the magic teddy bear and we'll let you go. We know you know something; we heard you and your sis discussing it, so brushing us off won't work." She and Lois peered intently at him. "Okay, so what's this about?"

He smirked. "Just some toy that she wants for—"

Lois socked him on the jaw. His head snapped back. "Don't give us that bullcrap! You two both agreed that the teddy's worth millions of dollars. Hey! You know we don't fool around where money's concerned."

Doug's smirk had fled his face. Several of his teeth felt broken. Lois punched like a heavyweight. "I-I-I . . ." he stuttered groggily.

"He still thinks this is a movie and he'll have a last minute escape," Vera spat. She began unbuckling her pants. "Let's do the bastard like you said. I've got a good load in me."

"Nowhere near what I've got, sis," Lois said. She regarded Doug pityingly. "The only way I managed to not crap myself while running back here was by remembering I didn't have any spare clothes."

Doug stared in incomprehension as Lois picked up the transparent plastic bag she'd returned with from the back of the store. She opened it out on the floor and squatted over it with her back to him. In disgust, he watched her squeeze out a long unbroken (almost two feet long) log of shit into the bag. She paused a moment after the brown length dropped off from her anus, then grunted and strained, fingers digging into her knees, till she squeezed off another smaller log of excrement.

Heaving an exaggerated sigh of relief, she rose and turned to Doug. "That's all for you."

Then she walked over to him and rubbed her backside clean on his hair.

Doug surfaced fast from his daze. "Oh, no. You're not feeding me that shit! I tell you girls I don't know anything!"

Vera giggled. Pants down around her ankles, she was regarding Lois's steaming pile of excrement with something like awe. "Damn! I never knew you had that much in you."

"Fear works wonders for the bowels, honey. Now, hurry up."

"Sure thing." Vera squatted over the shit in the bag and squirted out a largely liquid yellow mass over Lois's initial deposit. The feces seemed to spurt forever from her anus.

"Damn!" Lois yelped. "That's more than I pumped out!"

"It isn't!"

"It is too—it's just watery, so it looks less."

Doug stared listlessly at the glistening mass of shit in the plastic bag—a paradise for houseflies. The brown expanse, pale liquid over dark solid, entranced him with a special kind of horror. For a moment it reminded him of a glazed donut, which in turned reminded him of Melanie Catchpole. It seemed so long ago, almost an eternity away, since he and Sylvia had been blithely planning how they'd kill Melanie and keep the teddy bear for themselves. That plan was all shot to bits now.

(Like the no-longer-enforceable plan, losing his hand also seemed a far-off event, something divorced from now, an occurrence which, but for the agony that intermittently flowed up his arm like water, might well have happened to someone else a long time ago.)

Vera walked over to Doug. She too cleaned off her anus on his hair. The stink of her added to his dread.

Lois retrieved the bag of poop from the floor. She shook it at Doug, mixing up its repulsive contents. "Of course, you know what comes now, honey, right?" She winked at him. "There's still time to change your mind."

He spat on the floor. "There's no way you're making me eat your shit."

Vera giggled. "Who said anything about *us* making you eat it?"

Lois grinned. "You're going to *want to*, honey. In fact, we'll have to practically beg you to stop. We're giving you the old plastic bag over the head treatment. You know, as in—'this bag is not a toy; keep away from infants'?"

Sudden understanding hit Doug. Before he could protest, Lois had expertly slipped the plastic bag over his head, filling his vision with shit. Skillfully, like she'd done it before, she pulled the bag's open end down around Doug's neck and twisted it tightly shut.

After a moment's stunned disbelief, Doug suddenly found himself surrounded in the most horrible stink imaginable. It seemed he'd been submerged into a toilet. The smell was everywhere, like it was seeping through the pores of his skin into his head. After at first instinctively closing his eyes on being smothered, he opened them again to behold a solid brown clump (clearly Lois's) obscuring his right-eye vision. The brown log was draped down from his hair over his nose and lips. Trying to maneuver his mouth away from it brought his lips into contact with bitter-tasting wetness which he couldn't see. His vision was obscured in patches by green-flecked yellow smears running down the inside of the bag.

And, there was no air. That was the worst thing of all—there was no air. He held his breath for as long as he could: thirty seconds became forty-five, then fifty-five, one minute and ten . . .

Forgetting himself when his lungs felt like they were burning, he dragged in gulps of air, gagging when Lois and Vera's excrement flooded his throat instead.

He gaped out at Vera, who stood pointing at him and laughing her head off.

He spat the shit out, sucked in more 'breath.' Thick excrement flooded up his nostrils. He sneezed it out, then gasped it back in again, helpless to do anything as the feces slid down his throat, threatening to make him vomit. The only thing in his power now was to refrain from reflexly chewing on the shit in his mouth.

I can't fucking breathe! he thought desperately. *I need to breathe! Breathe! I need air!!!*

Dark spots were forming before Doug's eyes; his head felt woolly. He blinked several times, then, almost passing out, saw Vera leaning forward, peering concernedly at him. *Fuck!* he thought, his mouth and nose full of shit. *I'm drowning to death!*

A moment later, the bag of excrement was slid back up over his head. Only half aware where he was, he instantly gulped in deep breaths, not caring that he was swallowing shit to take them.

"He's almost unconscious." Vera's voice sounded very far away.

"Wake him up. No, don't touch him! You don't want his mess on you, do you? There's no water in here."

"Shit, I forgot that. Well I need to pee anyway."

A boot was placed on his thigh. Then a hot stinky stream splashed his face. "Hey, Dougie, wake up!"

"Don't use it all up," Lois cautioned. "If he keeps playing hardball, we might need to wake him again."

The urinating in his face stopped. "Sorry, my bad," Vera giggled.

Doug roused. "That the best you bitches can do?" he spat.

Vera rolled her eyes. Behind him, Lois said, "Okay, let's go again. We're in no hurry. Besides, we've shit to spare. And after that . . ." she winked at Vera, "we'll get to cutting on you."

Outside, a few black birds streamed past. "Those things are damn creepy," Vera said.

Lois shuddered. "I saw some in the alley just before—" Like she didn't want to relive the memory, she switched the subject back inside: "Dougie, for God's sake, be reasonable and we'll let you go take a well-deserved bath." She giggled. "Man, you need to get a load of yourself now. You smell like . . . shit! *Our* shit!"

That cracked Vera up. "Do it," she told her sister through tears of laughter. "Show the bastard we mean business."

The plastic bag went back down over Doug's head. Again he squirmed in the women's excrement; holding his breath, then swallowing down and snorting back up their mingled brown mess when his burning lungs screamed for relief. Again he fought not to puke so he didn't choke on it. Again dark dots clouded his vision. Again the bag—its contents now half-depleted—was slid off his head just before he passed out. And yet again, he was revived by a stream of Vera's urine in his face.

"You ready to talk now?" Vera asked as he gulped air.

"Go to hell," Doug gasped. "I'm not telling you two anything."

"Even if we fucking kill you? What use is money if you're dead?"

Lois walked round in front of Doug. "Maybe he likes our taste." She held up the poop-bag for Vera's inspection. "He likes you more—most of your serving's in his belly now. Much less of mine."

Vera wrinkled her nose at the crap-covered man facing them, his brown hair saturated with their waste. Damn, he stank! "It's a hot night. I think he was thirsty, not hungry."

"Yeah, could be that. Yours is much more liquid."

"Will you two psycho bitches stop ranting about your excrement like it's food and untie me this instant!?"

"Ooh, look—the big badass baby boy is angry with us!"

"Ooh . . . is our baby throwing a tantrum?"

Doug stared at them defiantly. They stared back at him perplexed.

Lois shook the plastic bag at him. "Why won't you simply talk? It's boring to keep doing this; we want to go home and make love."

Doug smirked. "You're nowhere close to besting me. I know the only thing keeping me alive now is my *not* talking. If I dare tell you about the teddy, you'll simply off me and—"

"We're not greedy," Lois interrupted. "We'll settle for a share of the profits."

"The lioness's share," Vera added. "But at least you'll have a little . . . maybe even enough to stitch your hand back on." She ran her tongue over her lips. "C'mon, Dougie, trust us. O.K.?"

He shook his head, spat out a chunk of shit. "Not as far as I can fling both of you handcuffed together. Think up a better deal, one that guarantees I stay alive. Till then, I'm not saying nada. You'll damn well kill me if I do."

Now, Doug felt he had the sisters where he wanted them. His voice held much of his normal ruthless confidence.

Vera scowled at Lois. "This is a goddam waste of time, you know."

Lois nodded. "Yeah. Imagine feeding him all that poop for nothing." She sighed. "And you know what? I've just realized we don't even need Dougie."

Vera's eyes widened. "What you talking 'bout?"

Lois grinned at her sister. "We've both forgotten that Dougie here isn't the only one who knows the answers." She smiled at Doug. "We're totally reasonable women. You don't want to tell us about the teddy bear? That's cool with us. We'll just follow your plus-sized girlfriend Melanie instead. She'll lead us to where we want to go." She drew her gun, placed its muzzle under Doug's chin. "Okay, tough guy; you have our express permission to take your fucking secret to the grave with you."

"No, no . . ." Doug protested, his eyes widening in horror. "I'll talk!"

"Too late, honey," Lois said quietly. "This is like a hot date. You should have put out after dinner; even if it did taste like crap."

She pulled the trigger, splattering Doug's head and brains everywhere. Literally everywhere—over the aisles, mannequins and boxes.

"Fuck!" Vera said as Doug's headless body went limp. "He really made a mess of things."

CHAPTER 23

Vera pulled her pants up. Lois wiped a smearing of feces off her hands with a tissue.

"It's odd how one so easily overlooks the obvious sometimes," Vera said, zipping up. "How I forgot about cutie-pie back at the bank I'll never know."

Lois threw the tissue away. "Heat of the moment, sis." She pointed to Doug's corpse. "Any need to hide this?"

"Nah, let's go. We need to go see his ex."

"Ex?"

A cold laugh. "Well they definitely aren't dating anymore."

Lois burst out laughing. "Ooh, sis, you crack me up!" She paused in her mirth, brushed blonde hair out of her gray eyes. "What's the rush? We'll pick cutie-pie up in the morning."

Vera smoothed down her top. She frowned. "You sure that's a good decision? She bolts, and we're back to square one again."

Lois laughed. "You worry too much, sis. Uh uh—she'll be there. You heard Dougie and green-eyes plotting to kill her; so he obviously didn't tell her where he was headed. She won't know where to look for him, so she'll wait till she's certain he won't be back home to her sweet, tight, pussy."

"Sweet? Tight? You've really got the hots for that woman, haven't you?"

"Honey, that ass of hers is so massive, I want to die and bury myself in it. Must be heaven inside there."

"Lois, darling, we're going to torture and kill her."

A demure giggle. "When did that ever make any difference?"

Vera grinned at the headless, shit-covered corpse in the chair. "You make a valid point." She nodded toward the door. "Let's go.

115

The way your face is flushed, you need some sisterly keeping tonight."

"You've no idea what my pus—"

Both sisters gasped. Falling from out of view, a flock of the black birds swooped down in front of the clothing store, then looped back up again.

"Those birds—"

The loop was seemingly endless, the morph birds falling and rising ceaselessly.

Then a stream of birds broke from the bottom of the loop and flew in through the storefront window, right at the sisters.

Both women instantly threw up their hands to shield their eyes. Both were suddenly aware of the birds passing through them—a feeling of painless discomfort. Both dropped their hands and swung round to look behind them at where the birds were headed.

The stream of morph birds splattered on Doug's corpse and were gone, absorbed into his flesh.

"They went through us," Lois sputtered.

"And into *him*," Vera confirmed.

"We're inanely stating the obvious; you know that, right?"

"We're immensely perplexed and wondering what will happen next."

Both nodded. Both kept watching.

What happened next was that a lot of rats suddenly erupted out of Doug's body, ripping through the duct tape securing him to the chair. The mass of rats—all dead, rotting, and stinking worse than the excrement coating the corpse—kept spilling from it, tearing gaping holes through Doug's skin; plummeting down like a furry waterfall.

The rodent fall stopped. All that remained of Doug's body now was shredded empty skin, flimsy like a burst balloon. All around the chair were piled the festering carcasses of black and brown rats, many swollen by death to twice normal size. Lots of them were burst open, their innards seeping out in a vile display.

Lois and Vera stared speechless at one another, then both spun to look outside, where the black birds still looped down from the heavens and back up again like a dangling ribbon of liquorice.

Another stream of birds blew in through the shop window and through them. These struck several garment racks.

Yanking Lois after her, Vera headed for the door. "Let's frigging go. I know we seem immune to this, but—"

A spiky green tentacle flailed at them from a suddenly-transformed garment rack.

They ducked the tentacle, made it to the front door, then looked back at what had attacked them. From where had previously been just empty space between a metal-and-plastic frame, six blue eyes now glowed back amidst greenish flesh. The flung tentacle hung in midair, dribbling come-like liquid from its tip.

On the floor by the chair, another of the creature's tentacles—this one with a massive cilia-rimmed maw in its tip—was busily vacuuming up the dead rats Doug had become. The swallowed rodents formed large visible lumps along its length as they travelled into the creature.

Lois fired two shots at the creature. The only effect was that it developed another six blue eyes at the point where she'd shot it.

"Run!" Vera screamed on glimpsing a second, much larger tentacle coiling up behind the monster-rack to lash at them.

They leapt out onto the sidewalk. Vera slammed the door. The next moment the giant tentacle smashed through it, spraying glass over them.

They backed off. Lois fired at the tentacle, the gunshots thunder in the hot night. Another six eyes immediately developed from the wound, and the tentacle swung towards them, squirting liquid. They leapt away from the opalescent gush as it flew through the air. It splattered the concrete, bubbling like acid. Drops that touched their clothes ate holes through the fabric.

Both Chameleon Sisters turned and dashed down the road, back towards the Webster Bank, as around them the night transformed the world.

"It's like we're having a nightmare!" Lois gasped as they passed another dangling loop of morph birds.

"Hopefully we are," Vera panted back, dragging her down a side street. "Then we're sure to wake up come morning."

CHAPTER 24

The ginger Queen woke earlier than usual. Unable to find sleep again, she left James's side and made her way downstairs to her slaughter room (formerly the rear guest bedroom in she and James's 75 Patricia Circle duplex). There, she sat regally poised in a chair, her perfect figure wrapped in a long green kimono, her feet snug in fluffy pink slippers, and watched her executioners prepare breakfast.

"Please no!"

The protest brought its maker no salvation. With a wet 'thunk' flesh separated from flesh: the head fell; the body ceased struggling against its captors' pale hands. Now it just jerked in place. And then even that futile unconscious resistance to its inevitable collapse to total inertia ceased.

Oh, blood! Sweet gushing blood!

The thick rich smell filled the Queen's nostrils. She sniffed it in deeply, savoring its tang of life departed. (The Queen always felt she could taste the spirits of dead humans in their remains. Ingesting them made her stronger, she believed.)

This latest corpse was a young man's. Now his lopped-off head bobbed in the blood basin. The executioner, a short bald man with a thick orange beard, bent and retrieved the head, then placed it with others in a basket. Next, two ginger helpers lifted the corpse off the slaughter slab and slung it atop a pile of similarly headless bodies.

The Queen frowned at the executioner. "How many left?"

He bowed low. "Two, your Majesty."

"Good, very good." She licked her lips, ran fingers through her hair and over her ears. "Send a tray up to the royal bedroom. Ensure there's enough pieces of liver in it this time."

"Yes, your Majesty."

She turned to leave the slaughter room, then paused. The next victim, a fat blonde woman wearing a torn blue dress, was being brought in by the executioner's assistants.

"Noooo!" the blonde screamed as both men dragged her toward the bloody slab.

The gingers halted their violently thrashing charge beside their queen. They bowed. The Queen smiled at the terrified blonde. "Oh, you un-transformed make oh so much noise."

"Fucking let me go!" The blonde shrieked, eyes wide with fear. "You can't just—!"

"Oh, but *we can* just eat you," the Queen interrupted, spearing the blonde deep in her tongue with her index finger. Like one performing a tongue piercing, she dug the sharp claw right through the thick meat. Blood welled up from the wound. The woman stood mute and trembling between queen and subjects, held captive now by the pain in her mouth.

"Yes, *we can* fucking eat you," the Queen reprised softly. "You're all so delicious after all." On those words she yanked fiercely on the speared tongue, ripping it completely out of the blonde's mouth.

The blonde froze as pain wholly paralyzed her. She'd never experienced agony like this before; didn't think it existed. This was worse even than when she'd had her twins. Her entire mouth and throat felt destroyed. Blood pouring over her lips, she stared at her tongue in the ginger Queen's grasp.

The beautiful monarch was examining the lingua as if it expecting it to speak to her. She was heedless of the blood streaming down her arm and staining the sleeve of her robe.

"It's so little," she told the blonde finally, "and yet you make such a huge racket."

Eyes screaming her agony, the blonde now began gagging on her own blood.

"Quick!" said the executioner. "Get her up on the block before she chokes to death! I need to drain her."

His assistants pulled the woman over to the slaughter slab. Now she hardly protested; she was too busy trying to breathe.

The Queen shook the blonde's ripped-out tongue at the executioner. "I'll take this with me now—a little something to nibble on. Now remember what I said about my breakfast . . . ensure there's sufficient liver."

He nodded; she departed. Behind her, another wet 'thunk' announced the separation of the fat woman's head from her body.

***

James woke up when the Queen reentered the bedroom.

She grinned at him, her big yellow teeth all on display. "Good morning, darling, I just went to see how breakfast was doing."

He yawned, ran fingers through his sparse hair. His pale ruthless eyes regarded her with amusement. "Yours, of course, not mine. And what's that you're carrying?"

She shrugged. "Just a tidbit. You don't mind me eating in bed, do you? I won't get fat."

He shrugged (She was joking with him—ginger women somehow never got fat. She claimed they ate 'healthy.'), then looked at the wall clock. "What time is it?"

She followed his gaze. The clock showed half-past-four.

He frowned. "You're up very early, dear."

She undid, then dropped her kimono. She stood facing him, hands on hips, pelvis thrust slightly forward, back arched slightly so her small breasts lifted to stunning effect. "I couldn't get back to sleep after a noise woke me."

James regarded the ginger Queen—the flawless face, the equally flawless body. And in the crook of her thighs, nestled like a spring amidst her orange pubic hair, the perfection of her sex. *I made a good deal when I made her,* he thought smugly. *I'm lucky she agreed to ball me instead of eating me. With her on my side now, Bigelow Jenkins has all the chance of a snowflake in Hell of keeping hold of his Indian Orchard and Boston Road neighborhoods.*

Eyes riveted on his now-flushed face, the ginger Queen took slow, measured strides toward the bed. She hid her delight when James began licking his lips. She kept her poise regal, drank in his lustful admiration of her figure. His desire for her was a heady sexual wine; by the time she reached the bed she was soaking between the legs, glittering trails of her sexual juices streaming down her white thighs.

"Come," James said, reaching out hands to her. "I fucking want you." His voice was hoarse.

"You *always* want me. But that's only right—exactly how it should be." She dallied a moment, raising the severed tongue in her hand to

120

her mouth and nibbling on its end. The fresh human meat tasted sweet. She sucked on it awhile, her orange gaze holding James transfixed in eyelight.

James flung away the bedclothes and pointed to his erection, the rocket-stiff penis throbbing like it wanted to blast off his body and bury itself in her loins. "C'mon, darling, suck on this instead. It tastes better."

She giggled, then got into bed, lay back, and spread her thighs wide. "No, darling. *You* lick *me* . . ." she held the blonde's severed tongue out to him, "with this."

James regarded the bloody organ. "You can't be serious."

She scraped a claw over her fangs. "Of course I am."

James just managed not to roll his eyes.

She caught his gaze and held it, her eyes demanding that he satisfy her how she desired. Then she laughed, and fluttered her long lashes at him. "Please do it, darling."

Sighing, James took the severed tongue from her.

He knelt between her milky thighs. The Queen spread herself as wide as she could. She smiled up at him. "Don't look so upset."

He grunted, still aroused despite his distaste. She had a pretty vulva. The arrangement of her sexual folds was almost floral—her semicircular inner labia curled wetly outward like petals. The clitoris peeked from beneath its hood like a nun wearing a pink wimple. The purple pee-hole, the white smeared vagina cavern; the musky stink of her arousal, a cloying perfume in his nostrils . . .

He ran the severed tongue over her dripping sex. She moaned with passion, raised her hands to twist her hard little nipples. "That feels just lovely—do it again."

He continued sliding the tongue up and down her wet crevice. Each time he reached the top, he flicked the organ over her clitoris, left, right, left, right, like it was still attached to its erstwhile owner. He wondered for a moment who that unfortunate person had been, then shrugged off any twinges of conscience—one broke eggs to make an omelet. (At the moment, James could care less where the gingers got those they ate, so long as it wasn't any member of his gang. Of course, he realized that once he and the Queen had taken over the whole city, he'd need to set a quota, else soon there'd be no one left alive in Springfield to rule over.)

The Queen moaned. "Oh, that's really nice! Now, put it in me quick!"

James heaved a sigh of relief at this madness being over. He dropped the horrid tongue and grabbed his swollen penis instead.

"No," she moaned, "I mean put the tongue in my pussy!"

James winced. His erection felt like it would explode on him. He let go of it, picked up the tongue again.

"Yes, yes!" the Queen moaned, her face flushed, her pupils dilated from her intense passion. She reached down and spread her labia wide, lifted her hips so her vagina gaped at him. "Put it in!"

James slid the tongue in. Right down to the bottom of her. Only the shreds of flesh where it had been ripped from its owner's throat remained outside. He twisted the pink meat; the Queen purred like a cat. He slid it out again; her eyes rolled back in her head and she began panting. Realizing his lover's orgasm was very close, James began a gentle in-and-out rhythm with the tongue. (Now his irritation lifted; he knew his luck that she was so easy to satisfy. True, she was quite the nympho, but she came so fast each time it was a delight to fuck her. She did wonders for James's ego, made him feel a total stud. It was part of the reason that he loved her.)

"Aaaarrggh!" The ginger Queen came. She stiffened. Her mouth gaped wide, lips curled back over sharp bared fangs. Her orange eyes stared into space. Her whole body trembled; her legs shook, her sex flooded with white secretion.

James twirled the tongue back and forth inside her vagina. His other hand rubbed her clitoris fast, squeezing and pinching it. The Queen came and came, then went limp, her breath spurting from her in heavy gasps.

"Oh fuck, darling," she moaned after a time, "that was fantastic."

"And a one-off," James said grimly. "No more second-hand-cunnilingus."

The Queen clamped her thighs tight together to keep the tongue inside her sex. She gazed languidly at James's resolute expression. "Now, darling, don't be like that. It *was* fun." She pointed to his swollen penis. "Do me up the ass now; nice and hard like you love."

She knew that would calm him down, and it did. She turned on her side, presenting her buttocks to him. Looking over her shoulder she grinned at the lust on his face as he hastily smeared his penis with Vaseline. Sweat was dripping off his forehead.

"Oh, honey, that feels just right," she groaned as two of his fingers entered her anus, lubing her up with Vaseline also. It felt good, the way he smeared the jelly deep inside her, twisting his fingers around in her rectum.

She felt euphoric, like she was floating away on clouds. Then she felt James's chest on her back, his hairy body tickling her satin skin. Next came the feel of his stiff manhood between her buttocks, then of the round penis head pushing against her anus. She pushed back against the penis, drawing in a deep breath as it spread her tight hole and popped inside her body.

James grunted with the penetration. He slid his penis as deep into her anus as it would go.

"Relax inside me, darling," the Queen said, his breath hot on her neck. She reached a hand back, dug her claws into his hairy buttocks, stopping his withdrawal. "Take your time. My ass isn't going anywhere."

James remained stiff and hard inside her. It was torture, but a delicious torture. The walls of her rectum choked his penis, strangled it, gripped it nice and firmly; wonderfully.

The Queen reached down between her legs and jerked the tongue from her vagina. A thrill blazed through her loins as it came free. She raised the severed organ to her face, regarded it curiously. It was smeared over with her white secretions. She bit into the tongue, ripped a chunk out of it and chewed. *Just delicious, and coated with me.* She pushed her buttocks back at James. "Okay, darling, now give it to me."

James made a strangled sound in his throat. "I thought you'd never ask." He began fucking her ass, stroking deep and firm.

While he fucked her, the Queen ate the tongue, savoring its meat. She couldn't concentrate on the food, however: the in/out motion of the penis in her rear was intensely stimulating, not to be ignored. She reached her free hand down and rubbed herself, moaning as she felt another orgasm building in her crotch.

"Slow down a bit, darling!" she gasped between chews of tongue meat. "Let's try and come together!"

"Better you speed up, darling," James grunted back. "I'm practically here already—my balls feel like grenades with the safety pins pulled." But he froze in her ass again. His eyes were shut; he felt like he was dissolving into her sweet rectal tissue.

"I love you, darling," the Queen mumbled around her mouthful of meat, grinding her buttocks against his crotch. She rubbed her clitoris harder. "You're so considera—"

Her golden eyes widened as a black bird flew in through one wall of the bedroom and out the other. Then another followed.

She froze, turned her head back to stare at James. "What was that?"

He opened his eyes. "What?"

"Two birds just flew through our room."

James looked around and saw nothing. "Darling, there's nothing here."

The Queen insisted, "I saw the damn things." She spat red spittle over the bed's edge. "Oh, just forget it," she snapped, angry at being unable to prove her claim.

He shrugged, began stroking in her anus again, rolling his penis in the soft rectal warmth. "Let's just fuck, my love—if I don't come in you soon, I'll die in your ass."

The ginger Queen sighed. "Oh, you put it so nicely." She relaxed, raised the half-eaten tongue to her lips again, took another bite and chewed, dipped her free hand between her white thighs again. James pushed her orange hair out of his eyes, then shut them and stroked deeply in her backside, sliding his hands around her to caress her breasts.

Four black birds now flew into the bedroom, then another six. Soon the room was full of them. The Queen didn't stop either eating or having sex. James clearly hadn't seen the birds and she wanted to be certain this time that they weren't going anywhere before she alerted him to their presence. Besides, she could already feel her climax rising from her crotch and spreading through her. No way were these things going to mess her orgasm up. Still, the birds looked odd, like they were made of liquid. One flew close to her face; it seemed to have gears in it. *Gears? How can a bird have gears?* Oh . . . but her climax was on her now.

"Oh God—I'm coming!" James gushed, suddenly opening his eyes wide. "What the hell . . . ?"

"I told you!" the Queen moaned," swallowing the last of the tongue. Then: "Oh fucking fuck my ass, darling!" she gasped, biting down on her lower lip to keep from screaming as her own orgasm commandeered her.

"They seem harmless enough," James managed to comment as he ejaculated hot jets of semen up the Queen's backside.

Then the morph birds ceased their aimless floating through the air and dove at the climaxing couple.

"Shit!" James yelped in horror.

***

The ginger Queen was aware of the birds hitting her and passing through her, just like they'd gone through the wall. There was no pain, it was pleasant even; those that flew through her breasts made them tingle nicely.

But her darling James? With a soft pop, his penis exited her body. Then she heard him groaning in pain. She spun around to look at him, his come draining unheeded from her spread anus.

The Queen was instantly worried, then frightened. James writhed in agony as the black birds vanished into him. Like bombs the birds hit him, first spattering on his hairy skin, then dissolving into it.

But that wasn't all that scared the Queen: James's body was changing. It was becoming larger and turning green in color. The transformation was fast; soon she could see what he was becoming. Once she did, she leapt off the bed and backed away quickly from it.

Croc god, was the best description that came to her mind as her erstwhile lover got down from the bed and stood facing her.

James now looked like the mingling of a man and a monster crocodile. He towered almost eight feet high, his head brushing the ceiling. Though still roughly human-shaped, he had a huge crocodile's head, and that reptile's armored skin, short thick limbs, and clawed feet. A thick scaly tail dangled between his legs, sweeping the floor behind him.

The crocodile man regarded the ginger Queen with yellow reptile eyes, then opened his vast long snout rimmed with huge white teeth.

He roared at her; a horrible mind-numbing sound.

Realizing she was in danger of being eaten, the Queen stepped hastily backward towards the bedroom door. She didn't dare turn her back on 'James.' No! This monster clearly wasn't her beloved James anymore. Her eyes filled with tears. *My darling is gone? Those birds changed him into this creature? Oh no!*

Carefully, never taking her eyes off the eight-feet-high mutant facing her, she felt behind her for the door.

She found it, only then the door burst open and several ginger guards charged into the room.

"Your Majesty!" one yelled. "We have to get you and the boss out of here! The house is changing, and . . ." He fell silent on noticing the crocodile man. "What the hell is—"

The flame-haired guard never completed his question. Moving at incredible speed, the transformed James grabbed him up and bit into him. Bit *through* him: that first bite severed the man in half at the waist. Blood foaming over his massive jaws, the reptile man wolfed down the guard's head and shoulders, then belched a red mist.

The ginger Queen began shivering like she was deathly cold. As the croc monster swallowed the rest of the first guard and grabbed another, she turned and fled the bedroom.

So intent was she on her flight downstairs and outside, she never even noticed the flowers now growing from the corridor walls.

PART 3:
CATCHING A FRIGHT

CHAPTER 25

Melanie Nemesis Catchpole jerked awake.

She looked around the office. *Doug's still not back? Shit, something must have happened to him.*

She quickly roused herself from the sofa. *I have to go looking for him. But where?* Even while thinking this, however, her feminine intuition assured her she'd be wasting her time searching. *Doug has to be dead. He wouldn't remain outside after everything that happened in the night.*

The *weird* shit that happened.

Her breasts felt strange, heavier than normal. In alarm, remembering the nuts she'd eaten, she hastily undid her shirt (this second time she'd slept fully clothed, ready to either fight or flee) and freed them from her bra.

Oh shit!

While asleep, her nut allergy had been hard at work. Both her breasts now had fingers sticking out where their nipples should be. The left breast had two, the right, three, one of them a thumb. In a sudden growth spurt, the thumb grew a little larger.

Groaning, Melanie examined herself all over. No, she didn't have a penis (it had happened before), or a bushy tail, or extra eyes anywhere. Just the fingers growing from her breasts. Waving fingers.

She was relieved—the effect should wear off by tomorrow. She peered at the nut canister. *But . . . I'm supposed to keep eating these, right?* Sighing, she picked it up and shook a pile of the mingled cashews, pecans, almonds, Brazil nuts and walnuts into her palm.

(She was particularly peeved that The Fixer had given her a 'Deluxe Nuts' jar, which had zero-percent peanuts in it [an omission normally considered a bonus]; or was it that peanuts didn't help against the weirdness, only tree nuts did? Whichever it was, Melanie was once again struck by a recurring sense of irony about her allergy—most people's nut allergies operated the other way around: they couldn't eat peanuts but found 'tree nuts' little or no bother . . .)

She threw the nut mixture into her mouth, chewed and swallowed, jerking her head back theatrically so her black hair swung behind her.

Her left breast instantly grew a thumb of its own.

She shrugged, tucked her breasts into restraint again. *Better safe than sorry—I'm protected against the weirdness now.*

***

Melanie unlocked the door to the inner office and peeked out. Outside looked exactly as she'd left it—grassy plains, slogan-marked sheep, odd buildings and black clouds in the distance.

She locked the door again, crossed to the French windows and pulled back the drapes. She froze, staring in shock.

The French windows were gone. What faced her now was a pale expanse of crinkled skin with large gray hairs in it.

She backed away towards the sofa. Now she realized that the whole front wall had the same old-person-flesh texture to it.

Quickly, not pondering the transformation (it was par for the course now after all that The Fixer had shown her in the night), she gathered up her stuff. The green nut canister went in a side jacket pocket for easy reach. Thankfully it wasn't too thick. It bulged a bit, but wouldn't prove a nuisance.

She left the room by its side door.

***

Outside, she was met by another shock. There was no landing, no stairs. What had been a five-story building was now apparently a bungalow.

Melanie cringed at the implications: *What if Doug and I had roomed on one of the lower floors? Where the hell are they now? Damn, I'm getting out of here before this building alters further! The only question is: front door or back door?*

Both exits had transoms through which bold sunlight shone. Melanie decided to go out the front way. Hopefully it still connected to downtown Springfield. If it did, she'd try to find her way to 1111 Parker Street and look for the magic teddy bear. If Doug was still alive, she expected him to try and rendezvous with her at the warehouses.

Making long strides for the front door, she reached inside her jacket for the teddy bear's picture. Then froze with her hand in her pocket.

Ahead of her two shadows solidified into Lois and Vera Smith. Both women were frowning and pointing guns at her. Both were covered with layers of dust; it was in their hair, their eyelashes . . . everywhere.

"Hey, hon," Lois said grimly. "We were just coming to wake you up."

Vera nodded. "Yeah."

Melanie couldn't resist a question: "Why are you both so . . . dirty?"

Lois spat. "We were sleeping downstairs in the lobby . . . then the ceiling fell in and we had to run up the stairs . . . and they kept disappearing behind us . . ." She brushed a spider out of her hair. "We just made it up here, and next thing we know, the fucking stairway door disappears—"

"Fuck reliving the great escape," Vera growled. "We're up here now."

Melanie asked, "Did you see Doug . . . downstairs?"

A wink passed between the sisters. Then Lois said, "Hell no—we were too busy running for our lives."

Vera added, "He isn't back yet?"

Melanie considered Vera's statement. *Girl, if you didn't see him, how d'you know he left here?* She let it ride for the moment. "Okay, both of you—why are you pointing your guns at me? I'm not responsible for collapsing the frigging building, am I?"

Lois replied, "We want the 411 about a teddy bear that you're looking for."

Melanie frowned. "Teddy bear? What teddy bear?"

Vera stepped up close to Melanie, stuck her gun in Melanie's ear. "Wrong fucking answer, bitch. Don't be a douche like Doug was, or we'll rinse our pussies with you."

Melanie's gaze narrowed. "I thought you said you *hadn't* seen Doug. Okay, where the hell is he?"

Vera giggled. "Oops, my bad—you got us there. Let's just say you two ain't dating anymore."

Lois added: "Arrrgh, men just make me so angry sometimes. Dougie was planning to kill you once you got the teddy bear. And from your touching concern for him, he'd clearly already gotten way past third base with you. Definitely struck a home run in your diamond; maybe even hit a series of them."

Melanie rolled her eyes. "You expect *me* to believe *you*?"

Vera nodded. "Uh huh. Oh yeah, and by the way, my kid sister here thinks you're super cute."

Melanie scowled. "You two murdered Doug?"

Lois sniggered. "We fed him dinner—*it* killed him. If you don't start talking fast, we'll serve you breakfast."

Vera rapped her gun painfully against Melanie's temple. "Trust us—you won't like breakfast. So start talking."

Lois quipped, "Honey, we're temporarily arctophiles—now tell us all about Teddy, and I don't mean Kennedy."

Melanie considered the Chameleon Sisters' ruthless faces. They clearly meant business. She figured their story about Doug planning her death was a lie, however. But they'd killed him . . . coldly . . . callously . . . He'd likely died while they were torturing the secret of the teddy from him, which is why they wanted her now. A hard ball of hatred for Lois and Vera formed in her belly.

"O.K.," she said, pulling her hand from her jacket and holding out the photo of the teddy bear. "This is what you want."

Lois snapped the picture from her grasp. "*This thing* is worth millions? Is it stuffed full of diamonds or what?" She pouted in puzzlement. "And why is it humping a banana?"

Melanie shrugged.

Vera took the picture from her sister, glanced it over, then stared pointedly at Melanie. "Dougie said it was magic. What kind of magic? Start explaining in detail. For your own good, just tell us the damn truth."

Melanie nodded. "O.K., but let's move outside first. You don't want the building collapsing on us, do you?" As confirmation of this possibility, the corridor walls rumbled.

(Melanie was calculating hard. The Chameleon sisters hadn't disarmed her, but neither had they even once moved their guns off her. Once outside the house, she'd make her move. She rehearsed her attack in her mind: *Pull gun, dive sideways to the right, twist and roll in midair, firing while still falling. I'll pop both bitches in the middle of their frigging heads, scatter their brains everywhere. They'll be dead before my back touches the ground.)*

Lois looked suspiciously at Melanie. "Hey, how much do you know about all this weird shit going on?" Then she looked perplexed. "And why have your nipples suddenly gotten so big?" Lois was leaning against the wall. In her sudden confusion, the entire left side of her body had turned the wall's exact cream color.

Vera rolled her eyes. "Sis, lay off the seduction, wilya? We're transacting business here."

Lois nodded. "Yeah, yeah. Her tits *are* much larger though."

"Whatever. Just don't start touch-testing."

Lois scowled at Melanie. "So, answer my damn question: what do you know about those weird black birds and the world changing?"

"Nothing. Only that if we remain in here we'll all likely get flattened." A twitching in her left bra cup announced the growth of yet another nipple-finger.

The corridor rumbled again. Melanie plucked the teddy bear photo from Vera's fingers—

"Hey!"

—and put it away in her pocket again. She stared Vera down. "You don't need it. I'm taking you to the teddy's location, right?"

Vera regarded Melanie with a frigid smile, then ran slim fingers over Melanie's heavy backside. "Just remember this, darling—you attempt to run, you'll get an ass-full of bullets. I mean—I'll pump so much fucking lead in your rear you'll think you're getting butt implants." She waved her gun towards the front door. "Okay, let's go."

***

Lois went first, Vera brought up the rear. Walking between both blondes, Melanie revised her plan.

Okay, now I'll boot Lois out of the way . . . shoot Vera first, Lois second—she'll be stunned from hitting—

She instantly revised her plan again. A large shadow had moved across the transom. Something was out there, something BIG. Melanie smiled grimly. Neither of the sisters seemed to have realized the danger. *I'll kick Lois towards whatever's out there, then turn fast and grapple with Vera while she's still shocked.*

Lois opened the door.

The monster standing outside the building was so shocking that Melanie instantly abandoned all her offensive plans.

What faced them was a gray/brown creature like a hill of rocks shaped into a caricature of a man. The stone monster was close to fifteen feet tall, with rolling granite eyes like grindstones. The rocks forming it ground against each other like angrily gnashing teeth. Melanie instantly noted the dark crimson stain that rimmed the monster's jagged mouth and had dripped down its neck onto its rocky breast. Her conclusion? This fucking thing was a clear danger to all three of them.

(Beyond the monster, Melanie momentarily glimpsed the windowless blue airplane casting lightning down at a burning rooftop.)

Lois spun round. Her eyes were wide with terror and she was trembling. "It's the monster, Vera! The one that ate Doug's sister green-eyes! It's gotten bigger!" Without realizing it, she'd begun pissing herself again.

Lois was still standing in the entranceway, the door unable to close because her body blocked it. Gnashing its bloody teeth in infernal excitement, the stone monster strode forward, stretching out a hand to grab her.

Alerted by the sound of its motion, Lois spun back around again. She saw the huge stone fingers reaching for her and promptly fainted. She collapsed in the doorway, head inside, legs outside, her gun bouncing down off the steps and away.

Next moment, the monster's huge fingers clenched shut in the empty space she'd recently occupied.

Melanie now reacted on instinct. *We needed to shut the damn door!* Leaping forward, she grabbed the swooned Lois and dragged her inside the corridor. Vera instantly slammed the door shut and locked it. Together, they pulled Lois well away from the entrance. Halfway down the cream-colored corridor, they paused to get over their shock. Each woman stared at the other, their hearts pumping like they'd burst.

Outside, the stone monster growled its frustration. Then the door dented as the creature struck it. Another blow flung wood splinters everywhere.

"We ain't getting out that way," Vera said drily. Gun dangling by her side, she grinned at Melanie. "Thanks for saving my sis; I owe you one." Her grin broadened. "Hey—don't tell me you fancy her too!"

Melanie had had totally enough of the Chameleon Sisters' bullshit. It wasn't the sapphic allusion (she could care less about that), she simply utterly detested both women now.

She hit Vera, a low hard punch to the gut that forced all the air from Vera's lungs in a single exhalation.

Gasping for air, her eyes wide with the sudden pain, Vera swung her gun up to shoot Melanie. "I'll f-f-fucking kill you for that, y-y-you fat bitch!"

Melanie karate-chopped her wrist. Yelping, Vera dropped the gun. Melanie hit her again, this time a short right to the jaw. Vera rolled with the punch, came up with her fists in a boxer's stance. There was blood on her lips. Her beautiful brown eyes were cold with hatred. She spat out words like they was poisonous: "And here I was thinking we'd just become besties. Now *we are* going to kill you."

"You're a piece of crap," Melanie spat back. "I'd rather make friends with a diamondback." She too raised her fists. Anger flowed through her like blood. She intended smashing Vera Smith's face so far into her skull, it would come out the back of her head.

Behind both women, the door was now completely disintegrated, a mess of shattered wood. The stone monster was reaching in at them. Its gray fingers however stopped about six feet short of where there were. The creature growled, spitting dust, clutching at air, leaving angry scratches in the cream corridor wall, which had now begun throbbing again.

Melanie flung a punch at Vera's head. Vera ducked it, flung a counter punch that slid off Melanie's forearm and hit her left breast.

Vera's eyes turned perplexed. "Hey—why the hell are your nipples hard? You want to fuck me, is that it? Stupid in-the-closet slut!"

"What are you fucking ranting about?" Then Melanie remembered the fingers growing from her breasts. She glared at Vera, who was giving her a smug, knowing smile like she'd just outed her. Frowning, Melanie feinted like she was going to throw her right hand, then swung up with her left instead, catching Vera flush on the jaw.

Vera's eyes rolled back up in her head; she toppled over backwards, unconscious.

Melanie bent over her. Yeah, Vera's lights were out alright; only the whites of her eyes now showed. Melanie squatted by the wall, catching her breath.

"Hey!" a cold voice said behind her. "Don't you dare move a muscle, and that includes your fucking kegels."

Reaching for her gun, Melanie spun around. *Fuck estrogen—I forgot Lois.*

Lois had pulled herself up against the wall. (Her back had once again matched itself to the cream paint.) She had two guns trained on Melanie. She waved the right-hand weapon.

"Now, honey, take your hand out of your pocket. Slowly. Bring out that gun and drop it on the floor. Try any heroine nonsense and I'll perforate your cute behind."

Melanie did as she was told, feeling naked as she put the weapon down.

"Kick it over here."

Melanie did so. Keeping an eye on her, Lois picked the gun off the floor and stuck it in her waistband.

Melanie stared beyond the busty blonde for a moment. The stone monster was still grasping in at them. Its grotesque knobbed face was pressed against the door jamb; its mouth—like a cave in a granite cliff-side—gaped open. Melanie was disgusted but intrigued. The interior of the creature's mouth was dark with caked blood; there were shards of bone stuck in the cracks of its stone tongue.

Lois waved her gun at Melanie. "Forget Frankenstone there." Then she caught the smell of herself. "Gosh—I pissed myself again."

Moving away from the wall, Lois smiled coyly at Melanie. "Okay, first, thanks for saving my ass. I've been figuring out why I'm not monster food now: You were right behind me—you *must have* pulled me away from the door. You could just have easily have kicked me outside."

"A mistake I deeply regret, believe me."

"Thanks anyway. I saw that fucking thing eat someone last night—hell of a way to die."

Melanie shrugged. "Worse than feeding Doug his fatal dinner?"

Lois smirked. "You're still angry about that? I told you—the asshole was no good."

Melanie rolled her eyes. "Girl, if we all went around killing douchebag boyfriends, there'd be no men left in the world."

"Whatever. Okay, move down the corridor," Lois instructed. "I want to see what you've done to Vera." She waved a gun at Melanie. "Go on, get further back so you can't rush me."

"Look, frigging just let me go; O.K.? I don't like you, you don't like me. This ain't high school—I ain't dyin' to hang out with the cool chicks."

Lois looked up from bending over her sister. "Shut up, hon. You're forgetting the magic teddy bear. That's ours now."

Melanie hadn't forgotten. She'd just hoped that after Lois's narrow escape from the stone creature at the door (which was still futilely trying to grab them—its fingers had now dug deep holes in the corridors walls) she'd be distracted from that interest for a while. Unfortunately, that was clearly not the case. *Looks like I'll need to bluff my way out.*

Frowning, she said, "You two girls wanna rumble with Bigelow Jenkins? A pair of little bitches wanna bite the big dog? That it? Ain't that more bone than you can chew?"

"The *big dog*? Biggs?" Lois raised a sarcastic eyebrow, then laughed. "Are you fucking joking? No, I forgot—you're from out of town, just a Jenny-come-lately with delusions of grandeur. Girl, don't fool yourself. Bigelow don't call no shots around here. Biggs is a pussy, so scared of James he shits at the sight of him." Then she smiled admiringly at Melanie. "Damn, honey—you sure as hell can punch. Few broads can put out Vera's lights like this. Few guys even." She regarded Melanie with an inquisitive gaze. "Why'd you beat her up anyway? You anti-lez?"

Melanie sighed. "This has nothing to do with sexuality. I simply don't like you girls . . . *you two* . . . get it? Even though you're both incredibly beautiful and look like the best thing going ever in bed." She gasped her frustration. "Is that so hard to understand? You're both cold callous capricious conniving cunts!" Her voice grew heated during the exposition, her face flushed.

A broad smile spread like sunshine over Lois's lovely lips. "You know anger makes you look incredibly sexy, right?" She gestured with a gun to Melanie, then pointed down at Vera. "Okay, come back over here. Grab her legs, I'll get her shoulders; then we'll take her out back."

Melanie complied. They lifted Vera and carried her off down the corridor. Around them, the house trembled like it was holding itself together by sheer effort of will.

Behind them, the stone monster growled loudly. It now began ripping out chunks of the front door frame in its fervor to reach them.

CHAPTER 26

The world outside the back door was a nightmare. It was nothing like the soft grassy pasture Melanie had seen through the office door inside. (*And where is that place now?* she wondered for a moment. Totally impossible to tell. It could be through the next door they reached. It could be twenty or two hundred miles away.)

They put Vera down on the sidewalk.

Lois gasped at the sights around them. "You've got to be fisting me!"

"I wish I was," Melanie retorted without sarcasm.

They'd emerged onto a street, that, even by the normal standards of an O-Zone, was fucked-up to the max. The house opposite them, for instance, had human ears growing out of its concrete walls. Two buildings to its left stood a skyscraper studded with massive human feet instead of windows. The feet moved sluggishly, their bared soles displayed like billboards. Several other houses looked to be covered with feathers, like they were actually monster birds roosting.

And the ground itself? Some parts of both road and sidewalks were normal, other areas were covered with thick bristling hair; yet other portions of the road were scaly, like parts of a giant reptile's back.

A loud growling sounded behind them. Melanie and Lois spun around, now realizing that in their shock they'd left their exit open. The noise came from the corridor. Melanie peeked inside and recoiled. The stone monster had now forced its head and shoulders inside the cream passageway and was squirming its way at them.

"It looks like a dildo sliding along a vagina," Lois quipped. She looked at Melanie, her eyes scared. "It's a persistent son-of-a-bitch. We'd better get out of here before it makes it through to us."

Melanie hadn't yet taken her eyes off the monster forcing its way towards them. "Yes, let's," she agreed.

She shut the door, which instantly disappeared. She and Lois stared at each other.

"Now, there's an anticlimax," Lois said.

"The corridor exit just moved somewhere else," Melanie said. She looked back around at their surroundings. "I'm uncertain, however, if that's good or bad for us."

Lois said nothing. She shared Melanie's thoughts. What faced them everywhere they turned was pure insane absurdity. Like the car down the road that was covered in barking dog heads, and something that looked like a giant wheeled cockroach rolling up a wall next door. Like the two-headed woman peeking out from a window in the house opposite (the one with the ears). Like the way several houses farther off seemed covered in human skin of varying colors . . . Like some buildings' odd angles of elevation (some leaning at forty-five degrees), and the stairs and ladders that rose into the sky to terminate at doors that just hung there in space . . .

"This doesn't even look like the O anymore," Lois gasped. She pointed a trembling hand skyward to where Bizarro floated in its brown familiarity. "*This* is like being up *there*."

Melanie recalled The Fixer's explanation. "It's a mingling. Bizarro come down to Earth. The parallands are blending with the here and now." She grinned at Lois. "Cheer up, hon; it only gets worse from here on."

Vera (who'd blended into gray invisibility while lying on the sidewalk) woke up then, rubbing her jaw and moaning. "Damn, bitch, where the hell did you learn to hit like that?" Then she saw where they were. "What . . . ?"

"Bout time you rejoined the awake," Lois said.

Still tenderly feeling her jaw, Vera staggered to her feet. From the waist down, her body was sidewalk-gray like she was made of stone. She regarded Melanie angrily, snatching a gun from Lois and pointing it at her.

She said, "What the hell do we do with her now?"

Melanie winced. "Are you girls still carrying on with this dominatrix nonsense? We're in deep shit here, you know."

"Shut up," Vera retorted. "Messed up or not, this is still the O-Zone; we're still looking for that teddy bear."

"Damn," Melanie said. "And I thought I knocked some sense into your empty head."

Vera's eyes hardened, her lips pursed tight with rage. "If you intend living past the next minute, I'll advise you against making any more cracks like that."

Melanie turned her gaze to Lois, who nodded back. "Delightfully-padded ass or not, you're too much of a smartass."

"You two are missing the point here," Melanie said patiently.

Vera growled, "What damn point?"

"Look!" Melanie pointed, the sisters looked. About a mile off, over a HUGE blue-and-pink birthday cake (complete with pillar-sized lit candles), spiraled massive ink-dark formations. "Those are the birds that caused this crap," Melanie said. "For fuck's sake—don't you get it? This isn't the O-Zone any of us remember anymore." She stared Vera in the eye. "There's no way we're finding anything in here now. I mean, where the hell are we?"

Lois chewed on a fingertip, her face unsure. "You're saying we're lost?"

Melanie pointed to the skyscraper with bare feet growing out of it. "Have *you* any idea where we are?"

Lois mused on that. "Nah, but . . ." she made an expansive gesture with her gun, "all this has to end somewhere."

"Yeah," Vera seconded, though her voice was also uncertain. "You're forgetting something else."

"What?"

Vera pointed up behind Melanie. "That's Bizarro up there. A true landmark if ever there was one. So . . . we're still in the O." Finger up in the air, she traced the edge of the brown mass with an imaginary line. "All we need do is follow it and we'll be back out in the city in no time."

Lois scowled at Melanie. "I do believe you're trying to trick us out of some good money, honey."

"And that'll prove fatal," Vera added.

Melanie laughed coldly. "Look behind you. If we're in the O-Zone like you remember it . . . where's the other floating mass of shit?"

"Nice try, honey," Lois smirked. "But we're wise to that trick." She blew Melanie a kiss. "I'll keep my eyes on you if you don't mind."

Vera, however, turned around. She spent a long moment gasping up at the endless blue sky, with its swirling black birds, then spun back to face Melanie again. Her beautiful face was now pale like she'd seen several ghosts.

Seeing Vera's shock, Lois looked back also.

(Melanie didn't bother attacking the Chameleon Sisters now they were distracted. She figured that even a pair of total meatheads like these two had to have some brains somewhere, even if it was in their tight buttocks.)

Lois finished her own examination of the empty sky behind. On turning around again, she looked even paler than Vera did. She was trembling. In her confusion, her legs had faded out of view. "What the hell is that huge monument over there? The one with faces and tentacles all over it?"

"Convinced now?" Melanie asked softly.

Lois looked at her sister. Vera nodded. Both blondes nodded to Melanie. Vera, her breasts bouncing with her labored breathing, said, "Okay—for the moment it's a truce between us. We'll resume with the magic teddy bear later. Damn, you're right—we've no frigging idea where the hell we are; we three need to work together to figure a way out of here."

"And fast," Lois added nervously. "There might be more of those stone monsters around."

"Yeah," Melanie agreed drily, pleased that the sisters had seen reason at last. "Those black birds—call 'em morph birds—transform anything." Then her face creased up with pain. "Yeow!!!"

Her breasts hurt! It felt like something was tearing out of them. Melanie ripped her shirt open, spilling buttons everywhere. She freed her breasts from her bra.

Lois and Vera gaped. Lois's tongue dangled out of her mouth. It dropped and dropped, till finally it hung between her breasts, all the way down to her navel. She slowly drew it back up between her lips again.

"Oh my God!" Vera gasped, flinging fingers up to her mouth. "She's got hands for nipples!"

"I told you her tits were getting bigger," Lois whispered in a shocked voice.

Melanie was even more startled than the sisters. Each of the large hands now sticking out from her breasts seemed male—both were very hairy. Both clenched into fists, then spread their fingers wide again; clenched tight again.

Melanie staggered back and slumped against a wall. "Fuck!" she gasped in a sharp outburst of air. "That hurt like hell."

"Are you okay?" Lois asked. She moved to help Melanie stand upright. One of the breast-hands grabbed her arm and held on.

"I'm fine," Melanie said, rallying. She was oddly touched by Lois's concern. Maybe the woman wasn't all bad. Shit, even Vera was staring at her worriedly.

The breast-hand let go of Lois's arm. Lois draped the arm across Melanie's shoulders. (Lois found the breast-hands oddly erotic, her mind was already rife with imaginings of the lovely delicious things they could do to her body in bed. Like, for instance, squeezing both her own breasts at once while Melanie fingered her vagina and stroked her hair.)

Melanie felt her breasts gingerly, like she was examining them for cancer lumps. "There's a bone in here," she said. "A long one connecting to my ribcage, like—"

Then she noticed the scared look on Lois's and Vera's faces. Next, a shadow dropped over herself and the sisters, and she heard a faint humming sound overhead.

She whirled around. The blue experimental airplane hung overhead like a fallen cloud.

Lois and Vera leapt away from Melanie's side, raised their guns, and began shooting at the plane. It responded in violent kind. Bullets and bolts of lightning flashed past Melanie on both sides, trapping her between them. Without a firearm or any cover, Melanie could only watch and hope she survived. *Damn! I'm caught between the devil and deep shit here!* She was aware of masonry fragmenting behind her, and of the Chameleon Sisters hopping about to avoid being crisped.

"Shit!" Lois cussed.

More lighting flashes came from the plane, zigzagging from the black tentacle at its tail end.

Then, without warning, the tentacle lashed downward.

"Duck!" Vera yelled as the black whip flailed towards them.

"Yeah, get your ass flat on the ground! Now!"

Melanie Nemesis Catchpole *attempted* flinging herself down. She was later uncertain if her reflexes were simply too slow, or if the hands growing from her breasts were affecting her coordination, or if something from the plane had paralyzed her . . . whichever it was, she somehow didn't move as fast as usual. Even as she ducked forward, the black tentacle reached her. Moving with unbelievable speed, the metal appendage wrapped itself several times around her body and snapped her up off the ground, up into the air. Melanie found herself with her arms tightly bound to her sides, powerless to resist being carried off. And now, almost like they knew they could currently get away with whatever discomfort they caused her, the hands on her breasts began itching fiercely.

As she was borne higher and higher aloft, dragged away after the now departing aircraft, she could see the Chameleon Sisters staring up after her. Oddly, her last impression of them was that, psycho bitches or not, they were actually very worried about her.

CHAPTER 27

"Ain't that just the damnest thing ever!?" Vera Smith exclaimed, watching the blue airplane carry Melanie off beneath Bizarro. "And I was beginning to like that chick. She's got spunk for real."

Lois frowned after Melanie's tiny departing figure. "I do feel sorry for her, you know. She's like . . . oh so dead now."

"You can't be certain of that." Vera's voice held reproof.

"Okay, maybe not dead. But, don't kid yourself, sis—she ain't coming back through here, for certain. That airplane never returns people, it just keeps taking them."

"Maybe it takes them up to some fairytale land on Bizarro where they'll never grow old." Vera's voice held a note of wistful hope.

"Damn, you do like that lady, don't you?"

Vera grinned. "Last time a woman knocked me out was in . . . I don't remember." She looked pointedly at Lois. "Okay, so what do we do now?"

Lois scrunched up her face in thought. "You know, this hasn't worked out at all like we planned." She threw up her hands in exasperation. "I mean . . ." She sighed. "Sis, let's just get the fuck out of here; find a way out of this fucked-up O-Zone or wherever it is."

Vera frowned, her eyes narrowed. "You're saying that we should forget about finding the magic teddy bear?"

Lois nodded. "Screw the teddy bear. And I'm not just saying that because the world's changed around us."

"Why then?"

"Well, even if we do find our way back to our normal O, we've actually no idea where the damn teddy's supposed to be." She nodded at her sister's suddenly wide-eyed expression. "Yeah, sis, that's the one question we forgot to ask cutie pie Melanie—where the teddy bear was . . ." She pointed skyward, to where the blue plane had now vanished. "With her gone, so does our hope of making those millions of dollars."

Vera considered Lois's words for a long minute, while continuously smacking her forehead with a palm. "Dammit! I can't believe we could be so dumb!" Her anger turned her cheeks red.

Lois burst out laughing.

"What the hell's so funny? We just lost—"

Lois stepped in close and kissed her. Vera resisted for a moment, then yielded to the soft lips pressed deliciously on hers. The sisters dueled tongues for a while.

Lois pulled away when Vera slid hands under her T-shirt and began fondling her breasts. "Uh uh. Not here . . . and don't look so fucking hurt."

Vera pouted, reached for her again. "But you started it. Oh, c'mon, get me off—there's no one watching."

Lois pushed her off. "Wrong, hon. There's a two-headed woman in that building across the road with a ringside view."

Vera looked. She saw the two-headed woman duck into hiding. In the woman's place, a three-legged bird paced across the window. She sighed, looked longingly at Lois. "Okay, what now, sis?"

Lois pointed left, down the street. "Best we head that way. We'll trace Bizarro till it ends. Despite what our abducted honey said, reality has to resume somewhere."

Vera thought a bit, then nodded. "Yeah, you're right. Or we'll find a door that leads back to it." She grinned. "Either way, first fucking town we get to—"

"I'm gonna buy me a bedroom-full-a-whores, and get well screwed!" Lois finished. It was the sisters' normal refrain when they planned on a night of womanizing.

They set out left.

"Wow," Lois said, "Everything's so surreal around here now, I'm almost expecting to run into the cast of The Simpsons. I'd love to ask Marge what she ever saw in Homer."

"Damn, they smell unwashed," Vera said as they passed the skyscraper with feet sticking out of it. "What do they call this place— the Athlete's Foot Building?"

Lois regarded the massive projecting appendages, each the size of an automobile. Each foot was implanted into the building at its ankle, the flesh–concrete joining seamless and natural-looking. The feet moved, some violently like they were kicking something. Strange insects that seemed made of Lego pieces crawled over the feet nearest the sisters.

Lois shuddered. "You know, sis, we're being very foolish here."

Vera regarded her in surprise. "What do you mean?"

Lois pointed. "We're walking in broad daylight, and not even camouflaging ourselves at all. I know we've not seen any gingers so far, but . . ."

Vera got the point. From that point on, the Chameleon Sisters walked close to each building they reached, their voluptuous forms automatically changing color to blend with each successive wall so it was impossible to tell that they were passing by.

CHAPTER 28

Bound in the metal tentacle, Melanie was swung up towards the plane. Right at the moment she expected to shatter her head against the shiny blue undercarriage, a hatch slid open in it and she was borne inside the aircraft.

The first thing she noticed was the smell! A foul stench ambushed her as she entered the plane. Like there were a million corpses nearby.

Melanie was set down on her feet in a large stinking chamber. The black tentacle unwrapped from around her body and slithered away. She had a moment's view of houses passing far below, then the hatch slid shut.

A cold blue light filled the plane's interior.

The terrible stench still disoriented Melanie. She looked around at her surroundings (a large chamber like a cabin without seats and a shut door at one end) and instantly recoiled in disgust and horror, fighting intense nausea.

The source of the obscene smell was now plain.

Fuck! She was surrounded by corpses. Rotting bodies in varying stages of decomposition were piled everywhere. In places the moldering dead were stacked ceiling-high against the plastic cabin walls.

A few of the dead were gingers, but most were human; women and men the aircraft had clearly violently transported from life to death. All were stripped naked, their shredded clothes randomly strewn about their bodies.

Worse, all the corpses were half-eaten, large expanses of flesh ripped from them, the tearing clearly the work of tooth and claw. Most corpses had all their large muscle meat—that of the thighs and upper arms—missing, while, save for the complete removal of their chest muscles, their torsos were intact, their bellies swollen pregnant-taut with putrefaction. Many of the necks were slashed; the rips were untidy, clearly made by claws. Other bodies had their torsos ripped open, the skin slashed in equally telltale parallel lines. Both corpses and floor were coated with a morbid sludge of congealed blood, vomit, fat, and excrement.

Those areas of the cabin walls not obscured by stacked bodies were maculated with bright red splotches of blood, and occasional smears of rancid yellow fat.

Melanie turned in a slow circle, surveying the carnage with rising horror. How many bodies were piled around her? She calculated there had to be a least two hundred dead people in the blue-lit cabin.

She fought to calm herself; tried to think clearly. To do so was almost impossible—the harrowing sight of the abused corpses, the heat created by their decay . . . above all their obscene smell, like she'd been accidentally interred in a war grave . . .

Some of the corpses had clearly been here for weeks, their maggot-coating bore testament to their age. Other bodies were new, only recently mauled. Those right beside Melanie were only days old at most. One seemed freshly killed, the blood pooled by it still a bright vivid crimson—tellingly, the dead woman still had uneaten thighs. The faces of the most recently deceased wore expressions of intense crap-your-pants horror.

Melanie's desire to puke returned magnified.

A sudden farting sound gave Melanie a fright; her heart leapt up into her mouth. She gasped on seeing what had made the sound: Coated in yellow pus, a hand-sized white roach was emerging from a nearby man's bloated torso through a hole in his navel. The farting noise was gas escaping the punctured belly. The roach dragged a large purple chunk of liver after it. Behind this first roach emerged several more, each one similarly smeared with pus, each also liver-laden. The corpse deflated as the insects left it, till finally it was flat.

Melanie gave in to her desire to throw up. She splattered both insects and corpse with vomit. The roaches instantly scattered, discarding their pieces of meat. Then, when Melanie was done upchucking, they returned to retrieve them.

The vomiting calmed Melanie down. Afterward, it felt like she'd puked out her terror, her dread. She felt stronger. She gathered the shreds of her tattered nerves about her, stitched them back into a cloak of courage. This wasn't her first meeting with death by any means; it was just that this mass murder surrounding her was so . . . so . . . unexpected. Being spirited away so abruptly, she'd expected to encounter aliens, scientists, Area 51 geeks . . . anything but—she stared into the bulging eyes of a young brunette who'd clearly bled to death when both her arms were torn off at the shoulders—anything but this.

"Damn!" she muttered. "And here we were all thinking this was a fucking research plane."

She felt the aircraft's throbbing as it flew on, though it made almost no noise. (She recalled that from the outside, the blue aircraft had seemed to have no engines.) Considering the smell, she considered this a blessing.

Her jacket and shirt were still open, her breasts hanging free over her bra. The hands growing from her breasts had balled into tight fists like they sensed her mental turmoil and wanted to fight someone on her behalf. Melanie decided the strange appendages were the least of her current problems. Ignoring them (at least they'd stopped itching), and leaving her breasts free (no way would they fit back in her bra now), she set her mind to work on the puzzle this ghastly airplane represented.

(She removed her glasses, let them dangle on their silver chain on her chest. This immediately proved a bad decision—the breast hands grabbed at them, distracting her thoughts—so she stowed the specs away in a pocket. At close ranges like this she didn't need them anyway—she wore them continually from sheer habit.)

Her first calm thoughts, however, almost brought a return of her panic:

Whoever . . . whatever . . . did this knows I'm aboard, and will shortly be coming to check on . . . to eat . . . me! And, oh no, that's so not happening!

She took a personal weapons inventory and winced. All she had now were the two time bombs clipped to her belt. No gun—Lois had disarmed her. Even worse, either during her fight with Vera or while being carried off through the air, she'd lost her knife. Apart from some money (three grand in C-notes which she'd brought along from Biggs's advance payment), the only other things on her were her picture of the magic teddy, Mary's black windup key, and her half-empty canister of Emerald nuts.

Mentally she cursed both Chameleon Sisters. Her time bombs weren't any good in this situation—both were easily powerful enough to blow this aircraft apart, but they couldn't be triggered while she was still aboard it. So she needed to find an alternative, and fast. She could almost hear the murderer's footsteps approaching, stomping ravenously towards her, bearing evil tidings of her death and subsequent mutilation.

Shit! I need a weapon!

She got feverishly to work searching the cabin, rooting amidst the dead for a weapon. It was a gruesome, sickening task: navigating between the corpse piles while doing her best not to slip on their sludge of putrefaction, then pulling or pushing aside decaying flesh to reach the clothes or belt or pouch it concealed, then checking if those held anything useful. And time and again coming away empty-handed. Twice sacs burst in corpses she moved, spraying fetid gas in her face, the evilness of the spewed vapor leaving her half-faint. Still, realizing her life was on the line, she staggered on to the next body. Several times she startled nests of the white fist-sized roaches living in corpses' bellies. One belligerent nest of roaches attacked her en-masse, and she spent five minutes swatting them off and stomping them into mush, sustaining several painful bites to her hands and face in the process. After that, however, like the stink of their dead fellows was a cautionary musk on her, no other roach nests attacked her.

She searched the corpses for twenty minutes, finally reaching the disturbing conclusion that whoever had killed them had either first intentionally removed all their weapons, or, that like herself, maybe the captives had never had any in the first place.

She slumped by a clear patch of wall. Sitting with her back on decay-warmed plastic, she considered her dire situation. *No weapons? I need to be able to defend myself. I'll be damned if anyone's adding me to this pile of human refuse.* Her eyes searched the chamber desperately, panic now threatening to smother her. *How do I defend myself? How? How? This compartment doesn't even have anything metal that I can break off! I need a fucking weapon, dammit! Where do I find one!*

Ironically, her answer lay right in front of her. By an odd quirk of fate, the corpse lying directly opposite Mel—an old one that boiled with grubs—had two broken legs. Both fractures were to the thighbones just above the knees, and each also crossed the bone obliquely—the slant leaving the edges of the break sharp and ending it in a point.

Once she'd calmed down somewhat, Melanie realized that the corpse's broken thighbones would make perfect spears.

Hopeful of survival now, she got up and quickly twisted them off the corpse. (While she worked, the corpse spilled maggots everywhere, but she got the job done.)

Thus armed, she took up a vantage point behind the nearest pile of bodies to the cabin door to await whoever/whatever had captured her and dropped her in this charnel vault.

CHAPTER 29

Five minutes later, the cabin door opened. Light from the corridor beyond flung a weird shadow into the cabin, then an animal entered.

It took Melanie a few moments to come to terms with what she was seeing. *It's a grizzly bear! A grizzly? Up here in the air?*

The huge yellow-brown animal shuffled in on all fours, swaying as it came. Snuffling loudly, it walked past Melanie's place of concealment, toward the middle of the cabin where the freshest corpses lay.

Melanie didn't attack it immediately; she was too perplexed by its being in an aircraft. She padded quietly after it, watching. *This grizzly can't be the culprit*, she reasoned. *It has to be a pet; likely the pilot's. The sick son-of-a-bitch is kidnapping people for the bear's food!*

The grizzly bear reached the new corpses. Suddenly it stood upright, then, in a clearly human gesture, scratched its head.

"Where's the newest one the tentacle brought in?" it growled in unaccented English. "She was tantalizing well-fleshed, unlike those two skinny blondes who were all breasts and hair and no meat; her thighs looked just scrumptious." Raising its head high, the grizzly bear looked around for its newest captive. "Where is she now? That woman was as choice a morsel as I've ever seen."

While horrified by its words, Melanie instantly grasped the implications of the fact that the bear could talk, and intelligently at that. It meant the grizzly was in all likelihood the pilot of this aircraft.

A bone spear in each hand, she charged the bear before its gaze swung to her. Standing upright, it towered over her five-feet-five-inch frame. She aimed the bones for its upper belly, to strike up under its ribs, into its heart. The bear was still turning toward her; it would be in just the right position when she reached it.

The grizzly sensed her motion just before she struck. Startled, it leapt back. Melanie ended up stabbing it in its lower belly instead. The amount of fat padding the animal's midriff ensured both punctures did very little damage. It screamed, then swiped at her. Jerking her spears out again, she rolled away across the filthy floor, stopping against a corpse with grub-filled eye sockets.

She leapt up instantly. The bear had now dropped down on all fours. Blood dripped from where she'd stabbed it.

The look of hunger in the bear's eyes made her shiver. It bared its teeth at her, black lips curled back. "I wondered where you'd gotten to," it growled, walking towards her.

Now that the element of surprise was taken from her, Melanie was extremely cautious. It wasn't so much the bear itself that worried her, as the floor. Covered as it was with corpses and slime, she knew she had to be constantly careful where she stepped. One misstep would prove fatal.

The floor didn't bother the bear, however. Though clearly wary of her two bone spears (which now dripped with its blood), it nonetheless padded steadily forward toward Melanie. Almost reaching her, it grabbed a recent corpse's leg—that of the woman with yet uneaten thighs—and effortlessly ripped it off her body. Then it stood to its full height again—its head touching the cabin ceiling—and using its teeth, tore meat off the severed leg.

It chewed, swallowed, then laughed at Melanie. "You'll taste much better than she does."

(The bear stank. It stank greatly, its musk clearly distinguishable amidst the already overwhelming olfactory offense of the corpses. The smell of everything was an additional opponent Melanie had to fight. The cabin seemed almost to lack air! Like she was constantly choking in stink she couldn't not breathe.)

Melanie regarded the bear coldly. "What the hell is this about? You're just travelling the O-Zone eating people?"

The grizzly took a second bite of thigh, then flung the leg away over its shoulder. It shook its shaggy frame. "You humans are delicious—the best meat by far. Unlike my friend L'il Ted, I'm not vegetarian. Veggie living sucks ass. What the hell's the point of life without a little meat, eh? That's what I always say."

Melanie winced at the info: *There's another bear on board? Hopefully, its name 'L'il Ted' means it's actually little, not like that 'Little John' character in Robin Hood who was the biggest of the gang.*

"Hey—I resent that!" she replied. "I'm a vegetarian. It doesn't suck ass. It's a healthier—"

The bear laughed loudly. "Ah, you're just a wussy, scared of seeing blood. Next thing, you'll be preaching some reincarnation, sanctity-of-all-life bullshite!" It laughed louder still, as if it had made the funniest joke ever.

Melanie reared up angrily. The fists growing from her breasts were bunched so tight now their knuckles were white. "I'm going to spill *your* blood, asshole" she spat at the bear.

"Asshole?" The grizzly visibly swelled with anger, its brown fur bristling. "You called me an 'asshole?'" It swiped the air with a claw. "You stupid bitch, I'm going to impale you on those bones you're holding!"

Melanie waved the bone spears at the bear. "Okay, so let's dance, asshole."

The bear dropped to all fours again and charged her. Melanie had anticipated its rush. She leapt out of its way, stabbing it in the side as it went past. She hit hard with her right spear, aiming again for its heart. The bone, however, slammed in between the bear's ribs and stuck there; was yanked from her grasp as the animal turned and bore down on her again.

"Grrrrr!" the bear roared. "I'm gonna eat you!"

Backing away from its rush, Melanie slipped and fell. Just managing to keep hold of the remaining bone spear, she landed hard on her back, her head smacking against a corpse's skull. She lay stunned, fighting to clear her head.

Her slip had taken her sideways out of the bear's attack, however. It slammed muzzle-first into an immensely bloated dead female abdomen. The taut belly burst under the impact, first sucking in the bear's head, then, when the animal withdrew its head, spilling the big white roaches everywhere. After the roaches spilled out a half-eaten almost-full-term human fetus.

The bear angrily brushed the roaches off its head, then it spun to face Melanie again, its eyes red and deadly.

"Ah yes, there you are!"

Melanie, still dazed, smirked at the bear as it squashed bugs against its shaggy fur. The world seemed to spin in her head. She staggered to her feet, gesturing around at the piled corpses. "Hey, asshole, haven't you ever heard of garbage disposal?"

"Fuck you—I like the smell in here!" The grizzly launched itself at her again. The spear between its ribs stuck out like a switch one could use to turn it on or off.

Melanie held her single remaining bone spear out in front of her. Too woozy from hitting her head to attack, this was the one defense she could see working.

Claws ripping down, the bear slammed into her like a football player making a tackle. She felt it gasp as it struck the spear, the bone slipping off its ribs to lodge deep in its belly.

Melanie and the bear crashed together into the side of a corpse pile, it on top of her. Again she smacked her head against a skull.

A mass of dislodged maggots spilling down into her hair, Melanie hoped she'd done enough to kill the bear. It lay motionless, completely covering her. Pain tore up and down her left side where the bear had slashed her open.

Moving sluggishly, she began fighting to extricate herself from under its bulk.

Then the bear moved. It got off her and stood up.

"And now you're all washed up," it said. "And so I'll just eat you."

The bear reared up to its full height. Melanie's second bone spear had run it clean through from front to back, but she'd clearly missed any vital organs. Though blood spilled from the puncture, drenching the light brown fur, the bear still moved with ease. Its eyes shone with a horrid vitality, and worse . . . an amplified hunger.

Melanie winced as her pain increased. *I stabbed it twice and yet it's not dead?*

The bear didn't bother to remove the bones piercing its body. Instead, it bent over Melanie's prone form. It clouted her head to stun her. Then it grabbed the hand growing from her left breast, and, in a spray of blood, ripped it off her chest.

Despite being half unconscious, Melanie screamed as the hand came free. The pain, the pain, the fucking pain!

Laughing, the bear messily ate the hand. Melanie stared dully up at it, at her blood dribbling down over its lips. Then she peered down at her chest, where the hand's removal was marked by a jagged circle that burnt like she'd been branded.

Fuck! There goes my nipple—I need plastic surgery, she thought inanely.

The bear bolted down the hand. Then, it reached down and ripped off Melanie's right breast-hand as well, laughing at her screams. It regarded her tormented face with amusement, waved the severed crimson-dripping extremity before her fevered gaze. "I don't normally torture my food," it said, "but in your case, I'm willing to make an exception." Still bent over her, it flung the hand into its mouth and chewed; the crunch of shattering bones sounded like gunshots.

It began stripping Melanie naked. "Now let's have a proper look at these super-meaty thighs of yours."

Squirming, Melanie kept her legs firmly pressed together. (Her chest was a mass of pain now, two waves of utter agony that continuously rolled together then parted.) The grizzly clouted her again; she relaxed her body. Stars whirling in her head, she felt it pull her trousers off.

"Oh, yes," the bear said, feeling her thighs. "Just incredible, and not fatty at all."

"Shut the fuck up," Melanie groaned. "Don't objectify my assets."

"Oh, I haven't even gotten to your ass yet," the grizzly bear laughed back. It reached up and stroked her face with a stinky, bloody paw. "Oh, my pretty, you're a feisty one aren't you? Even though you're well and truly beaten you've still some fight left in you. Well we'll see—"

Then it froze and frowned, the human expression clear on its animal face. "Where the hell did you get this?"

"Get what?" Melanie had no idea what the bear was talking about. The pain in her mutilated breasts and its blows to her head had her half comatose now. She was fading in and out, fighting with all her heart to stay awake, knowing that next time she blacked out she'd be dead—just another flesh lump on one of the grizzly's corpse piles.

"Hey, I'm fucking talking to you—where did you get this?"

Melanie blacked out, then was instantly awake again. It felt like every kind of pain in the world was converged in her body. She realized that the grizzly bear was shaking her. Its horrible smell wrapped her like a sheet.

"What do you want to know?" she murmured at it.

It thrust something before her bleary eyes. Melanie squinted, saw that it was the picture of the magic teddy she'd been hired to retrieve. Her vision faded out, then in again.

She forced a grin at the grizzly's adamant glare. Somehow the blood—her blood—on its jaws made the animal seem comical to her. "Don't tell me you want it too? Everybody does. This teddy bear seems the most valuable object in New England at the moment."

"This is my friend L'il Ted!" the grizzly screamed, shaking the photo at her. "He's down there and I'm up here all alone and . . . !"

Melanie couldn't believe what happened next.

First, the horrible grizzly bear broke down in tears—actually started crying—and then . . .

Like it had been zapped with a magic spell, the grizzly bear altered . . .

Melanie now found herself staring at an ordinary teddy bear; large and fuzzy brown with a black face and shiny glass eyes. The sort of cute thing six-year-old girls drool over.

"What's your connection to L'il Ted?" the teddy bear asked politely, in a worried voice. "Please tell me."

Oh, this one can talk too, Melanie thought dully.

"I was hired to . . ." she began, then the pain ravaging her body became too much, and she passed out cold. As she dropped through successive layers of darkness, she felt the teddy shaking her to wake her up. But she knew it was useless. This time, she was out for the count.

CHAPTER 30

Melanie woke up by degrees. Eyes shut, she breathed in deep, was surprised that her breasts no longer burnt with agony. The air smelt better—the disgusting, all-pervading charnel house stink of death no longer assaulted her. She smelt bear, however.

Two out of three ain't to be sniffed at, she decided. *At least I'm still alive. And where there's life, hope isn't too far off.*

She opened her eyes. The world faded in and out of focus several times before presenting a concrete form to her. Then she saw the grizzly. It sat in a chair facing her, licking its bloody chops. Across the bear's lap lay a tray piled with meat and skin.

The bear wasn't yet aware she'd woken. She looked around.

She was in a lab with sterile white walls, strapped down on a bed with its head area levered up so she was half-sitting. She was naked. Suddenly alarmed as the bear raised a chunk of meat to its mouth, she checked her body for damage. She heaved a sigh of relief—all her limbs were intact, the meat on the tray wasn't hers.

The only oddities about her body were the two silver cones that now topped her breasts. Both cones ended in sharp points. Each one completely covered the damaged areas where the hands had been ripped off; their rims hugged her milky skin like they'd been welded to it. The cones tingled—a nice sensation. A definite improvement over the previous pain like her lungs were being ripped out.

The wounds down her left side where the bear had slashed her open had also been stitched up, and treated with some salve that killed the pain.

She coughed. "Hey!"

The grizzly looked up from selecting a fresh piece of meat from the tray.

"Ah, you're awake," it said. It stood up, dropped the tray on a table, then—

Melanie just gaped.

—Altered into a cute little teddy bear again.

Melanie now recalled the conversation they'd been having when she'd passed out. What had it been saying? Oh, yes . . . this teddy, or grizzly(?) was friends with the one she'd been sent to find.

The teddy bear climbed back up into its chair. Then it sat looking at Melanie. She noticed it was holding a slim white device with a red dial.

"What's this about?" Melanie asked it. "Why do you keep changing form? And what do you want with me now?"

The teddy bear smiled sadly. "First let me introduce myself properly. "My name's Big Ted. L'il Ted and I were both made by The Fixer, and—"

"The cold black guy who dresses like a mortician?"

Big Ted nodded. "Yes, the same one. We were his assistants, but we escaped from his black suitcase, stole his aircraft and flew away in it."

Melanie considered this. It explained why The Fixer had seemed desperate to catch the plane and also why it had also seemed to be fleeing from him.

"But . . . why'd you run away? The Fixer seems a nice sort of guy."

Big Ted bristled. "Too nice, much too nice."

Melanie was about asking what it meant when it preempted her question: "The Fixer wanted us to be goody-two-shoes, to be vegetarians—"

"There's nothing wrong with being vegeta—"

"Meat tastes better." It was a pronouncement of tried-and-tested fact, not a debatable statement.

"I don't get it." She didn't. "Working for The Fixer, how in the world would you know what meat tastes like without ever—" Then she remembered how The Fixer had disposed of Mary's removed innards and understanding hit her like a bullet to the brain. She stared horrified at the teddy bear. "You two started eating the organs The Fixer was dumping inside his black suitcase, didn't you?"

Big Ted nodded. "We were tired of bananas—that's all he ever fed us. Bananas. Imagine yellow fruit for breakfast, lunch, dinner . . ."

The teddy leapt up on the chair, its body shaking like it was enraged.

Melanie saw where she'd stabbed it—the rips in its shaggy mohair coat were darned over with gold thread. "So, one day, L'il Ted suggested we try some human liver for a change. It tasted horrible when we were in teddy form, but once we transformed ourselves to real animals, it was delicious. Supremely delicious."

"So why leave? You could simply have remained with The Fixer. It's not like he's got anything doing with the discarded parts."

Big Ted sighed. "You don't understand. There's wasn't enough of it. No, that's not the real reason. He caught us eating meat and threatened to deactivate us . . ."

Deactivate. The word built hope in Melanie. Hope . . . if she could just deactivate this little monster here.

She said, "So now you two travel around the O-Zone feeding on people." It was impossible to keep her bitterness out of her voice.

Big Ted laughed. "At least we did until L'il Ted developed a conscience. The little wussy decided he didn't want to eat meat anymore . . . we had a spell when we kept snaring pregnant women . . . one stupid bitch gave birth while we were ripping her leg off; the kid squirted out like a bloody torpedo, hit L'il Ted in the balls. It was a traumatic experience for sure—completely put him off meat for good . . . I, however, found the brat delicious." The teddy bear stopped speaking for a moment and regarded Melanie intently, its shiny eyes managing to convey menace despite their deadness. "And so now, on to you, lady: What are you doing with L'il Ted's photograph? You mentioned you were hired. Hired by who?"

Melanie dallied in replying. She couldn't rid her mind of the horrible image of the pregnant woman giving birth while having a limb ripped off. *And then this creature—this monster—ate her baby?*

"Answer me!" Big Ted growled, twisting the red dial on the white device it held.

The next moment Melanie's body was wracked with horrendous pain. The pain first froze her stiff, then . . . it felt like she was being stabbed everywhere by a million knives. Her head, eyes, nose . . . her teeth, legs, arms, her belly . . . all HURT with simultaneously discernable agonies. Her vagina felt like it was being chainsawed. Her arm and legs felt like they were being pulped with hammers. Her innards felt like someone was dissolving them in acid.

Her body arched violently up off the bed, instantly snapping the buckles of the two leather straps restraining her waist. Her spine—

itself now simply a furnace-hot pole of pain running the length of her back—stretched like it would explode into its individual vertebrae . . . Were it not for the cuffs holding her hands and feet in place, she'd have launched herself through the air to escape the agony. She felt like she was dying forever, like one damned in the flames of Hell.

At some point she was able to localize the torment as coming from her breasts, from the two metal cones that now capped them.

Sniggering, Big Ted twisted the red dial counterclockwise. The pain instantly cut out. Melanie collapsed back gasping.

"No more!" she moaned in horror. "No more!"

Big Ted laughed, waves of mirth rippling its fur. "Not yet, lady. Once more, just so you know I'm not fooling around here." It twisted the red dial violently clockwise.

"Noooo!" Melanie screamed as the horrible pain began again.

This second time was much worse. Her eyes felt like they were exploding—her color vision turned black-and-white, then monochromed to shades of grey. Her brain fritzed. White noise plugged her ears, ringing them like cathedral bells. Her body . . . she felt like she was being ground up in a liquidizer. Impossibly, she could feel blades slicing through her at speed, while simultaneously a hammer reduced her to mulch and she was also dissolved away in acid. She was unaware when her anus relaxed and ejected thick clumps of shit, nor of the yellow arcs of urine she was copiously squirting through the air. Nor of the vomit streaming from her mouth, truncating her endless scream. Nor of how fiercely she was perspiring. She ceased puking. Her eyes stared at nothing; could see nothing. Her mouth remained open, no sound issuing from it. Her tongue felt like it was being repeatedly sliced in pieces; all the teeth were being yanked from her jaws with pliers, her root canals filed without anesthetic. Her body arched off the bed again, liquid excrement plopping down from her buttocks, piss squirting in jets at her painfully curled toes, toes that felt like they were being fried in oil. Her vagina felt like she was birthing the baby with the largest head ever. And yet still more and more pain blew from her breasts through her body, destroying her, and yet, at the same time refusing to overload and kill her. Seemingly inexhaustible pain. Unbelievable pain.

The pain switched off again. Melanie once again collapsed onto the bed. In stages her mind rebuilt itself; her vision became corporeal (nothingness coalesced into optical phantoms that finally resolved into the world around); her ears heard silence again.

She became aware of laughter.

"How did that feel?" Big Ted asked. "I'll tell you how it works, though you've likely figured it out yourself already—the silver caps on your breasts contain special electrodes that transmit horrible sensations to all the pain centers in your body." It shook the white device at her. "And of course, this remote control . . ."

Melanie gaped at the teddy bear, still disbelieving what had just happened to her. The pain was gone, the shock remained. Her body felt so weak that for all intents and purposes, it might just as well as have not been there. She felt emptied of her humanity, more abused even than if she'd been raped. She became vaguely aware that she'd shit and pissed and vomited all over herself. *Oh yes,* she thought with intense conviction, *I am going to kill this teddy bear if it's the last thing I ever do in my life.*

"Why?" she gasped. "Why do this to me?"

"You weren't talking fast enough." Then it laughed. "No—it's just fun. I enjoy watching you humans squirm and beg." Its voice turned solemn. "Okay, now tell me everything." It pointed the white remote control at her. "Just so you know—I only turned it up halfway."

Melanie couldn't even consider what more than halfway would feel like. Lying in the mess of her own bodily wastes, she talked and talked and talked, answering all the teddy's questions. It wanted replies, she gave them promptly, her eyes ever flickering to the innocuous-seeming white device with its red dial.

Big Ted didn't want to know a lot, but everything it did—she told it.

"Okay, that's all," Big Ted said finally.

Melanie heaved a sigh of relief when it put the remote control aside.

"Now," Big Ted said, "I'm going to loosen your restraints. After you've cleaned yourself up, we'll talk further." It began undoing the cuffs around her wrists and ankles.

Once it had freed her, Melanie put all her strength into getting off the bed. Big Ted made no attempt to pick up the remote control again. Staring at the device as it lay on the chair, Melanie didn't question the toy's oversight. She didn't even recognize this as an opportunity to kill the evil teddy bear—it could easily become its grizzly version again and tear her apart. All she saw was a chance to prevent herself suffering that terrible cascade of agonies again. She had to destroy that remote control unit, no matter what.

"Now go and wash yourself," Big Ted ordered, a broad smile on its fuzzy face. It pointed to a door on her right. "The bathroom's that way. Hurry up. Once you no longer stink of poop, we've business to discuss."

Instead Melanie lurched to the chair and grabbed up the remote control.

Before she could smash it to the floor, however, pain flared up in her breasts and ripped through her body again. She instantly dropped the remote control.

"Noooo!" she screamed, collapsing to the floor and writhing as the agony flooded her.

This pain, however, wasn't as bad as her previous two experiences. Though she felt like she was being incinerated, she was conscious of everything around her. She saw Big Ted peering down at her.

"Turn it off, please!" she begged.

"You'll behave yourself now?" The voice was amused. "No more stupid attempts to destroy things?"

"Yes! Yes!" she gasped. "Stop it! Please!"

The teddy bear nodded, then said, "Okay, plane, turn it off. I believe she's learnt her lesson."

The pain stopped. Melanie lay panting, her breasts rising and falling.

Big Ted picked the red/white remote control up off the floor where she'd dropped it. "Just remember: the airplane's computer is monitoring all your actions up here, no matter where you are, and . . . it can control those breast caps too. So, if you try any nonsense, like for instance, trying to take the caps off, next time . . ."

Leaving the threat hanging, Big Ted walked away to the lab door and exited.

Melanie watched it leave. Then she painfully got to her feet and entered the bathroom. She was certain as fuck now that she was killing Big Ted no matter what it took.

CHAPTER 31

"You're going to find L'il Ted for me," Big Ted growled. "I'm not asking—I'm telling you. You'll do it, or else . . ."

Melanie nodded cautiously. She knew the 'or else' meant at least, more of the pain, at worse, being eaten by Big Ted. Her breasts tingled with agonized memory; she was uncertain which fate was worse.

She was dressed again. She'd retrieved her pants, belt, and boots from the 'slaughter cabin.' Her jacket, her shirt (along with the money in her pocket), and her brassiere, however, had been shredded beyond repair during her earlier fight with Big Ted. Among the stripped clothes of the dead, she'd found a gray zip-up running jacket. It was a bit tight around the bust, but she'd make do. Her two bombs were still fastened to her belt (Big Ted clearly having no idea what they were). Mary's key, and the Emerald Nuts canister (which had thankfully survived the fight) were safely secured in pockets.

She and Big Ted currently sat facing each other in another cabin, this one arranged with tables laden with gleaming black equipment reminiscent of The Fixer. The bear was back in its stinky grizzly form, and noisily finishing off the heaped tray of human meat and skin it had been eating when Melanie awakened earlier. Melanie impassively watched it gorge itself. She was now well beyond disgust for the magic creature—in her gut she nursed a black ball of hatred for Big Ted like it was a pregnancy.

"We ran out of damned bananas," Big Ted explained between mouthfuls of meat, "so L'il Ted went down to get some more. And apparently, someone caught him down there."

Melanie regarded the grizzly warily. Now that she'd puked out all yesterday's meals and this morning's breakfast of nuts, and seeming shat out the entirety of whatever food she'd previously eaten in her

165

lifetime, she felt incredibly weak. (All she had in her belly now was some water she'd drank in the bathroom.) She however didn't feel starved. Like in the case of a mystic who'd been fasting for a long time, her hunger floated around her gut like a sort of negative nourishment. (*Or maybe*, she considered, *maybe the horrendous pain I recently experienced has paralyzed whatever nerves remind my body to eat.*)

She chose her words carefully now, ever conscious of the agony that awaited if the bear thought she was being flippant.

"I'm confused here," she said. "Bigelow told me L'il Ted was shipped in from out of town. How come you're saying it was here all along?"

Big Ted belched. "No. The bananas were in a truck. L'il Ted gets into it, and the truck starts up and leaves town. It's already well on its way to Hartford before L'il Ted realizes what's going on. Me too. And I was cautious about zapping the truck with L'il Ted in it . . ."

The grizzly bear fell silent like the memory hurt to relate; Melanie considered its words. Its explanation made sense; the rest of the story was easy to figure out: On reaching Hartford, the trucker had found a talking teddy bear in the back of his vehicle. Clearly too, L'il Ted had let itself be taken captive without a fight—Bigelow hadn't mentioned any violent transformation . . .

Melanie asked, "What's L'il Ted's transformed shape?"

"He's a timber wolf. Why do you ask?"

A wolf? "I'm wondering why it didn't fight and escape; how they caught it so easily."

The grizzly bared teeth. "He was full of guilt feelings over how eating human meat was bad and we ought to stop. Probably figured he was doing the right thing by surrendering. The little veggie—"

Melanie cut it off. "Yeah, and the other thing—how'd it get deactivated? How does this deactivation thing work?"

Big Ted clearly didn't like how she'd interrupted it. Melanie tensed as the grizzly's right paw inched towards the red/white remote control, then it changed its mind. It put the meat tray—empty now except for some skin scraps—aside, then fiddled about in its left ear like it was looking for something. Melanie heard a soft strangely familiar click, and then Big Ted held out something for her inspection.

She tried not to let her surprise show. What Big Ted held was a black key just like the one The Fixer had fitted Mary with. Melanie pulled out the black key in her pocket and compared the two. Both were exactly alike, like they'd come from the same mold.

Big Ted was surprised too. "Where did you get that?"

"I found it in the dust somewhere." She wasn't bothered about lying; there was no way for the grizzly to check her story.

Big Ted took her words at face value. "L'il Ted and I are windup creatures. Each of us had a key. But when we fled The Fixer, I lost my key, must've got knocked off somewhere . . ." It pointed to Melanie's black key. "That's most likely it you've got there." It scowled again. "After that I had to share L'il Ted's key with him, we'd each wind the other up every two days. So . . ."

"So the key was with you when your friend was 'abducted,' and once it ran down . . . deactivated . . . that was it—no way to power L'il Ted up again."

The grizzly bear grinned a lot of pointy teeth. "And now he's back. And *you* are going to power him up for me." It turned from staring at Melanie to regarding the scraps of skin on the tray, stirring them with a claw. It wrinkled its nose at them, then like a balloon deflating, compacted itself into its teddy bear form again.

Melanie rolled her eyes. "Okay, I'll do it—it's not like I have any choice, right?"

"You're very astute. Consider this a trade: your life in exchange for my getting L'il Ted back—just use that key you're holding to reactivate him." It stuck its own black key into its ear, pushed it in till with a click the key disappeared, then grinned at Melanie. "Deal?"

She nodded, pocketed her own key again. "Just tell me what frigging warehouse L'il Ted's in and drop me off there."

Big Ted scowled, its black eyes reflecting her face. "Unfortunately, there's a new complication. L'il Ted isn't in the warehouse anymore."

Melanie regarded the teddy bear coolly. "Where is it then?"

"He's in the Eyeful Tower."

"In France? How the heck did it get from here to there?"

"Eyeful . . . E-y-e-f-u-l . . . Eyeful Tower. Get it?"

"No."

"Are you trying to be difficult again? There's a lot more pain where the last dose came from, you know."

She shook her head. "I've just never heard of an Eyeful Tower in my life."

Big Ted considered that, then growled, "Plane, show her the Eyeful Tower."

The metal wall to Melanie's right dissolved into a colored video screen. Against the background of a sky that thronged with clouds of morph birds, the screen showed a tower seemingly made of pink meat. The pink tower was covered with massive eyes. Blue, green, hazel, albino red, brown, black, gray . . . cat-slit eyes, piss-yellow reptilian . . . all sorts of eyes that blinked and stared everywhere.

"I can't imagine how it got its name," Melanie said drily.

"I think it's a converted skyscraper," Big Ted said. "Those black birds that are everywhere now must have altered it to its current shape."

Melanie regarded the strange eye-covered tower. It made her shudder with revulsion. "Are you certain L'il Ted's in that gross place?"

"As certain as I am that you're going to die a horrible death if you fail to get him back for me." Big Ted spread its felt paws wide, its expression extremely smug. "Let me explain something to you, woman. You can't escape from me. No matter where you flee to . . ." it grabbed up the remote control, "I'll be able to reach you there and thrill you with pain." It laughed nastily. "Better still, the airplane can sense any attempt you make to remove those lovely shiny breast electrodes I fitted you with . . . and I don't think I need to tell you what happens then . . . So do what I'm ordering you to and I'll remove the electrodes from your breasts and let you go free. Or else . . ."

Melanie winced. Each time she slipped back into the pleasant delusion that this was a normal toy bear facing her, it hit her with this sadistic nonsense. And this new info particularly sucked: *The airplane's tracking me?* (She'd been thinking she might be able to remove the electrodes once on the ground again.) *Well we'll see*, she thought. *I'm playing your game for now, you toy son-of-a-bitch, but . . .*

Big Ted continued: "Now listen. The airplane's computer has determined that L'il Ted is in a chamber in the Eyeful Tower's basement. He's still in his box and still deactivated. It also says that the tower is full of those horrible cannibal mutants—the gingers."

Melanie winced. "Full of gingers, huh?" She found it amusing, Big Ted calling the gingers 'horrible cannibals.'

"Yes. The Eyeful Tower seems to be their new base of operations."

She laughed; her whole situation suddenly seemed utterly hilarious. "I'm stuck between a rock and a hard place here, right? Okay, what weapons do you have on board?"

"Weapons?"

She smiled pityingly at the teddy bear. "Yes, *weapons*. Or are you seriously expecting me to take on a tower-full of cannibals with my bare hands?"

(She just resisted adding 'you asshole' to the statement. Big Ted's oversight of something so obvious raised hope in Melanie that she could get out of this alive. And she needed a fucking plan. She was as sure as orgasm followed masturbation that this damned teddy bear planned on eating her once she'd freed its cuddly timber wolf friend.)

"Yes, yes, of course," Big Ted said. "There's quite a large cache of weapons aboard that I removed from captive's bodies so others couldn't use them. Grabbing up the pain remote, it leapt down from its chair—"Please follow me,"—then plodded stolidly from the cabin.

Wishing she could smash an axe through it from head to crotch, Melanie followed Big Ted to inspect the weapons store.

PART 4:
THE EYEFUL TOWER
OR
THE FRENCH KISS
GOODNIGHT

CHAPTER 32

Armed with a Glock G30S pistol in a hip holster and a sheathed hunting knife, Melanie was dropped off two hundred meters from the Eyeful Tower. (There'd been other weapons on the plane, including a pump action shotgun, but only the Glock had had a full clip of ammunition. She'd even found a spare clip for it.)

She watched the blue plane snare someone else—a tall thin man.

Damn, she thought, as the misfortunate victim—shortly to be Big Ted's lunch—was borne off, *I'm hungry too.* It was a morbid thought, but one she couldn't help having. She was also as weary as dead bones. With no immediate possibility of taking a rest, however, she shrugged her tiredness off, behaved like she wasn't. Her clawed left side stung too, but she could ignore that.

She headed off up the street towards her destination, now just visible over the rooftops

Everywhere was transformed now; it was like she dreamed. She walked past flesh houses topped with hair, past one studded with working clocks, past another with thousands of stinky monster sausages growing out of it. Another house had elephant tusks projecting from its brick walls.

Several cars, each covered with dark rhino-like hide, walked up and down the street on short grey stumpy legs. Their tires rolled aimlessly at their sides. Through their windows, Melanie watched their steering wheels spin left and right as though ghosts turned them.

Overhead, the sky was a clear blue dotted with black and white clouds, the black being masses of morph birds.

Bizarro hung far, far off overhead to her left, a feces-painted sky horizon. The single brown mass's distance (where before its separations had floated within walkable space of each other) was evidence to Melanie that something was now wrong with everything, that nothing was normal any more, that anything could be a terminal danger.

It was midday, the sun beaming down like it approved of the change to the world.

She walked with fast strides. Without a bra or shirt to harness their motion, her big breasts bobbed boisterously beneath the running jacket (which was only really comfortable anyway unzipped almost to nipple level).

The ground was black and shiny. It was transparent. Inside parts of it, she saw massive gears whirling, like the road was an immense engine she trod over.

She walked by a house that had become a chicken. It stood on two scaly yellow legs and was covered with reddish-brown feathers. Above its open windows fluttered large wings. A cartoon-like head and beak projected from the roof and pecked the air.

Opposite the chicken house was one that seemed to be made of cats, like someone had built a million felines into a mansion. From a top floor window of this mansion, a pretty old woman waved down at Melanie.

The sights hurt her mind. She wore her glasses again now; the distance looked just as weird as her nearfield.

She paced quickly past the freaky houses, keeping her eyes fixed on the ground, on the dark spinning wheels that filled its depths.

An all-to-familiar sound alerted her to look up again.

Like airborne oil slick, a swarm of morph birds had swooped down into the street, were headed straight at her. She hastily opened her green canister and downed a mouthful of nuts. She winced as the tell-tale allergic buzz hit her, scant seconds before the liquid birds went through her. She winced with relief once they were out her back side. She turned and watched them go; they splattered en masse onto a street sign. 'Brewster Street' the sign read. The sign instantly grew brown insect legs all along its length, fell to the ground and walked off, thankfully away from her.

That danger past, she realized that her head and hands now felt odd. Checking, she discovered she'd lost both her little fingers. Both her ears had vanished too. She ran her remaining fingers over the sides of her head. Her earholes were still there, which was a relief. *It would be suicidal if I couldn't hear,* she thought; then, permitting herself a little vanity, mentally added: *And my hair will cover my missing ears.* Still, she was troubled. *What if my eyes had vanished? What then? Oh, I hate this damned nut allergy!*

She realized, however, that losing body parts (or growing additional ones) for a day or two was immensely better than having the morph birds irreversibly screw her body up. And the nuts *had* taken the edge off her hunger.

She also realized that she'd been slacking. And this definitely wasn't time to slack. This was time to focus her attentions and energies, though she still had no idea how she'd break into the Eyeful Tower. And neither—she looked back; Big Ted's airplane was a distant blue cross—did her current sadistic employer.

Gun held ready to blast any attacker, she considered one of the paradoxes of this case: Despite its carnivorous bluster, Big Ted was scared shitless of The Fixer.

"Why not drop me closer to the tower?" she'd enquired. "Or even . . . even, just hover beside it . . . swing me in through a window, then once I'm done, retrieve me the same way?" She'd grinned. "It's how the US army get the job done."

"No!" Big Ted had instantly yelped like it was in pain. "No, The Fixer is always close at hand! He'll capture me!"

"But . . . you don't know—"

Big Ted had grabbed the pain remote and zapped her again. End of discussion.

Remembering how generous Big Ted was with dishing out agony to her filled Melanie's mouth with bile. She wasn't called 'Nemesis' for nothing. That satanic teddy bear would pay for all the pain it had caused her, and pay big.

She bit down on her rage, cleared her mind, tried to think calmly. Concentration was hard, and it wasn't just her anger distracting her. She looked down at her breasts, at the shiny metal cones that topped each smooth milky expanse. In an irritating development, they tingled pleasantly now: Big Ted's great plan to keep her sweet. The metal caps were currently feeding pleasure sensations through her breasts.

She'd protested: "I don't want to be fucking aroused!"

Big Ted had waved off her concerns. "You won't be aroused, you'll just feel nice. I'm not all bad, you know."

And so now here she was, breasts tingling nicely like sexy, meaty male lips were sucking on her missing nipples.

She did have some leeway in which to maneuver, however. Here on the ground, Big Ted's control over her was limited. The plane could track her movement via the breast caps (Big Ted claimed to a range of a hundred miles), and would instantly know if she tried to remove them (resulting in it zapping her with a permanently paralyzing dose of pain), but that was all. Out of the aircraft's direct line of sight, Big Ted had no idea what she was up to. And the plane wasn't hanging around for The Fixer to find it.

For a moment, a dim hope struck Melanie: *I might run into The Fixer, with his accompanying cold zone. It'll be a moment's work for him to get these shitty breast electrodes off me, and then we'll both work out how to take down Big Ted and take over the plane.*

She quickly realized the folly of such hope: *For one thing, Big Ted is so fucking scared of his black-cloaked master that no way would he have currently dropped me off anywhere near him. And second, The Fixer himself, ignorant of his creation's plans, will be intent on following the plane away from my drop-off point. So at the moment . . . he isn't anywhere near me.*

She scowled. *Damn! I really do fucking have to go through with this nonsense! On my own initiative, I have to make it through a building-full of gingers!*

She managed a wry grin. *And I'm sure the real reason Big Ted refused us doing the logical and straightforward simply-hover-by-the-fucking-Eyeful-Tower-and-retrieve-L'il-Ted-operation is because he's scared stiff of the 'horrible cannibal mutants' somehow swarming up into his stolen plane and eating him. Fucking bullying sadistic coward asshole!*

The entire situation was impossible. The only way Melanie presently saw of getting L'il Ted out of the Eyeful Tower was by blowing the entire building sky-high with the time bombs on her belt.

***

Without warning, the landscape altered, and Melanie was walking through an expanse of honeysuckle plants around which violet hummingbirds flittered. After the rotting-corpse stink of the airplane, the sweet honeysuckle smell was a nice lift. The ground was still transparent black, but now, green grass grew in the dark burnished flooring, and huge white flowers also.

Several 'political' sheep rested beneath the honeysuckle plants. One—sporting a picture of President Nixon—kept its eyes on her all the while she crossed towards it.

On her right, beyond the honeysuckles and sheep, was a large wooded patch of the black glass earth. The ground dipped in that direction, affording Melanie clear panoramic view of the area. Massive elms and birches, dogwoods, cedars and juniper trees, hop hornbeams and maples, hazelnut and mulberry trees grew into the distance in stupendous profusion, their leaves all shades of vibrant green, almost like that part of the transformed landscape had been reserved as a park. The calm sedate feeling seemed perfect, an antidote to her ravaged body and emotions. That was, until she looked more closely up into a nearby cherry tree, part of a brilliantly flowering pink cluster, across the branches of which frolicked a group of squirrels. In addition to being hairless, all the rodents were covered with human ears.

Out here, her view of her destination was blocked by several story buildings, one of them with an array of different animal legs growing out of its brick sides. In addition, the building had huge live turtles replacing its windows. The bright-green amphibians, secured in place by the rears of their shells, kicked and wagged their heads as they regarded Melanie and the surrounding world.

The building behind it was either coated with, or built from, fish. All kinds of them. The myriad pisceans were stuck back-to-back and stacked four stories high. Bright orange tentacles descending from the building's roof stroked the fishes' bodies while they moved their mouths and gills like they breathed the air.

Melanie stopped looking up after that. Ignoring the sheep with political slogans scrolling across their backs that kept bumping against her legs, she crossed briskly to where the street continued.

Once between the houses again, she kept her eyes firmly focused ahead, now and then glancing down into the abysmal black depths she trod over. (The road's seeming engines were a comforting normalcy to view.) She did not wish to see the oddities she passed; like the house built from human legs bolted together, or the one seemingly built from stacked (and still-living) raccoons. Or the one with Paris Hilton's face as its frontage. (She'd never really liked Paris, anyway. Not even the one in France: The one time she'd been there, her boyfriend had fallen from the Eiffel Tower and broken his neck.)

Eyes on the road like this, she totally missed the emergence of the black sheep with the blue paralland symbol on its back from an alley across the street.

The black sheep stared curiously at Melanie as she passed. On a flicker of ovine recognition, it set off after her like she was its shepherdess; only—exactly eleven steps later—to be promptly licked up off the sidewalk by the Paris Hilton house's sticky tongue, and eaten whole. The black sheep bleated softly as Paris Hilton ate it. It dripped oil and pooped a stream of glassine beads and bolts. Paris Hilton swallowed, burped, then grinned like she'd just come.

The sheep might have never been.

At the exact moment of the black sheep's passing, Melanie's attention was caught by a sound a short distance ahead. The sound of wheels. Not of a car or motorbike, but a jagged metallic bounce like someone was pushing a cart. The loud and grating noise issued from the side street she was about reaching.

She paused. Pulling her gun (having only three fingers now subtly altered her grip), she waited for the cart to emerge.

CHAPTER 33

The cart rolled into view. It was yellow—a wide, wooden, six-wheeled affair. It contained a massive pink snake.

Melanie leapt back, raised her gun to fire. This snake was larger than any anaconda she'd ever seen on TV. If it so much as twitched in her direction . . . she wasn't taking any chances.

Then the man pushing the cart emerged around the corner. Melanie instantly recognized him.

Though Joe the Bartender had a stubbly beard now, he was just as thin and unkempt as before, and his eyes were just as bloodshot.

She lowered the gun. "Hey!" she said.

Startled, Joe stopped. He relaxed on recognizing her too. "Melanie . . . Melanie Catchpole? What are *you* doing here?" He lowered his voice. "It's very dangerous, there's gingers everywhere."

She waved the question off. "What's with the snake, Joe?"

He sighed loudly and stepped back from the cart. Melanie gasped; her mouth hung open. The end of the pink snake disappeared into the crotch of Joe's jeans. Actually, Joe's pants didn't have a crotch region anymore—the entire area below the belt and above the legs was cut out to enable the massive flesh-toned serpent join seamlessly to his body.

Melanie finally managed to shut her mouth. "Joe, don't fucking tell me that this thing's your penis. What in the heck happened to you?" She had a good idea, however.

Joe looked close to sobbing. "It is my dick, Melanie. I was reading in my room one night about three months ago, when suddenly all these black birds flew in through the wall and entered my body. Then it got bigger and bigger and bigger and . . ." Joe burst into tears. "I always wanted a bigger dick, but this . . . this is just . . ." The water streamed from his eyes. His sobs wracked his thin frame like he was having an earthquake.

Melanie said nothing; she couldn't find the right words. She holstered her pistol and looked. While Joe wept and wept, she examined the monster penis rolled up in the cart. Considering the cart's depth, the throbbing organ had to be at least twenty feet long, and it was a foot-and-a-half thick. She located the glans—the slit in the immense bulbous head would easily admit her foot. (Joe was uncircumcised; his foreskin lay draped like a purple blanket over the pink meat.) For a moment she wondered how in the world Joe's heart (and the sleazy bartender had never looked the picture of health to begin with) managed to pump blood through the monster organ— its veins were super fat, some as thick as her wrist. She concluded that maybe the penis had its own heart, possibly housed somewhere in Joe's belly, which did seem more swollen that she remembered. She didn't bother trying to work out how he ate enough for both himself and his oversized organ. Also, if Joe still had testicles, they were hidden well away below the massive penile trunk.

And . . . did Joe just say this happened three months ago? I've been time-warped as well?

Joe got over his funk. He wiped his eyes, stared miserably at her. Seeing him like this, Melanie found it impossible to hate him for what he'd done to his daughter. He looked absolutely finished (and that even before considering his horrible transformation—the monstrous serpentine manhood protruding from his groin). And yet, she reasoned, this utterly dislikeable man had to have *a lot* of character—a tempered-steel spine—not to have simply committed suicide already.

"I'm still looking for Mary," Joe said. "You haven't seen her, have you? I mean you and Doug said that once you came back you'd help me find her, but you never came back. And it was that same night that everything went to shit. You seen my kid anywhere?"

The question stumped Melanie. For a moment, her resentment of Joe came to the forefront of her mind, and she saw herself blowing his brains out with her gun, then sitting astride his chest, and, using a set of pliers, yanking his teeth from his dead jaws one at a time . . . Then the ugly vision faded, and she was left feeling empty.

"Have you seen Mary anywhere?" Joe repeated. His question wasn't demanding or belligerent, it was depressingly sad; worried yet borderline hopeful.

Melanie considered telling Joe the cold brutal truth: *Hey, asshole dad! This weird crap all around us is your fucking emotionally-abused kid! She was eaten and blown up, and this is the result! See what you've done, shithead!? You've fucked up an entire town, hopefully not the entire country, or world! Yes, asshole, everything you're seeing, unbelievable as it is, is the result of you messing up your daughter's head, then bleeding her for drinks to boot! I mean, selling her blood for drinks? Where the hell do you get off, huh!? And concerning your hypertrophied prick? You got off fucking lightly there, you son-of-a-bitch. You should have penises growing out of your tongue and your nose and your brain!!*

She couldn't do it. Joe looked like the news would crush him. "No," she said as gently as she could, "I haven't seen her."

Joe shrunk a little more into himself, then he grinned. "That's good, I guess. If you haven't seen her, she's likely still alive. I'll find her; I'm gonna keep searching till I find that child of mine." His eyes suddenly glowed with pleasure. "Mary's all I have in this world. I love my little girl to death, you do know that? I fucking do! And I'll find her even if it kills me, even if it damns me to damned Hell." He smiled at Melanie. "I think she's still alive; no way she can be dead, right? My girl was a survivor."

Melanie just managed to hold back tears. She nodded, thinking: *You poor, poor, poor fool, Joe.* She couldn't even dislike him anymore; the simplicity of his faith immunized him from her disdain. She was however forced to review one opinion: *No, dead Mary wasn't the dumbest person on planet Earth—her father is.* Despite her dubious new-found respect for the bartender, her conviction in this was absolute: she'd never met anyone more foolish in her entire life. *Damn, what a massive dick this man is,* she thought, *and he's even got the dick to prove it.*

"Keep looking, Joe," she finally replied, absentmindedly patting his monster penis. "Mary's likely out there looking for you too. She could be anywhere . . . *everywhere* even."

Joe didn't catch her irony. "Shit!" he suddenly yelped, the happy, expectant glow fading from his face like he'd just tasted wormwood. He hushed his voice. "It ain't good that you're out here in the open like this, Melanie. The fucking gingers are everywhere now! For a start, let's get off this main street. Side streets are much safer."

With an ease clearly born of much practice, Joe spun the yellow cart containing his hypertrophied penis around and rolled it quickly back the way he'd been coming from.

"Follow me," he whispered over his shoulder.

CHAPTER 34

Melanie and Joe had taken only a few paces forward when two gingers stepped out from a hairy doorway a short distance off. The cannibal pair stood in the road awaiting them.

Melanie winced, then stroked her gun's grip. "We go forward," she told Joe. "Those two attack us, I'll blow them both down to Philly."

"O.K.," Joe replied as they kept walking. "But remember, we're right next to the Eyeful Tower. The gun noise will attract other gingers."

Melanie considered that. Joe was right. But they couldn't turn and run now—the two mutants (who were stronger and faster than humans anyway) would be on them like stink on a polecat.

She'd have to do this the hard way.

She pursed her lips. "It's okay, I've got a knife too."

Joe heaved a loud sigh.

Melanie stepped up by the cart. She slid her pistol out of sight between two coils of Joe's penis. Best the gingers thought she was unarmed. The weapon's grip projected between the loops of pink skin in case she still needed it.

She rested a hand on the hilt of her knife. She doubted the sight of it would alarm the gingers, which was in her favor.

They'd almost reached the waiting pair now. *It's utterly disgusting,* Melanie thought, *how those two cannibals just stand there, expectant of our guaranteed arrival, like we're parcels the USPS is delivering. Like they imagine they've somehow hypnotized Joe and myself into being lunch and we've absolutely no say in the matter.*

Up close, Melanie recognized one of the waiting cannibals as Cody, the fat man who'd masterminded blowing Mary's clockwork guts sky-high. Like he was on his way to work, Cody wore a navy-blue three-piece-suit and a striped gray tie. Shiny black shoes. His companion was an attractive woman in a purple pantsuit and ankle boots.

The pair's leeched-looking white skin, flaming orange hair, and the horrible bloodlust in their orange eyes was completely at variance with their sartorial elegance.

"They look like a pimped-up pair of ghouls," Melanie whispered to Joe.

"That's the thing about the gingers," Joe whispered back. "They dress to kill."

Melanie didn't appreciate the comment. *And why isn't Joe scared of these fucking mutants? Something isn't right here—Joe isn't showing the slightest sign of fear.* Come to think of it, Joe sounded almost admiring of the gingers.

Then she made an oblique mental connection. *How strange*, she thought, *to be stuck here with the two biggest douches on Earth at exactly the same time*. It struck her as particularly ironic how neither Joe nor Cody realized that the current state of everything around them was the result of their combined stupidity.

"Remember," Joe whispered as they reached the gingers. "No shooting."

Melanie didn't reply. She just stared at the cannibals, biding her time to attack.

Cody kept staring at Melanie like he knew her from somewhere but couldn't place her face. Melanie was impressed by how both gingers were wearing nice perfume.

The ginger woman grinned at Joe, pointed to his massive coiled-up penis. "Hey, Monster Cock! You found another one, eh?"

(Melanie was again surprised by how the gingers' teeth were all so big—this woman's massive yellow dentition looked like it needed more space that her pretty mouth to fit into. Each of her canines, for instance, was the size of one of Melanie's index fingers. And now she was worried too: *Did she just call Joe 'Monster Cock?' She knows him? And what does she mean: 'another one?')*

Joe smiled affectedly. "Nah, Sue. She ain't one of those. She's a friend who's—"

"Hey!" Cody interrupted. "I know this bitch!"

Melanie protested, "I've never seen you before in my life!"

"Oh, hell yes, I know you," Cody said with more confidence.

Sue rolled her eyes. "You're always saying that, Cody! Once you see a plump chick, you go gaga at the thought of how she'll taste."

"She really is a friend of mine!" Joe pleaded. "I'm taking her to see the Queen for employment."

"No she's not," Cody said emphatically. "I *know* her." He regarded Sue with a piercing gaze. "Remember . . . three months ago, up north on Kathleen Street . . . she's the one who ran into the store to escape us, then vanished. She was with a guy. You were jacking off for fun against the glass."

Sue's eyes widened. "*She's* the one?"

Cody grinned. "Yeah, just check out the thighs and ass on her— like a human version of American Fried Chicken." He bared his fangs. "Let's eat the bitch, Sue!"

"Will the two of you stop fucking objectifying me!?" Melanie snapped. Being described that way infuriated her even more than the thought that they wanted to eat her.

"No!" Joe yelped. "You can't eat her!"

"Shut the fuck up!" Cody thundered. "Stay out of this. I'm just cancelling out a three-month-old hunger . . ."

Three months? Melanie pondered again. *It was just yesterday noon . . . I think.* She was tenser than a bowstring now. Her hand gripped the knife hilt, just waiting . . .

". . . The fact that her majesty says we can't touch you don't mean shit now, Joe. Okay?"

Sue laughed, licking her lips while she regarded Melanie. "Besides, Joe, don't be a fucking hypocrite. You're just like us, anyway."

"I'm not!" Joe insisted. "I'm not like you at all."

"Tell that to the fucking morph birds," Cody said. Baring his teeth like a vampire, he leapt at Melanie.

Melanie's tension broke; she uncoiled like a spring. Almost before Cody realized what had happened, she'd drawn her knife, stepped out of the way of his rush, and slashed his throat open from ear to ear. He turned to gape at her, blood rushing down over his suit and tie. He stood a moment, then crumbled, crimson jets still spurting from his neck. His protests over his dying came in garbled grunts like bubbling stream water.

Melanie turned her attention to Sue. She smiled. "Let's dance, honey."

Sue gaped at Melanie. Her mouth was wide open, her yellow fangs all out—she'd been poised to leap at Melanie and rip into her flesh. Now, however, she cast a shocked gaze over Cody's lifeless body.

Melanie strode towards Sue. The ginger woman's nerve broke; her shock turned to terror. She spun around and dashed off, running like the Devil was after her.

"She's gonna call the others," Joe said.

"No she isn't," Melanie replied, cool amusement in her voice. In a fluid motion she flung her knife after the fleeing cannibal woman.

The knife struck Sue in the back of her head. She froze for a moment, took three steps forward, then collapsed onto the road, her arms and legs jerking wildly. Then she stopped moving.

Melanie walked towards Sue. The dead woman lay on her side. The point of the knife's blade stuck out of her face between her eyes. Placing a boot on Sue's head, Melanie yanked the knife out again. Bright blood followed the blade's extraction. She walked ahead of its spread back to Joe.

He was staring at her in awe. "Damn! I've never seen anyone handle the gingers like that before."

Melanie scowled. "These bitches are pussies. Try the eaters if you want real conflict. Now those yellow bastards are *real* cannibals."

Joe nodded sagely.

"We need to move the bodies," she said. "Leaving them out here is asking for trouble."

"No need," Joe said. "They're children of the O. It takes care of its dead."

Melanie saw that it was true. Already, to the creaking of hinges, long tentacles were emerging from the doors and windows of the houses flanking them. The tentacles, long and warty, several with legs of their own even, made straight lines for the two corpses. Reaching them, each secreted lines of bubbling white liquid over the bodies, an acid that instantly dissolved straight down through their flesh, cutting them apart. Some of the tentacles even had mouths that drank up the spilled blood.

Then, each one dragging a part of Cody or Sue along with it, the tentacles all retreated again into their parent houses.

With a cascaded slamming of doors and windows, the street was silent, motionless, and empty again.

"Damn," Melanie said. "The houses even ate their clothes."

"It's the way of the new O," Joe said. "Nothing is ever wasted here.

Melanie retrieved her gun, which had slipped down between the coils of the monster penis. Something about the way the organ throbbed around her arm felt nicely reassuring.

She holstered the firearm, then stared coldly at Joe.

"What?" he asked, his face suddenly ashen, his gaze not leaving the bloody knife in her right hand.

She finally smiled, her piercing gaze losing its edge. "You and me are about having a long talk, Joe. From what you and the gingers were saying just now, there's a whole lot of stuff that you've not yet told me about this place. Part of it having to do with why the gingers left your punk ass alive."

"Yes of course," Joe said. "But let's get out of the road before more of them arrive."

Melanie had to laugh. "I don't get why you're so terrified of them. "They fucking seem to like you, man."

Joe winced and began wheeling his penis away. He went fast like he was angry. Melanie had to run to catch up to him.

"Okay," she asked as they went, "for one thing, what's this deal with the ginger Queen ordering them to lay off you?"

Now Joe really looked angry. "You heard Sue, didn't you? They— the damned gingers—all call me Monster Cock!"

Melanie looked at Joe's massive penis, so HUGE he had to cart it around, and guffawed. "You know, most men would take that as a compliment."

Joe burst into tears again. "First I lose Mary and now *this*. Everyone makes fun of me, everyone!"

It was horrible watching him cry, tears dribbling down his hairy cheeks while his penis throbbed angrily. Melanie put an arm around Joe. "I'm sorry, okay? It was wrong of me to laugh at you."

He wiped his eyes with the back of his hand. "The only reason I'm alive is because the ginger Queen considers me a national treasure. A frigging joke. I present myself in the Eyeful Tower three times a week and then she has her servants unroll my penis and measure its length and girth. 'It'd be a total waste of a good man if we ate you,' she jokes, 'unless we can figure out a way to eat you and keep your penis alive. America needs men like you.'"

Melanie figured she'd best change the topic. She said, "Joe, just fill me in on what's new in the O-Zone. I seem to have been away way too long for comfort."

CHAPTER 35

Melanie followed Joe down that street and across another until they reached a final alley, this one too narrow to permit the passage of cars. The houses lining it all had skin walls, some of them very hairy. Occasionally one had a large hand (much bigger than a person) projecting from its wall.

"Ensure you never get close to the hands," Joe cautioned as he wheeled his penis around one. "The houses don't seem intelligent, but if a hand catches you, it'll clench tight, frigging burst you open." He shuddered. "I've seen it happen. Wasn't a pretty sight."

"I can imagine." Straight ahead of them, through the space of the alley's end, she could now see the right side of the Eyeful Tower. It looked like an erect cousin of Joe's penis . . . one studded with eyes.

During their walking conversation, Joe had explained that the entirety of Springfield was now seemingly an O-Zone. No, it was worse than an O—as she could clearly see, it was now like actually living permanently up on Bizarro. He wasn't sure of its spread however. There were reports of this new fucked-up-ness (some were calling it SNAFU, others the FUZ, a.k.a. the Fucked-Up-Zone) extending (its rough shape an inverted triangle) as far north as Holyoke, west to Russell, down south to Windsor Locks in Connecticut's Hartford County, and east to Palmer, and Ware (up in Hampshire County), ending just around the boundaries of the Ware River.

Stranger still, there were streets one took now (according to Joe, Melanie was really lucky he'd found her when he did), that led to even odder places than this new, transformed O. One such route, for instance, led to a street that went on forever, and a hotel (ostensibly situated in New York) with 'X' number of floors . . .

188

"Everything's screwed-up now like you'd never believe," Joe had explained. He'd pointed to his huge penis. "I mean, I've got it bad, but you should see some other guys." He laughed. "Like Biggs, for instance . . ." He couldn't stop laughing.

Melanie asked. "Bigelow Jenkins?"

Joe laughed louder. "One and the same. Biggs is now a giant head stuck on the side of a cow." He slapped his thighs. "Imagine that—a fucking piebald prize Holstein! Worse still, he's conscious—I mean he can talk and all—and he's still trying to run the city. Biggs lives in a pasture up north now and even when they're milking his cow, you'll hear him barking out orders to subordinates, telling them how particular drug shipments have to gotten out on time . . ."

Melanie was glad when Joe seemingly ran out of wind then. Her mind boggled. Bigelow Jenkins, a head on a cow?

"I'm starving," she told Joe to change the topic. "You got anything to eat on you?"

He nodded and stopped the cart. He felt around inside it, lifting and shifting the humongous coils of penis till he found what he was looking for.

He held both items out for Melanie's inspection. One was a small blue/yellow pack.

"Planters Chipotle Peanuts okay?" His other hand held a can of Samuel Adams Boston Lager. He grinned. "You don't really expect an ex-barkeep to have anything else on hand, do you?"

Melanie gratefully accepted both from him. "It's a relief to finally have something to eat that I'm not allergic to," she said, ripping the peanut pack open.

While she chewed, she noticed Joe staring at her oddly.

"I've been wondering how you escaped the black birds transforming you," he said softly. "But they did you too. Your ears are gone."

She nodded after a swallow of hastily munched peanuts, chased the mouthful down with a gulp of warm beer. (The peanuts were hot, spicy with the jalapeño, but she hardly noticed; the malty-tasting warm brewski was just the right antidote to the cayenne pepper.) For the moment, his deduction was as good an explanation as the truth. Besides—she stole a glance at his penis—it was well too late for a dose of nuts to do Joe any good.

She raised a hand so he could see it only had three fingers.

He nodded sadly. "And your breasts too."

"Huh?" She looked down. Her jacket had unzipped itself, likely during her skirmish with the gingers. Her breasts dangled free. The silver cones topping them glinted like they were wet.

Looking back up at Joe's face, she was gripped by immense disgust. The man's sleazy gaze was riveted on her bared chest. Spittle dripped from his lips as his eyes roved over the abundant expanse of her milky white flesh. It was creepy: Because of the tingles of pleasure the metal electrodes were feeding through her breasts, it felt to Melanie almost like Joe's bloodshot eyes were stroking her absent nipples. Melanie wasn't shy or a prude by any definition, but still she shuddered. It was a horrible feeling, like being raped by vision. She glanced at Joe's penis; the massive meat snake now squirmed in its cart like it wanted to fuck her. She wasn't bothered about this last bit—even pumping all the blood in Joe's spindly frame into it couldn't erect such a monster. Still, she hated the way the cock's veins throbbed with desire.

(And revoltingly—she'd only just noticed this now, maybe as a result of the organ's excitement—parts of the huge penis's underside appeared to have tentacles growing out of it. Or maybe it was just shifting creases of the organ's pink skin that she was mistaking for prehensile appendages. She couldn't be sure what she was viewing, but . . . total 'ugh' either way . . .)

She glared at Joe, her glasses enlarging her eyes into angry pools.

Joe didn't care. "You've got two of the most wonderful milk-factories I've ever seen, Melanie. I'd just love to give you something to suckle with them." He laughed sadly. "But like you see, I'm much more than the man I used to be." His eyes stroked her breasts, teasing every luscious curve. "But, oh wowee!"

Melanie suddenly felt chilled. The air in the alley was cool, but it was much more than that. Joe's fixed stare now seemed morbid, like he was sizing her up, a housewife regarding meat in a shop. But what was worse? She'd just understood his last statement. *This douchebag's actually talking about making me pregnant? He wants another daughter to fuck up? What damn nerve!*

She choked down her urge to choke Joe, who was now sweating heavily as he stared. She found it odd too, how she didn't simply end this awkward, unpleasant situation by zipping her jacket closed over her breasts. Like she both liked and disliked the attention. Or, like she expected Joe to do the decent thing—look away politely now her feminine assets were exposed to the world. *Yeah right; like smelly unshaven Joe here has ever done anything polite or decent in his life.*

Joe stared right on at Melanie's chest.

"I need to get into the Eyeful Tower, Joe."

"Huh?" Joe didn't look up. Instead, lips partly open, he ran his tongue between his cracked teeth. His breath came in short loud snorts.

Melanie grabbed his head by the ears and forcibly tilted his face up to hers. It felt like she was raising a stone monument. The dandruff-laden head lifted slowly, Joe peeling his gaze away from her massive mammary endowment only with the most excruciating difficulty. (Beside them both, Joe's penis squirmed—its coils looping out of the cart like a mythical sea serpent's—as if protesting the removal of some pleasant stimulus.)

Finally, they made eye contact of a sort. "I said: I need to enter the Eyeful Tower."

That got Joe's attention. The lust instantly faded from his eyes, was replaced by intense nervousness. His penis slumped back into the yellow cart and lay quiescent. He pointed down the alley at the visible portion of the Eyeful Tower. "W-w-what do y-y-you want in there?"

She walked off towards it. "Let's get closer first. I'll tell you, but I want to get a good look at the thing."

Shaking, Joe wheeled the cart after her.

They found a shadowed vantage point just inside the alley entrance. Even so concealed, Melanie didn't really feel safe, however. Barely a meter behind them, the fingertips of a massive hand projecting from the stone walls swiped the air, trying to grab them. Each of the hand's attempts stirred up a wind in the alley that blew up her hair. With that so close, it was impossible to relax.

(Fortuitously, with only a small unreeling of his penis, Joe's cart had stowed away out of sight inside the demolished wall opposite the grasping hand. He looked ridiculous standing there, a skinny man with a pink anaconda thicker than his body twisting sideways from his groin to vanish into the darkness beside them. Melanie imagined she could hear Joe's cock hunting rats in the gloom.)

"So we're here now," Joe prompted, still sounding scared. "What the heck d'you want to go in *there* for?"

Melanie told Joe all about the teddy bears in the blue airplane.

While speaking, she studied the Eyeful Tower. It was only thirty yards away now, across a plaza of black transparent stone in which grew mutated pines, elms, and oaks with long tentacles for branches.

Like Big Ted had suggested, Melanie figured the tower had initially been a skyscraper—an apartment building—the hundreds of massive eyes dotting its meaty pink surface were spaced with window regularity. Each eye looked about six feet wide. The eyes—blue, brown, green, hazel, albino—swiveled in their sockets, all gazing up, down, and sideways in no coordinated order. Occasionally, a number of them blinked. Some of the orbs were weeping, torrents of water streaming down from them over lower-level eyes. One or two eyes were horribly rheumy with age; several had cataracts; several more were as bloodshot at Joe's . . .

Like external elevators, monster blue veins throbbed between the ranks of eyes; large bulges pulsed up and down their lengths like laden cages in transit.

A satanic halo, concentric rings of morph birds looped around the tower's top. The black rings spread out wide across the sky like they were being frightened away, then contracted in tightly again, like the tower's meat held birdseed they couldn't resist. Then they once more rippled off beneath the white clouds.

And worst of all, the Eyeful Tower throbbed like it was alive, jiggled and twitched like it was being stimulated. Melanie found it horrible, an utterly abhorrent monument.

In and out of the doors at the Eyeful Tower's base streamed female and male gingers. Some bore human corpses over their shoulders, some dragged corpses after them, yet others rolled the bodies in on carts. One way or another, human dead flowed into the building in a constant stream of murder.

A large ear-covered truck rolled up to the Eyeful Tower. The bald, orange-bearded driver alighted and strolled round to the rear of the vehicle, let down the tailgate. The rear of the truck faced Melanie and Joe. It was stacked with human dead.

A brisk unloading began. This close up, Melanie and Joe could make out the damage that had reduced the bodies to coronary inertia—some were dotted with bullet wounds, others had slashed throats, three or four were headless (in one case, a decapitated brunette's scalp dangled like a horse-tail between the legs of the man ferrying her corpse). One little body seemed axed—its left half separated stickily from its right almost to the belly, with lobes of lung and coils of intestine spilling from the ghastly tearing. (As was to be expected in the currently prevalent state of oddity, few of the corpses looked normal. Most had extra limbs. Several had odd machines growing out of them. One woman seemed to have wheels between both her breasts and legs.)

Melanie wrenched her gaze from the horrible sights. "Okay Joe," she said, concluding her deadpan exposition/recital, "now you frigging know why I've got to get in there."

Joe was still staring at the cannibals offloading the truck. Melanie was shocked: his awestruck gaze was even more intense than when he'd been ogling her breasts. "The gingers ain't fooling around," he said in a quiet voice. "They're frightfully efficient at killing humans." One of his hands squeezed his penis where it vanished into the dimness of the broken wall.

Melanie hated the admiration in Joe's voice. He sounded scared of the mutants all right—damn terrified even—but . . . Something in his voice threatened to unnerve her.

Thankfully, the gruesome unloading finished then. With a sigh like he'd just ejaculated, Joe turned to Melanie. "Sorry, where were we?"

"You *were* listening, right? I mean: you heard all I said about rescuing the teddy trapped in the tower?"

He nodded quickly, his eyes once again shifty and furtive. "Yes, yes . . . I heard everything. I need to think."

Melanie was becoming very bothered by Joe's ceaseless mood swings. Now, he wasn't even looking at her breasts anymore. It seemed to her like he was obsessed with the human flesh he'd seen being offloaded, like . . . Then she remembered: *What was it that those two gingers I killed—Cody and Sue—said to Joe? 'Another one . . . you hypocrite . . . you're just like us?'*

She eyed him with suspicion. "Joe, have you been eating people too? Do the gingers feed you human flesh?"

He looked up at her quickly, his eyes surprised. "Oh, no, Melanie. It's just that . . . just that whenever I see the gingers, I wish I was one of them."

"Wish you were one of them? Are you fucking nuts?"

Joe looked down shamefacedly. "It's not like that."

"How the fuck is it?" If she didn't need Joe now (though she didn't even know if he could help her), Melanie was certain she'd have pulled her gun and shot him out of sheer anger. It seemed to her that whatever stupidity the world threw up, Joe enrolled in the vanguard of idiots out to promote it. "How the fuck is it, Joe?"

He looked up now, met her eyes evenly. His voice wavered but his words were potent with feeling: "I don't like being like this—a freak with a dick four times as long as my body. And I don't like being considered food." Not taking his eyes from hers, Joe pointed angrily out from their place of concealment. "Those cannibal shits, hate 'em or not, are running things around here. The morph birds don't affect them, they can come and go as they please. Most important: *they're* doing the hunting and killing, not the other way around." He paused, then finished: "So you see—I'd rather be *them* than *me.*"

Melanie's rage wilted in the heat of his glare. "I see," she said drily, then let it go. His explanation made sense. Too much sense—why be prey when you could be the predator? And Joe was even protected (she suppressed an involuntary fit of giggles at why he was so highly valued by the gingers); Melanie couldn't imagine what the average human around here felt like now—an endangered species?

"I've got it!" Joe yelped, cutting into her thoughts. "I know how to get you inside the Eyeful Tower safely!"

Melanie eyed him suspiciously, then nodded. "Lower your voice, but go on."

Joe pointed through the broken wall at his cart. "It's easy. I told you how the ginger Queen ordered me to present myself before her thrice a week so she can measure me, right?" His face squeezed up in distaste. "Between you and me, I think the bitch has gone nuts ever since James got transformed."

Despite her urgency, Melanie was intrigued by the digression. "James the O-Zone ruler? What happened to him?"

Joe laughed. "The changes hit him even worse than Biggs. James is a crocodile monster now. Massive scaly green thing, the kind you only expect to see in a prehistoric Nile Valley recreation. Bastard's got teeth like . . . Only thing is, her insane majesty still loves the prick so much, she's got him chained down in the tower basement." He pointed out at the streams of gingers entering the watching tower with their dead human burdens. "A lot of that meat is just to keep James alive."

The story made Melanie feel queasy. *Ah, so now there's a monster in the basement too, is there?* She removed her glasses, misted them with breath, cleaned and replaced them on the bridge of her nose. "Stick to the point," she urged Joe softly. "How does *your* getting in help *me* get in?"

He grinned, scratching his dirty beard. "Easy. I'll hide you underneath my penis. No one ever thinks to look inside my cart."

Melanie gaped at Joe's audacious suggestion. *Fuck!* she thought, *ridiculous as this sounds, it might actually work.*

She nodded at him. "Joe, you're a frigging genius. Let's do it."

CHAPTER 36

They retreated through the broken alley wall into the shrouded interior of a house.

Joe produced a flashlight that reduced the shadows. Melanie looked around—grossly mutated roaches scurried over the walls, jostling one another to escape the unfamiliar light.

"You're here at about the right time," Joe said. "I'm due to see the Queen in about an hour; I'll simply head across early to the Eyeful. We'll be in without any trouble, you'll see."

Melanie groaned. Joe was gazing intently at her chest and licking his lips again. *Hell, not my tits again. If you dare attempt to grope me, I'll—SHIT!!!*

Without warning, a massive jolt of pain had suddenly surged through her breasts, back to her spine and down into her belly. She bent over gasping. Then the pain was gone, and her breasts felt wonderful again. Too wonderful, like she'd shortly begin rubbing her crotch from the pleasure.

"You okay?" Joe asked worriedly.

"I'm fine," she groaned back. "Just a twinge."

That's a reminder, she realized as her breathing normalized. *Psycho Ted's getting impatient up there. So time to fucking do this. Shit! And Joe just said James is now a monster and secured in the basement, right? Do I have to get through him too?* She steeled herself grimly in her determination: *And so what if the beast in the basement gets in my way, decides to crash my fucking rescue party? . . . Well then, I'll simply have to shoot the fucker, won't I?*

Lips compressed into a narrow line, she straightened up. "Hurry up, Joe."

She needn't have spoken. Joe had already stood the light on a table, and was lifting the coils of his penis out of the cart. She winced; in this dimness she couldn't be certain, but it again seemed that the snake-cock had tentacles on its underside. *Shit! I have to lie under that fucking thing?*

Joe gasped at her from beneath a humongous loop of penis he'd hoisted up on his shoulders. "Hurry up yourself and climb in. This dick of mine is ridiculously heavy. I feel like it's about to crack my friggin' back!"

Safekeeping her glasses in a pocket, Melanie climbed into the cart and lay down on its metal floor. She instantly felt like she was choking. The air down there was thick with musk, like someone had sprayed it with a perfume made from essence of unwashed male crotch. She gagged, then drew in a shallow breath as she felt Joe slowly lower his penis onto her. Damn, it was heavy, even spread out over her body. It felt like a Sumo wrestler pinning her down. It felt hot. And yes, now she had her confirmation: the horrible organ did have tentacles, long fat feelers that crawled over her prone form like snakes. They slithered around and beneath her, filling all the space her body didn't occupy.

It was like lying in a bed of worms. The massive hot penis crushing down on her, the acrid male musk in her nostrils like she was a pimple on a testicle, the tentacles (some of which had now coiled themselves around her body in their quest for space); her experience was of the uttermost claustrophobia.

She firmed her resolve, this had to be gotten over with. She looked up through the massive coils. Joe was peering down at her.

Their eyes met. "You okay down there?" he called.

"Yes, yes, yes, fucking yes!" she growled back, her discomfort becoming anger. "Let's fucking go. . . please."

Joe didn't reply. Melanie thought he suddenly looked very pleased about something.

"Joe!" she called, but he still didn't answer. His eyes were now glazed over like he was concentrating on a puzzle.

Then Melanie felt the penis's tentacles tightening around her. She instantly realized that this wasn't random. All along her body they grabbed her tight, pinning her arms to her body, trapping her down in the cart.

"Fuck, Joe! What is this shit!? Let go of me!" Her hands were in front of her, clamped tightly against her breasts by the tentacles. She began fighting to free them, to reach down for her gun. "Joe, let me go!"

Joe silently shook his head. Melanie saw he was licking his lips. *It's a fucking trap!* she realized in panic. *He's suckered me in!*

Fear flooded her. The kind of horror she'd not experienced even up on the blue aircraft when she'd been surrounded by corpses. "Joe, fucking let me go this instant, you shithead! What is this nonsense!?"

Shaking his head again, Joe grinned down at her. His face was flushed, his eyes wide and staring. Saliva drooled from his lips. He began jabbering like an idiot: "Meat's meat, gonna eat gonna eat gonna eat gonna eat . . ."

He jabbered and driveled on. Melanie managed to get a hold on her panic. *He's going to eat me? Shit! Shit! Shit!* Using every ounce of strength she possessed, she slowly began forcing back the tentacles from her breasts. It was hard going, but she finally freed her right hand, slipped it out of the tentacles' clasp, and dropped it to her hip. Next step was drawing her gun. After that, one shot through the cart wall would kill Joe. *No, I won't kill this bastard, I'll maim him, then force him to watch while I cut his stinking manhood off his body a foot at a time . . .*

But she couldn't free her gun. Like greased bands of iron, two thick slimy tentacles were wrapped around both the Glock's grip and holster. Try all she might, she could neither part the tentacles nor slide them aside. Her panic returned magnified. It was now also becoming hard to breathe: removing her hand from her chest had allowed the tentacles to squeeze down harder . . .

"Gonna eat gonna eat meat's meat, baby!" Joe gushed on, "Wanna gonna eat eat gonna fucking eat MEAT Melanie, baby . . ." He was gripping the edge of the cart and leaping up and down.

Melanie reined in her fear again. *What the hell do I do now? I can't reach my knife—*

"Fuuuuccck!!!" she screamed then as something that burnt like fire splattered the back of her head. The pain didn't go away, instead it spread over her scalp, bubbling along, the agony threatening to drive her insane.

God no! What the hell is that!?

She twisted her face back to see what had burnt her. She had the barest glimpse of the huge penis-head spurting a transparent liquid at her and next moment was splashed in the eyes with it. The next instant her vision went blank as the acid corroded away both her eyes in their sockets. Completely blinded, she felt it peel the skin off her face and eat up her facial muscles.

Realizing that she was fucked beyond any relief, Melanie began screaming. Then another spurt of penis-acid burnt out her voice box and she could make no further verbalization of her terror. Her world became simply unrelenting agony and horror, and the asphyxiating smell of unwashed male crotch, until the acid burnt all the way through her skull and dissolved away her brain.

Melanie Nemesis Catchpole's death happened much sooner than she imagined it did, but she felt the agony of every microsecond of its occurrence.

CHAPTER 37

Joe watched his penis slowly eat up Melanie's corpse. The organ was extended in a wide curve around the room now. It fed like a snake: once it had burnt the meal's head off with acid, he had to pull it out of the cart and stretch it out over the ground, so no kinks in its length hindered a smooth ingestion.

(The penis's tentacles had all now retreated back into slits along its length.)

Melanie's body was about half gone now—she'd gone in neck-first; the penile ingress was stretched taut around the dead woman's immense hips, about to be stretched even tauter by her massive buttocks. Joe had stripped Melanie naked first. Reviewing the lovely expanse of her dead flesh now—*Damn, this girl has an incredible body! And just check out that cooter on her, and the size of those beef curtains! Oooh, I fucking just loooove girls with huge pussy lips!*—filled him with regret that he was going to eat and not fuck her. *Shit! How things have changed! Back when Mary was alive, I'd have . . .*

Thoughts of his missing daughter filled Joe with immense sadness. *I was a good father, wasn't I? So why'd she run off? No! My Mary was a good girl. She wasn't like her mother—didn't tramp off to suck dick for cash. My baby was kidnapped . . .* His lips pursed tight. *And when I fucking find the bastard who done it, I'll feed him to my dick too!*

Thinking of Mary was making Joe maudlin, so he returned his attention to watching his penis swallow his latest victim's remains. Melanie's huge ass was all the way in now. Just her legs to go—those thick meaty thighs, the white calves and ankles, the shapely feet with the cute octopus birthmark on the right one.

Joe smiled broadly. Feeding via his penis felt almost like getting a good blowjob, just one from which you didn't come. It was a nice buzz. He patted the thick pink trunk where it grew from his groin.

Yeah, just wonderful. (Joe no longer had any stomach. His penis connected directly to his guts—it ate and spread the food into the rest of him.)

Grinning as Melanie's legs vanished into his manhood, Joe looked across to the table with the flashlight, on which also rested the two weird metal objects he'd cut out of Melanie's breasts. (Joe's first impressions of the silver cones being some sort of micro metal bra— like pop singers and burlesque showgirls sometimes wore—had been proven wrong.)

Both objects looked like little opened-up umbrellas. Their metal poles had been embedded completely through her chest, fusing at the rear to her spine where a mass of white wires connected them to her spinal cord. Both glittered stain-proof, not a drop of blood on them. It had taken Joe a lot of work to cut them out of Melanie's body. But it had to be done—his penis wouldn't digest metal. Even those of her teeth with fillings had had to be extracted.

His grin faded; he regarded both objects with fear. When he'd been cutting them out, the umbrellas had kept shocking him. Made no sense at all. Maybe he'd take them to the ginger Queen. He'd feign ignorance as to both their origin and function—a shock or two should do the bitch some good. He knew shrinks used that method all the time to cure psychos—shock treatment it was called—and in Joe's book, any woman pining after a guy who'd turned into a croc definitely qualified as a nutter.

A loud slurping sound came from Joe's penis. He looked back over to it, saw the lips of the immense glans just shutting over Melanie's toes, then the foreskin cover the opening like drapes. Oh yeah, it was a great feeling. Now the corpse slowly travelled down the cock, its voluptuous curves stretching Joe's manhood deliciously.

Oh yeah, Joe thought, *I did right, remaining here in Springfield, MA. I could have left town back when the Chameleon Sisters offered me a ride in their truck, but I made the right choice in staying. This place is my home. "C'mon Joe,"* they said, *"it ain't safe around here no more. We'll look after you . . . just climb in the back, your dick'll fit without any trouble . . . we're heading west to California . . . L.A. . . . you can set up another WTF? bar there, create a sensation . . . We'll have lots of fun." But . . . but how'm I ever going to find Mary if I leave here, and besides . . .* he licked his lips at the now slowly shrinking bulge in his penis, *there's still lots of food! The Chameleon Sisters are likely in Los Angeles by now, partying it up . . . but them girls left way too early, if ya ask me . . .*

Walking backward, teasing a length of penis behind him, Joe found a dirty chair and sat. Dislodged from its perch on the chair's back, a large misshapen moth dropped by his boot. He stomped it; the insect splattered into green mush.

Joe picked up Melanie's clothes and searched her pockets, from time to time scratching his beard. Across from him, his manhood's enzymes digested her away entirely, absorbing her into its length. It took just ten minutes.

When Joe found the strange black key in Melanie's pocket, he paused. Just looking at it scared him, with its runes like magic symbols. It wasn't something he wanted anything to do with. (Joe had been so busy plotting how to eat Melanie that he'd not paid much attention to her explanation of her quest. His thoughts spinning sideways down devious pathways, he'd hardly heard a thing she said. Joe had totally blanked out the parts about Big Ted in the plane, and so had no idea that a teddy bear had implanted the 'umbrellas' in Melanie's body.) *She said it activates a teddy bear in the Eyeful Tower basement, right? Alright then, I'll hand it over to her beautiful ginger majesty along with the shocking umbrellas.*

He grinned at his penis. Melanie was totally gone now—the organ was a smooth round tube like before. Joe felt refreshed—strong as Hercules—as nutrients leeched from the dead woman surged through him.

Whistling happily, he began gathering his penis back into coils and loading it back into his yellow cart.

A roach with too many legs walked past him. He stamped it flat and kept working. Slowly, he filled the cart with his cock again.

Then, with no warning at all, the world chilled and Joe felt the irresistible cold fingers of an old terror squeeze his heart.

Shit! Joe quailed. *It's The Fixer! I've got to get the fuck out of here!*

CHAPTER 38

Joe had a total, unequivocal dread of The Fixer. Since that evening when the faceless black figure had walked into his bar, he'd been terrified of him.

Joe still recalled vividly how The Fixer's hand had extended across the counter and grabbed him by the throat. And the chill he'd felt when those black fingers touched him? Joe had been close to death before—he'd twice had heart attacks—but those were nothing compared to this. When The Fixer grabbed him by the throat, he'd seen flashes of a place beyond death, where sub-absolute-zero chill didn't freeze a body but burnt like fire, where a million years and a second were one and the same thing . . . And he'd known, known with every trembling scared cell of his sleazy being, that if The Fixer had really wanted to, he could banish Joe into that realm of eternal preternatural chill from which Joe would never escape, and where, with no judgment being pronounced or punishment delivered, the torment would be eternal and absolute.

Joe had been relieved that night to escape with only soiling his pants. Since then, since everything went to shit, he'd seen The Fixer on several occasions. Each time he'd avoided the black-cloaked figure with the suitcase like he was the bubonic plague in person. Just *seeing* The Fixer always filled Joe with immense guilt, even when he'd not eaten anyone. That place of absolute chill he'd seen had been worse than Hell . . .

And now? Now The Fixer was outside, coming down the alley towards Joe, Jack Frost the herald of his arrival.

The cold intensified in the room; outside, the alley walls coated over with ice. Soft steps sounded on the cobbles.

Panicking, Joe finished loading his penis into the cart and pushed it toward the hole in the wall. Every feeling of wellbeing had by now fled him; unreasoning terror compelled him to flee.

He got his cart through the broken wall just as the footsteps halted outside it. Joe saw he was trapped. The Fixer stood right beside him on his left. The temperature around them both compared to that of Leningrad in winter.

The Fixer put down his black suitcase. He tilted up his wide-brimmed hat. "I believe you've something belonging to me in your possession, Joseph," he said in that hoarse croak of his that so unnerved Joe.

"Wha-wha-what's that?" Joe managed to stutter.

"Don't play dumb with me. A black key of mine is presently in your keeping."

Joe was saved from replying right away because the immense hand growing out of the wall behind The Fixer reached out then and grabbed him in its hairy clutches.

Joe watched breathless with hope. Would the huge fist crush his dread interrogator?

The Fixer made no attempt to free himself. While he did nothing, however, a thick white coat of ice spread over the grasping hand. Within this frigid plating, the hand began visibly cracking, the deep fissures in its surface spreading and connecting like a forming web.

Finally the fist exploded outward. A dozen frozen chunks of meat landed around Joe and The Fixer.

"Give me the key, Joseph," The Fixer continued like nothing had happened.

"Sh-sh-sure," Joe stuttered.

Any proposed resistance Joe might have put up had been completely fractured along with the hand—behind The Fixer, just a bony stump now protruded from the wall. Joe hastily fiddled about in his trouser pocket and produced the black key. He handed it over with relief.

"I-I-I just found it somewhere, s-s-sir."

The Fixer took the key from Joe's trembling fingers. "I sense a departed soul; one I knew. Melanie Nemesis Catchpole is dead. Regrettably, irretrievably so." The man's 'face'—a fractured gray mirrorscape reflecting light from ten different sources, none of those the overhead sun—regarded Joe. "Tell me, Joseph—how did she die?"

Joe had no intention of replying that question. As a diversion, he quickly dug about inside his cart, shoving his penis roughly aside till he found the two umbrella-like electrodes. After a quick glance out the alley at the Eyeful Tower, he held these out to The Fixer. Joe was shivering, and not just from the cold mist now swirling around them. "I found these too, s-sir!"

The Fixer took the electrodes from Joe. "I sense that these were in Melanie's body, Joseph. But . . . tell me—was she up in my aircraft?"

The tone of the black-garbed figure's voice assured Joe he'd just made a mistake in handing the umbrellas over. Worse still, he imagined that several of the Eyeful Tower's eyes—four green ones on the left in particular—were now regarding him with suspicion. *Damn!* Joe thought, *how the hell am I getting outa this? I ain't telling him I just ate Melanie, and I honestly don't know about any airplane!*

He looked guiltily back at The Fixer, at the faceted opacity that served him for a face. *Shit, his mug looks like a gray diamond!*

"You're trying my patience, Joseph." The Fixer dropped the electrodes on his suitcase; they vanished through it.

"Well, Mr. Fixer sir, it's like this, see . . . I don't know about the plane, but see, Ms. Melanie . . . I met her and she gave me the key and the umbrellas, and she said there's a teddy bear in the Eyeful Tower she has to find—"

Joe froze then because The Fixer grabbed him by the throat. Once again, to Joe's immense horror, the dark man's hand had simply leapt across the space separating them. The Fixer's upper arm still dangled by his side; his forearm had lengthened across the gap between himself and Joe.

Joe cringed as once again uncanny cold spread from The Fixer's fingers, creeping like freezing worms up and down his body. He felt like spikes made of ice were being hammered into his protesting flesh. "Please don't hurt me, sir! I'll talk, I will!"

The Fixer laughed, only there was no mirth in the sound. Unable to pee himself because of the length of his penis, Joe felt his bowels loosening instead. He clamped down hard on his sphincter.

"I'm giving you *one* chance to tell me the truth, Joseph. Just one; and then . . . Now, tell me everything you know about Melanie Catchpole . . . including her death. And I mean *everything* . . ."

With no recourse or escape—Joe could already feel the freezing tentacles of the cold Hell beyond this zone of chill reaching for his soul—Joe talked and talked and talked. He told the truth, the whole truth, and nothing but. (It felt to Joe like The Fixer's fingers were yanking the words out of his voice box.) When he was done talking, he considered it a great accomplishment that he'd not befouled himself.

"Please don't kill me, sir!" Joe begged finally. "I was just hungry! I haven't eaten for days."

The Fixer let out a sigh. "You're a pathetic excuse for a person, Joseph. I should wring the life out of you, but . . ." he let go of Joe's neck, shortened his forearm back down to his side, "unfortunately for me—in your case at least—I can't kill anyone; it's simply not my nature." Sighing again, he turned toward the Eyeful Tower. "So L'il Ted is in *there*? In the *basement*? I'll have to pay her cannibal majesty a visit." He turned back toward Joe. "Though I hate to admit this, Joseph—I'm in your debt, you've just performed me a great service."

On that note, he adjusted his black hat, picked up his suitcase, and strode out of the alley toward the eye-studded building, his zone of cold accompanying him like a horny dog after a bitch in heat.

As the black figure departed, Joe sank to the alley floor, his penis uncoiling from the cart after him. He sat there on the slowly warming stones, considering his narrow escape. His frayed nerves calmed, his racing heartbeat slowed to normal. *What the heck did he mean—I've just done him a service? 'Cos of a teddy bear?*

A flock of morph birds flew low through the alley. Several passed right through Joe's penis and on through the stone wall.

Watching the black liquid birds flap past with their tiny clockwork gears whizzing, Joe was struck by sudden regret. A mournful look in his eyes, he gazed toward the Eyeful Tower, where his recent antagonist was no longer visible. It had just occurred to him that if only he could find the courage to ask the question, the dread Fixer might actually know where his daughter Mary was. *An' he might just tell me too—particularly now he claims he's in my debt.*

He finally brightened up, got to his feet. *One day I will ask him. At least I didn't crap myself this time. That's a start for sure.*

Wheeling his squirming monster penis ahead of him in its yellow cart, Joe headed off up the alley, away from the Eyeful Tower. Joe had the idea that with The Fixer about visiting her, the ginger

Queen—her royal insanity—wouldn't be too bothered if for once he missed their regular appointment.

Joe grinned a hideous row of cracked teeth. Yes, sirree—The Fixer tended to have that unsettling effect on people.

CHAPTER 39

In her bedroom on the third floor of the Eyeful Tower—a meat-walled chamber without eyes looking inward—the ginger Queen lay in bed masturbating with a severed human tongue. (Pleasuring herself with the glossae of the deceased was her current craze.) A bowl of the pink organs lay beside her bed. The tongues—half-submerged in blood—were still warm, all only just ripped from their hapless human owners.

The Queen rubbed the tip of the wet organ over her clitoris, relishing the shivers that coursed up through her limbs at the contact. *Oh oh oh!*

Around her, the bedroom walls rippled, seemingly in sympathy with her saccharine sexual sensations.

She picked out another tongue from the bowl and sucked the sweet blood off it. Then, spreading her toned white thighs wide till they were almost flat against the pale green sheets, she parted her labia and slid the tongue deep inside her sex. Her orange pubic hair looked like a forest fire between her legs, her splayed vagina the lake straining to put it out.

She stroked herself slowly with the tongues—the one penetrating her, the other rubbing her swollen clitoris. The lustful grimace on her beautiful face intensified as hot raw feeling boiled from her sex. She increased the speed of her in-and-out stroking. Her breasts tingled, her stiff rosy nipples felt exquisitely nice. It seemed like she floated on clouds.

She bared her fangs in ecstasy, bit her lower lip till blood spilled, twisted her head side to side, flung her long glossy orange hair across the pillows like she was scrubbing them with it.

Her orgasm was building up fast now. The strokes she made with the two tongues became violent. She scoured her clitoris like she intended rubbing it off her crotch. She dug the other tongue in as far as it would go; her legs left the bed, flailed in the air.

The feel of the obscene meaty piston travelling inside her slick sexual tube kicked her over the precipice of orgasm. She belly-flopped into a pool of pleasure; rose skyward on wings of bliss. The waves of her climax were like blows: she felt like her vagina was a fist slamming into the rest of her body, an erotic boxer pummeling her to a sexual pulp. She flung her hands up to gather and squeeze her breasts. She clamped her thighs tight around the tongue in her sex, ground them together deliciously while her orgasm ran its course.

Then, when the rage of her sensations was over, she lay back, completely disheveled, destroyed by pleasure. Staring at the skin ceiling, she ate the tongue she'd caressed her clitoris with. The other tongue remained in her sex; she liked the snug feel of it there.

As her afterglow subsided, so her thoughts darkened.

Since her lover James Richards had become a monster, the ginger Queen had grown very depressed. *There has to be a way to cure him*, she felt. *There just has to be . . . But how?* Her besotted love for James assured her that there was a fix, one she would certainly see if she wasn't staring so intently at it. *I have to get my darling back to normal*, she fumed desperately. *It's not just the sex I miss—that was of course nice—but I want to feel his arms around me again!*

The vestiges of her orgasm's pleasant feeling crumbled from around her like the rammed walls of a besieged castle.

At that moment when she felt her absolute lowest, a part of the Queen's bedroom wall directly opposite her bed opened up like a door and The Fixer walked in. There was no fanfare or announcement to his arrival, he was just suddenly there with her.

The Queen sat up in a startled rush. She shivered, and not just from the instant chilling the bedroom had experienced. The black-cloaked man with the suitcase filled her with apprehension. With deep anxiety. She didn't care for him at all—he neither obeyed her commands, nor respected her authority. Also, he wasn't human—couldn't be eaten. He apparently couldn't be killed either—several of her tribe reported having shot him to no effect whatever. *And he's so damned black, like someone carved the night into human form . . . and that face, oh that face!*

The meat wall sealed over behind The Fixer. He dropped his suitcase, stood there motionless. A sudden panic seized the Queen; it felt like he was drinking her dark thoughts into his face . . .

Then, angered by how completely unapologetic he seemed at having intruded on her privacy, she quelled her fear, found her voice. "How dare you barge into my bedroom like this? I'll have my guards remove you at once!"

"Good evening, your Majesty," The Fixer said equably, bypassing her anger. "We've important business to discuss." Frost swirled around the bedroom, the intense chill making both walls and monarch shiver.

"Business?" She now felt uneasy again. *Whatever he wants cannot be good.* Nervousness didn't make the ginger Queen modest, however. Spreading her legs in her visitor's full view, she retrieved the tongue filling her vagina, raised it to her lips and bit off half of it. She chewed a while, swallowed. She felt better afterward: the meat reminded her of the helplessness of those it had come from, confirmed that she was still in charge here. "What business?"

"You have an object of mine in your possession," he said. "I want it back."

She regarded him in confusion for a moment, then, turning to her bowl of severed vocal muscles, she dropped the half-eaten tongue amidst the other bloody lingua and got warily out of bed.

"Of course," she said in restrained tones, reaching for her clothes—a pair of denim cutoff pants and a purple shirt. "Whatever you want."

✳✳✳

"The Eyeful Tower was a warehouse before the changes," the ginger Queen informed The Fixer as they strode together along eye-studded corridors. Once she'd heard what her black visitor wanted back, her mood had improved greatly. Indeed, she felt quite chatty now, particularly since he'd done something so she no longer felt like she was freezing to death in his company. "This whole area . . ." she gestured out of a wide window whose frames were covered with thick eyelashes, "used to be southern Parker Street . . . the upper part of the Sixteen Acres neighborhood." She frowned prettily. "At least I think so."

"Do you approve of the changes?"

She shook her head. "Even though their extra limbs mean more meat for us, the humans don't taste as good anymore . . . it's like the nourishment they contain has been diluted to fill their new body parts. We could also do without the strange objects growing out of them. Would you believe that just this afternoon, a dead woman was brought in with a bicycle growing through her from neck to crotch? Imagine that—a bicycle. She'd apparently got around by falling forward on her wheels and pedaling herself." The Queen bared her teeth, teased free a tangled shred of tongue tendon. "Total crap. I severely reprimanded the man who'd caught her. I mean—who in the world eats bicycles?"

"West of here, in New York State, there are *huss*, beings that eat metal. Oddly enough, they look human. They're flesh and blood, but their jaws and bones are diamond. Mercury flows as blood in their veins."

She repressed a shudder. "Ugh. I'd hate to meet those creatures."

(They walked past several gingers who bowed respectfully to the Queen, while shivering in the frost of The Fixer's passing and wondering how it didn't affect her majesty.)

"You may not have a choice," he said. "Here, the parallands are blended with Earth now. More and more species that would ordinarily not interact will likely do so. I foresee these changes spreading as far west as Illinois. Ohio at the very least."

"Like we don't already have enough nonsense to deal with." Now the Queen wished she'd brought along a tongue to chew on, to relax her. The Fixer's words were disquieting. There was already a shortage of edible humans in Springfield (lots of gingers now ate beef sold by Bigelow Jenkins), and they'd shortly have to deal with monsters also?

They descended three flights of flesh stairs that wobbled beneath their feet. Entered the basement.

The Fixer said, "Though this explains how I never sensed its presence before, I do not understand how my teddy bear ended up here, underground."

The Queen shrugged. "You know how everything warped up. I think the whole original warehouse is the basement now, it's still stone. The Eyeful Tower grew over it like a tree." Now her mood dimmed again, depression began to weigh her down. She worried her bright hair with her claws. Here in the basement they'd shortly reach

James. Already the horrid musk of the reptile beast he'd become permeated the corridor, that stink of a predator's lair—terrible and fetid with the odors of brutal slaughter. The sound of the creature's restless prowling grew louder with their advance. (The fact that the cannibal Queen was herself a murderous predator was lost on her—this beast was something infinitely worse than she.)

They reached the row of six-inch-thick iron bars that separated James from the corridor. Now the Queen couldn't keep her tears from drenching her beautiful face. *James! James!* She froze, stared through the rusty grille at the crocodile monster—once her man!—stalking its realm of rotting meat.

The two gingers guarding the cage bowed quickly to her majesty, and then even more quickly, fled the basement, both hurrying to be away from The Fixer.

The cage was thirty-meters deep and twenty wide. Initially a suite of clerical offices, the connecting walls had all been knocked out. The remaining walls, ceiling, and floor were next doubly reinforced with tempered steel bars. (Afterwards, James had been lured down here by a trail of human corpses and locked in.)

Like it sensed her gaze, the creature looked up from prowling the cage floor across which it swept a woman's severed lower half to and fro. Spilled innards trailed its massive jaws, blood spattered its great rectangular head. The crocodilian was a total nightmare—a monstrous bulk dominating the cell. Forced down on its legs by the height of the roof, it stood eight feet tall at the shoulder, was as long as a pair of elephants placed end-to-end—a distortion of a monster reptile. Green scales like corrugated armor plate rippled over its form. Eyes the size of a human head, each one amber like it was full of old urine, with pupils like black daggers. Claws like rows of bloody scythes . . . Legs like support pillars. The massive beast had eight legs already; two more sets of limbs currently grew from its sides. Its tail was six meters long and thicker than the Queen's body.

The beast regarded those watching it like it was preparing to attack.

An evil wind of stink blew from the cell. There was no respite from the fumes of putrefaction. Like up in Big Ted's charnel plane, the monster's lair was piled with the rotted refuse of human slaughter—it preferred its food alive and screaming. Splattered blood covered the once-cream walls and ceiling. Broken human bones lay strewn across the cage, many lying inside wide pools of urine across which blue insects skittered. The monster's black excrement was piled in a far corner. Closer to the cage's bars lay an expanse of defleshed human skulls, all broken open so their brain contents could be sucked out. Around everything boiled maggots.

The stink of the defiled dead spilled relentlessly from the cage. The ginger Queen fought not to gag.

The Fixer stood beside the Queen, regarding the huge reptile. His interest was indicated by subtle shifts in the shading of his face, now it looked like a Rorschach test done in gray. He asked, "Who is . . . was this?"

She regarded him with confusion. "You don't know?"

"I know a little bit of everything, but not everything itself. I see more than most people do, but still, occasionally I miss the obvious."

"It's James!" Her voice escaped her as a tortured gasp. She felt like her heart would burst from her tormented emotions.

Like it recognized its one-time name, the massive reptile reared in its cage, its body swelling with its heavy breaths. It blinked like it was interested in their conversation.

"*James.*" The planes of The Fixer's face now all shifted. The many sheets of gray appeared to slide over one another like each searched for its correct alignment in his visage. The entire impossible expanse flickered with light that wasn't part of the normal color spectrum.

The Queen gazed intently at The Fixer, her eyes desperate and pleading. "Do something! Surely you can help him! You can't just leave him like this!"

The shifting of his facial planes stopped. "Nothing *can* be done. I would help you if I could."

"Nothing?" Her voice dangled limp as the legs of a hanged man.

"Absolutely nothing." The words were flat, final; perhaps holding a modicum of pity. The Queen couldn't tell.

The Fixer's next question bore a silver lining of compassion, however. "Why do you torture yourself so? Why do you keep him here?"

"I loved him; do you understand that?" Somewhere deep inside her, she felt her dark companion's understanding was important, like it would make her inescapable bitterness more palatable.

"Yes," The Fixer replied, "I do understand. In your case, however, such precious emotions will hurt you for a long time to come. A very long time." He gestured at the caged reptile. "That thing is immortal."

"Immortal?" She sank to her knees at the horrible truth, her hands gripping the metal bars for support. She stared in at the crocodile monster. It stared back without recognition. Then it spat at her, a mess composed in equal parts of slime and rotted meat.

Unable to escape the deluge, the ginger Queen found herself coated with befoulment. While pulling worm-ridden intestines from her flaming hair, clearing slime from her eyes, and crying her eyes out, she was aware of the Fixer helping her to her feet.

"Come," he said. "We must go on. I must have that teddy bear. My need is urgent."

The Queen stood, but shook her head. "No. I must remain here with James. My need for him is greater than yours is for your toy. I may be sick with love, but that's just how I am, the only way I know to be." She smiled sadly through the cage bars at the reptile within. "He will live *forever*? Then I must find a way to live forever as well, and maybe in our joint forevers I will find a cure somewhere. I cannot give up—there must be a cure somewhere."

She began crying again. Inside its cage, the crocodile monster turned away from the bars, went back to playing with the severed set of female legs.

The Fixer said nothing. After a while, the Queen dried her tears and pointed down the corridor. "The main warehouse storeroom is that way. If what you're looking for is down here, it'll be in there." Her eyes turned cold. "Now please go. Leave me alone with my grief."

The Fixer tipped his hat to her. "I will, your Majesty. I can already sense my teddy bear. Thank you for all your help. Of course, I'll let myself out afterwards."

She didn't reply.

The black figure picked up his suitcase and strode off, leaving her, a sad, dirtied woman, weeping by the monster's cage. Frozen in a cell of sorrow, she never even noticed how the world warmed up again once he'd gone.

CHAPTER 40

Once he entered the large storeroom at the corridor's end, The Fixer had no difficulty in finding L'il Ted's box. The carton, stacked on some empty wooden crates, gleamed before him like a lantern.

He dropped the carton into his suitcase, then departed, walking into the stone wall and floating up its substance like it was an elevator.

He stepped outside the Eyeful Tower into early evening sunshine.

While crossing the tower's plaza back to the alley where he'd found Joe, The Fixer reflected on the ginger Queen's behavior. Humanity, including those beings evolved/devolved from homo sapiens, were a paradoxical lot, he felt. Everyone lived in the comfort zone of their overriding illusion. *The cannibal Queen, for instance, slaughters innocent people like they're cattle to feed her own lust. She perceives nothing wrong with her actions, yet finds everything wrong with her boyfriend being unable to respond to her romantic overtures.*

***

Seated in the dim room where Melanie Nemesis Catchpole had died (he groaned loudly on seeing her glasses lying on a table), The Fixer pulled L'il Ted's carton out of his suitcase. Forming a knife from his right index finger, he cut the box open. After restoring his finger to normal, he pulled out the brown pug teddy bear, held it in his hands. He stroked L'il Ted's innocent-seeming form. Regret spilled through him.

Before anything else, The Fixer needed to know the answer to a question, an uncertainty that tugged at his conscience like puppet strings.

He got out the key taken from Joe from the folds of his cloak, stuck it in L'il Ted's left ear, and wound it up.

L'il Ted opened its eyes. This wasn't just figurative: though already 'open,' both glass orbs suddenly glimmered over with intelligence.

"Thank you, kind sir, for—"

On recognizing who'd awakened it, L'il Ted gave a yelp of fright. It instantly transformed into a timber wolf and attempted to flee. The Fixer had anticipated this happening, however—after winding up the teddy bear, he'd kept a firm grip on L'il Ted's left rear leg. The scratching, scrabbling wolf found itself trapped. Desperate, it spun around and bit at The Fixer.

The Fixer laughed coldly. "Your behavior conclusively answers one question of mine: you two *are* guilty as charged." His voice turned grimly severe: "Now, L'il Ted, convert back to your normal form or I will freeze you and smash you to pieces."

After a moment's seeming hesitation, The Fixer once again gripped a cute little pug teddy bear with light brown fur and a black face. Incongruously, the teddy bear was shaking with fright.

"Please, Boss, I'm sorry—it was Big Ted's fault."

The Fixer laughed again, his black cloak swirling around him. He shifted his grip up around L'il Ted's waist, his gloved fingers looping like a belt around the teddy bear. "I'm certain he will blame you too.

"It's true! It is!" L'il Ted squealed, its high squeaky voice a caricature of its creator's. "I never wanted to eat humans! But Big Ted said that if I didn't he'd rip me to bits!"

The Fixer considered the teddy's words. It was likely true—transformed, Big Ted was about four times larger than L'il Ted. He sighed. *I gave them animal forms so they'd feel real, not like mere machines. And now this . . .*

He said, "Blame is meaningless now—it matters nothing at all which of you began it. Now it ends—that is what's important. I will not have you two using my airplane to commit mass murder all over Hampden County."

"Yes, Boss," L'il Ted hastily agreed. "Of course." The little pug's fright practically radiated from it. Then it asked in a hopeful voice, "One thing, Boss?"

"Yes?"

"Do you have any bananas on you?"

Despite his dire mood, The Fixer laughed loud. Then he dipped a hand through the surface of his suitcase and pulled out a bunch of the yellow fruit.

L'il Ted snatched the bananas out of The Fixer's hand and began peeling one. "Thanks, Boss, these are why I came down again in the first place. I was tired of killing—"

"That's fine," came the dry interruption. "I created you two to eat bananas, but you began an orgy of slaughter. Now answer my question: Were you already corrupt, or did humanity corrupt you? Think very carefully before answering."

"C'mon, Boss, just give me a minute here."

The Fixer had to wait till L'il Ted had finished the entire bunch of bananas before receiving his answer. He waited. The teddy bear ate the fat yellow fruit lovingly, regarding each in a fairytale daze before popping it in its mouth and chewing loudly. It flung the peels across the room to where a large number of roaches lay dead, frozen stiff by the room's new sub-zero temperature.

Finally L'il Ted licked its lips. "Thanks, Boss. Ah . . . bananas, I'd almost forgotten what they tasted like. Sorry, Boss, what was your question again?"

The Fixer replied patiently, "Your killing spree. Was it nature or nurture? Did I make you this way—with seeds of evil in you—or did you just go bad, like fruit left in the sun too long?"

L'il Ted pondered the question a while. Finally it said, "Way I see it, Boss, our bad behavior is all your fault. You're responsible for everything we've done wrong."

The Fixer was taken aback. "What? How dare you accuse me of . . . ? You little fur-coated twerp! I fix—I repair—people, not destroy them!"

"Well, it's like this: You built us, right?"

"Yes . . . so . . . ?"

The teddy bear warmed to its theme. "So, if we screwed up, it's either that you intentionally built us flawed from the get-go, or you designed us to misbehave later."

"WHAT!!!? How dare you suggest such—!?"

"Or maybe . . ." L'il Ted interrupted triumphantly, the joy of its recent meal of bananas addling the better sense out of its brains, "maybe you're simply not as smart as you think you are, Boss—you simply can't build a good product. It's the truth, though—whatever

Big Ted and I did is on you. Don't blame us for what you either intentionally or not programmed us to." L'il Ted began laughing like it had told a joke.

The Fixer stared speechless at his creation. *I gave you two free will and you blame me for what you did with it? In what way am I responsible for your bad choices? I thought that was what 'free will' involved—deciding what to do, being responsible for your own actions. Would you prefer that I had left you both mindless automatons?*

He regarded the still loudly giggling pug teddy. "Stop laughing, L'il, this is not a joke."

Instead, L'il Ted laughed louder, leaning forward till its black face was under the shadow of The Fixer's hat, its nose almost touching the mirrored expanse of nothing the wide brim shaded. "Oh yes, it is funny, Boss! I've just realized that you're a joke! Big Ted and I always considered you smarter than us both, but clearly our opinions of you are well overrated!" It calmed. "You know, Boss, if you hadn't asked this 'nature versus nurture' question, I'd never have figured you out for the emotional dupe you are! So don't you go laying any guilt trips on me, okay!? Okay!? Whatever we've done wrong is whatever you wanted us to do! And besides—"

The Fixer didn't want to hear what L'il Ted's 'besides' was. With a gentle tap to its head he switched the teddy bear off, then flung it to the floor, well away from him, like it was something tainted and unclean.

For a long time afterward The Fixer sat in the room's darkness, his creation's words slicing at his conscience like knives. He stared at L'il Ted in horror. *The little monster blames me?* It made no sense to him. *It blames ME?*

Finally, he roused himself from his chair, walked over and picked up the deactivated teddy bear again. What had to be done . . . had to be done.

He formed his right index finger into a scalpel and slit L'il Ted's head open. Next, he transformed all five right hand fingers into an array of tools, strange spanners and corkscrew shapes, which he sunk into the black array of liquid gears that filled the teddy bear's head.

His left hand expanded into a black screen that displayed circuit diagrams alongside 3D technical drawings. The Fixer mentally scrolled through the images till the screen displayed a set that matched L'il Ted's head.

Working with grim purpose, The Fixer reprogrammed L'il Ted.

From time to time he stopped working and sighed deeply. He realized he'd been sighing a lot today.

***

Thirty minutes later, The Fixer was done with his task. He sealed up L'il Ted's head, then switched the teddy bear back on. He didn't attempt to restrain it—there was no need now.

"Wow, Boss," L'il Ted instantly said, like nothing had happened in the interim, "I mean what I said earlier, sir, I'm really, really sorry we got carried away like that—killing all those people . . ."

"It's alright; I've forgiven you. All is forgotten."

The fuzzy pug shook itself like it had fleas. Its voice dropped to a tortured whisper. "Thanks, Boss. But . . . I feel real bad about it now . . . what can I do to make amends?"

The Fixer sighed, poked a dark glove up through the ceiling. "Well, for a start, you can convince your big friend up there to return my airplane."

A frown formed on L'il Ted's felt lips. "Hmmm, yeah, Boss, you're right. It ain't good, him snatching up folks like that." Balancing on three legs, it pointed its left forepaw at The Fixer. "But what . . . what if Big Ted won't listen to me? He's headstrong."

"He *will* listen; don't worry your brains about that. He won't let me near enough the plane to board it, so *you'll* have to talk sense into him . . ."

L'il Ted began bouncing impatiently up and down. "Yes, yes, I'll do it. Let's go."

". . . And afterwards, we're cleaning that blasted airplane up! I can smell the corpses you've filled it with from down here. How could you?"

Unable to meet The Fixer's gaze, Li'l Ted turned guiltily toward the broken wall. "Let's go, Boss. Faster's better in this case."

The Fixer stood up. His face swirled about like wobbling mercury, like boiling silver. He shook a stern finger at the teddy bear. "No, L'il Ted. For the moment you remain inside here. I'll leave first. You know Big Ted won't bring the plane down as long as I'm around. Five minutes after I'm gone, walk out into the plaza opposite the Eyeful Tower and wait for him to pick you up. Do you understand?"

L'il Ted nodded fierce agreement. "Don't worry, Boss—I won't let you down!"

"Okay, I'll be waiting for you two—the plane can always find me."

On those words, The Fixer picked up his black suitcase, and with a wave backwards, walked off through a frozen wall.

He left L'il Ted feeling radiant at being forgiven and feverishly plotting what it would say to convince Big Ted to stop its madness.

***

Thirty minutes later, sitting on his suitcase on the roof of a house covered with hair, The Fixer heard the noises he'd been expecting. The shockwaves of accelerated air reached him, the sounds of his airplane blowing up

He turned and watched the explosion, a crimson flare that lit up Bizarro's underside. The orange flashes of the blue aircraft's detonation painted the sky like a premature sunset. Red and yellow incandescence streaked up at the brown mass, streaked down towards the earth, and blew sideways, at one point forming a vivid cross of flame.

The Fixer was immensely saddened. He'd not lied to L'il Ted—he had forgiven it—but there was no reparation for what his pair of teddy bears had done. No amends could be made—there'd been too much psychic pollution. The plane itself was a total write-off now— the dark being couldn't imagine himself working in such surroundings, where the trapped and tortured souls of murdered dead haunted the walls, screaming for justice, wailing for revenge . . .

So he'd reprogrammed L'il Ted to explode once it was up in the airplane with Big Ted.

And worse . . . while reprogramming it, The Fixer had been shocked—disgusted and disbelieving—by what he'd read in the teddy bear's psyche. His creatures had ripped and torn . . . slain . . . eaten . . . and had taken pleasure in doing so. Extreme pleasure. Men, women, children, mothers . . . babies . . .

At one point, The Fixer had hated himself intensely for setting this in motion (even though he knew he hadn't). In a paradox his conscience was yet to unravel, he *still* held himself responsible . . .

But that was done now. For good. The next pair of assistants he made would be perfect. Automations without free will. Like angels.

A motionless ebon carving, he watched his airplane fragment into blazing pieces. Notably, The Fixer's blue aircraft didn't fall out of the sky: Blown apart into its components, it dissolved into thick black clouds of smoke, which then converted into clouds of morph birds.

The Fixer was satisfied. There would be no waste. Everything would be recycled. Everything could be restarted, except the memories and the horrors his creations had subjected others to.

Finally, the mass of black liquid birds which the blue airplane, Big Ted, and L'il Ted had become flew out from beneath Bizarro to flock with their fellows in the darkening O-Zone sky.

It is done, The Fixer thought, standing up and picking up his suitcase. *The horror is over.*

Departing from his rooftop vantage point, the black-cloaked figure felt satisfaction and relief, but no pleasure. Indeed, he felt intense grief. His dark heart was deeply saddened.

If his gray impossible face had been human, The Fixer would have been crying, tears pouring like a waterfall from his eyes.

The End.

ABOUT THE AUTHOR

Wol-vriey is Nigerian, and quite tall.

He currently resides in a state of uneasy stalemate with his threatening-to-thin-beyond-redemption hair, and believes there actually are things that go bump in the night.

Wol-vriey recycles the ridiculous into reasonable reality for the reader.

His WEIRRRD philosophy?

WEIRRRD = Warp/Write Everything into Realistic Ridiculous Readable Distorted Dream Dimension Descriptions.

Wol-vriey blogs at:
http://oddityfarm.wordpress.com

WOL-VRIEY
BIZARRO AND TRANSGRESSIVE FICTION

BOSTON POSH

In 2028 AD, the USA is a nation ravaged by hungry dragons and dinosaurs. In Boston, Massachusetts, private eye Bud Malone is hired to rescue a kidnapped heiress. But nothing is as it seems.

Malone works to unravel a tangled web involving Boston Chinatown, a 200-year-old woman with a 9-year-old body, white robots, a human-liver-eating psychopath, a golem, a porcelain dragon, and a snake goddess with a crush on him. There's also a woman obsessed with chicken sex. Then Malone meets Posh Lane, a gorgeous call girl who's desperate to quit her pimp.

Romantic sparks ignite between Posh and Malone, but Posh's past suddenly catches up with her in a BIG way. To save Posh, Malone agrees to run a quest for Earth's new rulers, the Forks. But, Malone has no idea that agreeing to the Fork's odd request will send him on the weirdest trip he's ever been on in his life.

VAGINA MUNDI

Rachel Risk is a professional thief with super-strong hair that can stretch like tentacles to manipulate objects. Ashley Status has both a digitally augmented brain, and 'muscle-purses' in her arms and legs in which she stores inflatable objects—cars, guns, rocket launchers, etc.

When Raye is framed as the fall girl in a jewel robbery, the pair flee Chicago's vengeful robot gangsters and take refuge in the Hotel Bizarre, where the gorgeous 'vagina singer,' Femina, is performing for a week.

But the Hotel Bizarre is even stranger than its name suggests, and very soon Raye and Ash are involved in an deadly adventure, a struggle for survival the likes of which they'd never imagined possible—with loads of deviant sex, drugs, music, and violence at every turn. And just what is the old woman in the skin desert really doing with all those cats glued to her walls?

Vagina Mundi—a Bizarro Hymn in praise of WOMAN!

Burning Bulb
PUBLISHING

WOL-VRIEY
BIZARRO AND TRANSGRESSIVE FICTION

VEGAN VAMPIRE VAGINAS

The biggest bank heist in US history. And Tom Palmer can't remember pulling it off. And no, this isn't your standard case of amnesia. After a one-night-stand gone horribly wrong, Boston salesman Tom Palmer wakes up with a vagina implanted in his left hand. Then his day gets worse.

Tom is transported across space-time to a nightmare version of Boston, one where the Bizarro virus has transformed half the population into cannibals. Worst of all, Tom discovers that in this new Boston, he's the infamous gangster Pussypalm, wanted for robbing the Federal Reserve Bank of Boston a year ago. He also learns that the vagina in his hand is prophetic, i.e. it talks . . . after sex.

With 130 people left dead during his bank heist and six billion dollars missing, Tom knows he's living on borrowed time. It is in his best interests not to remember anything. Because once he does . . .

VEGAN ZOMBIE APOCALYPSE

In the post-apocalypse worlderness, zombies rule the earth. They're allergic to meat, and brains literally make them explode. Zombies now eat blood potatoes, parasitic tubers grown in the flesh of humancows corralled in maximum security farms. Two fugitives meet in the ancient ruins of Texas. The first is Soil 15-f, a womancow who's escaped her farm a week before she's due to be killed and her blood potato crop harvested. The second fugitive is Able Kane, former head necros food technician, now sentenced to death for heresy. But Soil is no ordinary humancow.

Unknown to herself, she's the vegan zombie agricultural revolution, and the zombies desperately want her back. And the necros equally desperately want Able Kane dead. He's fled with a forbidden discovery which will reshape the world for the worse if used. And Able is just hardheaded/misguided enough to use it.

Burning Bulb
PUBLISHING

OTHER GREAT TITLES FROM

Burning Bulb
PUBLISHING

WWW.BURNINGBULBPUBLISHING.COM

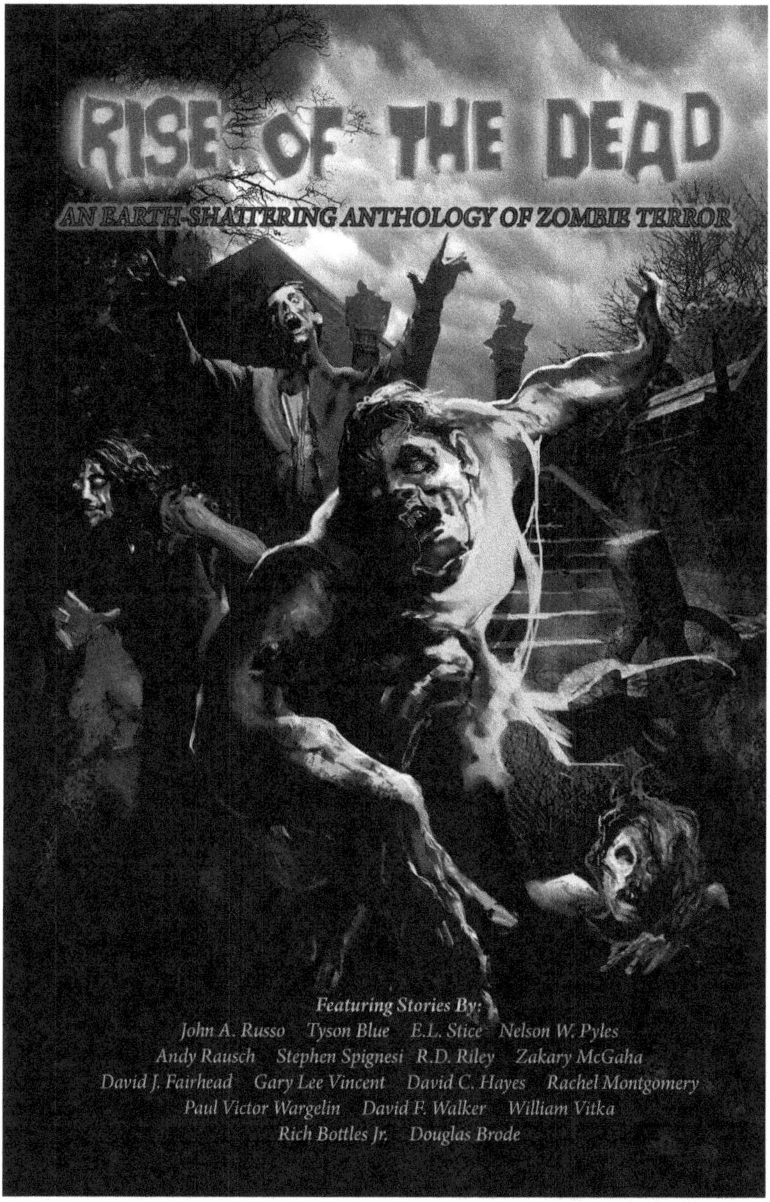
RISE OF THE DEAD
AN EARTH-SHATTERING ANTHOLOGY OF ZOMBIE TERROR
Featuring Stories By:
John A. Russo Tyson Blue E.L. Stice Nelson W. Pyles
Andy Rausch Stephen Spignesi R.D. Riley Zakary McGaha
David J. Fairhead Gary Lee Vincent David C. Hayes Rachel Montgomery
Paul Victor Wargelin David F. Walker William Vitka
Rich Bottles Jr. Douglas Brode

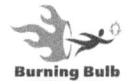

ANTHOLOGIES
BIZARRO AND TRANSGRESSIVE FICTION

THE BIG BOOK OF BIZARRO

The Big Book of Bizarro brings together the peculiar prose of an international cast of the most grotesquely-gonzo, genre-grinding modern writers who ever put pen to paper (or mouse to pad), including:

NIGHT OF THE LIVING DEAD horror writers John Russo & George Kosana; HUSTLER MAGAZINE erotica contributors Eva Hore, Andrée Lachapelle, & J. Troy Seate and established Bizarro genre authors D. Harlan Wilson, William Pauley III, Wol-vriey, Laird Long, Richard Godwin and so many more!

From Alien abductions to Zombie sex, The Big Book of Bizarro contains OVER FIFTY STORIES of the most outrélandish transgressive fiction that you'll ever lay your capricious and curious hands upon!

WARNING: This book may be one of the most controversial and dangerous books you'll ever read.

WESTWARD HOES

Nine outlaw writers rode into town from obscurity to pen nine tantalizing tales of horror and fantasy, and leaving once they branded their own personal marks on the weird western genre and became living legends of the American Frontier experience.

Like drunken Indian scouts, the writers fervidly tracked down and captured the Western genre, tore off its fashionable veneer and ravished its exposed essence.

So belly up to the bar with your favorite soiled dove and enjoy perusing these thrilling tales of Old West debauchery, danger and desire; compiled by the publisher of The Big Book of Bizarro and featuring the bizarro novella *Big Trouble in Little Ass* by Wol-vriey.

Burning Bulb
PUBLISHING

ANTHOLOGIES
BIZARRO AND TRANSGRESSIVE FICTION

THE BIG BOOK OF BIZARRO SPECIAL KINDLE EDITIONS

OTHER AWESOME COLLECTIONS

Burning Bulb
PUBLISHING

GARY LEE VINCENT'S
DARKENED
THE WEST VIRGINIA VAMPIRE SERIES

DARKENED HILLS

When evil descends on a small West Virginia town, who will survive?

Jonathan did not start out his life to become a rambler, it just worked out that way. William was a troubled youth with something to hide. Both were from Melas, a small town tucked away in the West Virginia hills... a town where disappearances are happening more and more frequently.

After the suicide of a wanted serial killer, the townsfolk thought the nightmare was over. But when a centuries-old vampire is discovered they find out the hard way it's just getting started. Dark secrets can only stay hidden for so long and when the devil comes to collect, there will be hell to pay. Can Jonathan and William find a way to stop the vampire before it's too late? Find out in *Darkened Hills!*

DARKENED HOLLOWS

In the heart-stopping sequel to the award-winning *Darkened Hills*, Jonathan and William must return to West Virginia to face possible criminal charges stemming from their last visit to the damned town of Melas, where both had narrowly escaped the clutches of a vampire seethe.

And as livestock start mysteriously getting murdered with all of their blood drained, worried farmers are searching for answers - leaving the local Sheriff and his deputy racing against time to learn the cause before a more violent crime is committed.

Burning Bulb
PUBLISHING

WWW. DARKENEDHILLS.COM

GARY LEE VINCENT'S
DARKENED
THE WEST VIRGINIA VAMPIRE SERIES

DARKENED WATERS

When the world goes to hell, the chosen must arise!

As Talman Cane orchestrates a flood of epic proportions in this third installment of the *Darkened* series the towns of Melas and Tarklin are caught completely off guard by the deluge. Hell-bent on finishing what they started, the evil brothers return to the lunatic asylum to take care of the witnesses and add to the ever-growing army of the undead.

Aided by Lucifer himself and the insane vampire demon Legion, the stage is set to channel all of the forces of hell to come forth. In an all-out race to survive, Jonathan, William, and Amanda soon discover they are up against impossible odds as Lucifer opens the Gateway to Hell, ushering in the zombie apocalypse and the End Times.

DARKENED SOULS

Melas and the Madison House are about to be rebuilt.
True evil is about to be reborne!

Young ex-priest and vampire-killer William is drawn back to the West Virginian town that almost killed him, where his vampire arch-enemy Victor Rothenstein still stalks the earth.

The town of Melas lies destroyed after the battle of the End of Days. But why is wealthy Jackie Nixon so eager to rebuild it using the bone dust of murdered souls?

Terrible evil has visited before, but the Gateway to Hell is about to be reopened in a horrific climax. And this time – it's personal.

WWW. DARKENEDHILLS.COM

Burning Bulb
PUBLISHING

WEST VIRGINIA-THEMED HUMORROROTICA
BY RICH BOTTLES JR.

HELLHOLE WEST VIRGINIA

From the heights of Mothman's perch high atop the Silver Bridge in Point Pleasant to the depths of Hellhole Cavern in Pendleton County, evil lurks within the shadows as the sun sets upon the haunted hills and hollows of West Virginia.

Bizarro author Rich Bottles Jr. blows the coffin lid off horror genre clichés with this tour de force cast of Eco-friendly vampires, beach-yearning zombies and sex-starved she-devils.

LUMBERJACKED

If you are easily offended or do not possess a truly depraved sense of humor, this story may not be the light summer reading fare you desire. As for the four feisty female freshmen stranded on top of West Virginia's third highest mountain, they have no choice but to experience the sick, twisted debauchery and perverted mayhem described deep inside the tight unbroken bindings of this horrific missive.

Lumberjacked takes the reader to a nightmarish world where character development and aesthetic integrity are prematurely cut short by the swinging axes of maniacal lumberjacks, who are hell bent on death and destruction in the remote forests of Appalachia. And at the climax, when paranoia crosses over to the paranormal, Lumberjacked makes Deliverance look like a family raft trip down the Lower Gauley.

THE MANACLED

What happens when twin brothers lease out the former West Virginia State Penitentiary with the false purpose of filming a documentary on supernatural phenomena, but their true intention is to make a pornographic movie?

Chaos ensues as the disturbed spirits of murdered convicts, along with the reanimated dead from the neighboring Indian Burial Mound, take their vengeance on the unwary and undressed trespassers.

Zombies, ghosts, mobsters and porn collide in this bizarro tale from horror author Rich Bottles Jr.

Burning Bulb
PUBLISHING

"THE BLAZING SADDLES OF SEX SATIRES!" – GEORGINA SPELVIN

THE BOOBY HATCH

It's a Zany Love Lab where
Looney Professors Measure Pleasure!

From Legendary Horror Writer
JOHN A. RUSSO

THE BOOBY HATCH

With NIGHT OF THE LIVING DEAD, John Russo helped
blaze a path in the horror genre that has never been equalled.
In this hillarious erotic novel, he blazes a path through the
wild, zany Sex Revolution of the 1970s.

Sweet, innocent Cherry Jankowski works for Joyful Novelties,
where she tests sex toys ranging from the ridiculous to the
sublime. But she can't find love or peace of mind and her
efforts are hampered by a Peeping Tom, an exhibitionist, a
cross-dressing boyfriend, a quack psychiatrist, and even her
own product-testing partner, Marcello Fettucini, who can't
get it up anymore and is scared of losing his job!

www.TheJohnRusso.com

Burning Bulb
PUBLISHING

NIGHT OF THE LIVING DEAD

Why does **Night of the Living Dead** hit with such chilling impact?
Is it because everyday people in a commonplace house are suddenly the
victims of a monstrous invasion? Or is it because the ghouls who surround
the house with grasping claws were once ordinary people, too?

Decide for yourself as you read, and the horror grips you. All the
cannibalism, suspense and frenzy of the smash-hit move are here in the
novel.

www.TheJohnRusso.com

Burning Bulb
PUBLISHING

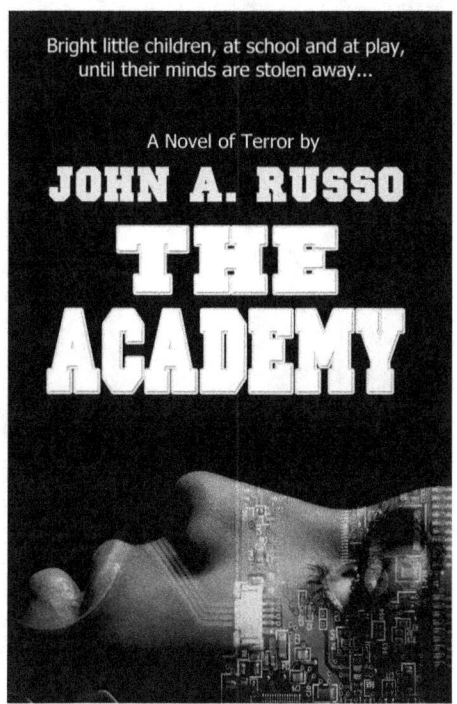

Bright little children, at school and at play, until their minds are stolen away...

A Novel of Terror by

JOHN A. RUSSO

THE ACADEMY

THE ACADEMY

The Academy. It's every parent's dream, turning their little darlings into geniuses, superachievers, perfect little children.

And if there's a problem, the Academy fixes that too. It's a simple operation. Just a little device. Then a teeny pink scar on a tender little skull . . .

One boy knows the secret. Now he wants his mind back. But it's much, much too late. Too late for anything but the ugly feelings. The bad feelings. The messy sexy feelings. The knife-cold hatred, the murderous rage, for total, screaming, blood-drenching revenge . . .

www.TheJohnRusso.com

Burning Bulb
PUBLISHING

"The most unique vampire story since 'SALEM'S LOT."
- George A. Romero

From Legendary Horror Writer
JOHN A. RUSSO

THE
AWAKENING

"A gripping plotline and good old-fashioned gothic horror."
- *Fangoria*

THE AWAKENING

> For two hundred years, he has rested. Now he rises. Now he will be satisfied. Nothing can stop him. No one can resist him.

Benjamin Latham is young and handsome, his eighteenth-century mind wakened to a bizarre twentieth-century world. And there is the need deep within . . . an animal need, frightening, murderous, unholy . . . a vital need that must be fed.

And with his need comes a power over men and women to do his bidding, to quiet his dark craving . . .

Until the murders begin. And the inquiries. All suggesting the same hideous truth.

Now Benjamin must find a sanctuary: a lover, a partner, a friend. Someone who can share his darkness. Someone he can lead to . . . The Awakening.

www.TheJohnRusso.com

Burning Bulb
PUBLISHING

DEALEY PLAZA

From legendary horror and suspense writer JOHN RUSSO comes a harrowing tale where no one is safe!

Dealey Plaza is one of the most notorious places in America, and when youthful conspiracy buffs go there in 1964 to stage their own reenactment of the Kennedy Assassination, four of them are brutally murdered ~ the first victims of a hate-filled legacy that continues for four more decades.

The survivors of that long-ago Dallas trip, each of them now icons of the American way of life, are about to be honored ~ or killed.

Who will live and who will die? Will it be country-western star Lori McCoy? Her loving husband? Her scheming ex-husband? Or the case-hardened FBI agent and longtime friend who risks his life trying to protect them?

www.DealeyPlazaBook.com

Burning Bulb
PUBLISHING

LIMB TO LIMB

SUCH A PRETTY GIRL . . .
Tiffany Blake was a beautiful long-limbed dancer with a glorious future and the backing of a rich benefactor. Then a monstrous accident severed her leg at the hip.

SUCH A COLD, CRUEL KNIFE . . .
And now her fellow dancers are disappearing without a trace. One by one they fall victim to a dark and deadly pattern of evil – caught by the bloody, brutal logic that would have them pay with their lovely bodies for the cruel fate of another . . .victims of the sadistic madman whose flashing knife will make them writhe a gruesome new dance.

www.TheJohnRusso.com

"A sense of infectious fun, straight from the author's pen."
— Nightmare Library

From Legendary Horror Writer
JOHN A. RUSSO

LIVING THINGS

"Russo carries his talent for the horrific neatly over into the novel form."
— West Coast Review of Books

LIVING THINGS

Beneath the shimmering Miami sun sprawls one of the Mafia's biggest empires, a glittering world of lavish beachfront mansions, neon-painted nightclubs, beautiful women, expensive cars—and absolute control over the state's billion-dollar drug trade. But, one by one, its ganglords and henchmen are falling prey to a new rival. His powers are fueled by monstrous ancient rituals; his hellish undead legions slaughter mobsters and innocent citizens alike, his unholy lust for power is virtually unstoppable.

Now a burned-out ex-detective and a brilliant anthropologist must enter a gruesome, nightmare world to fight this master of malevolence and illusion. Their time is short, their weapons few, and they face an ultimate, terrifying choice - annihilation or the loss of their souls to the eternal torment of those who never die. . .

www.TheJohnRusso.com

Burning Bulb
PUBLISHING

MAD WORLD BY ANDY RAUSCH

"*Mad World* is dark, twisted, no-holds-barred fun."
—Jason Starr, author of *Bust*, *Slide*, and *The Max*

EVERYONE'S PLAYING AN ANGLE IN THE CITY OF ANGELS

Mad World tells the stories of a black hitman who doubles as a university professor, a Catholic priest who longs to be a gangster, a would-be author from Kansas, a gay phone sex operator who claims he's straight, a group of rich twentysomethings playing a deadly game of life and death, a vicious Mafia boss, and a sleazy Hollywood movie director. As each of their stories intersect, the body count piles up and the action comes nonstop in this tense, white-knuckle thriller by first-time author Andy Rausch.

"A wild ride. If you like it gangster, *Mad World* delivers."
—Daniel Birch, author of *Get Some*

Burning Bulb
PUBLISHING

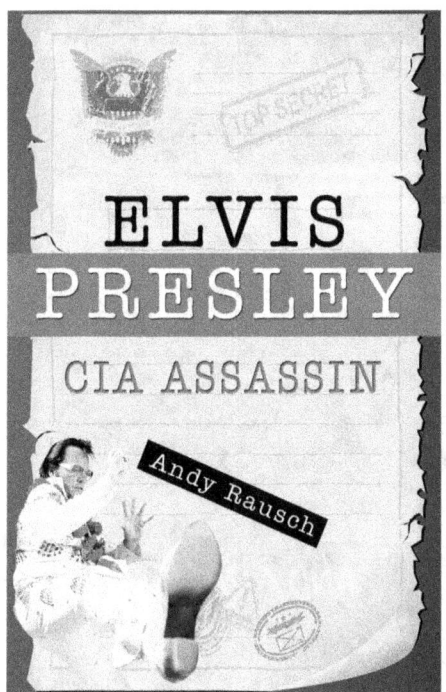

ELVIS PRESLEY, CIA ASSASSIN

"I can guarantee you. Read this book and you'll never look at Elvis the same way again!"
~ Douglas Brode, author of ELVIS CINEMA AND POPULAR CULTURE

SOON TO BE A MAJOR MOTION PICTURE

In 1970, singer Elvis Presley secretly met with President Richard Nixon. This new comedic novel imagines that Presley became a Central Intelligence Agency operative, eventually moving up through the ranks to become a skilled assassin.

Presented in an oral history fashion, the book tells us about Presley's secret transformation by the people who knew him best.

Did he fake his death in 1977? Was Presley involved with the Watergate scandal? The Iran hostage crisis? Communicating with aliens?

Read this book to find out the answers to these and many more questions.

Burning Bulb
PUBLISHING

BLOODLETTING: A TALE OF REVENGE BY ANDY RAUSCH

"Relentless… Addictive… The kind of nightmare you don't want
to wake up from."
—Heywood Gould, screenwriter of *Rolling Thunder*

He was just an average Joe. But when he finds his family held at
gunpoint by merciless thugs, he's told he must murder a Mafia
chieftain if he ever wishes to see his loved ones again.

Against all odds, Joe keeps his end of the bargain, but the criminals
don't. Now at his wits end, Joe is pushed beyond his breaking point
and forced to exact bloody revenge against those who've done him
and his family wrong in this powerful and violent novella by author
Andy Rausch (*Mad World*).

"Andy Rausch has a tight noir style that combines gritty, realistic drama
with a cinematic flair that makes for a powerful, compelling (somewhat
Stephen Kingesque), authentically visual reading experience."
—Stephen Spignesi, author of *Dialogues*

Burning Bulb
PUBLISHING

THE TAILSMAN

From the creators of *The Big Book of Bizarro* and *Westward Hoes* comes a new comic unlike anything you have ever seen!

He's hot on the trail, looking for some *tail...*

Sly Franko was a man of the West, a forger of the wild frontier. Like the Country Western song that would be written years after he died, the words, "Faster horses, younger women, and more money," seemed to be the anthem of this horn dog cowboy.

Franko would ride into town on a blazing saddle, find the closest saloon to wet the whistle, belly up to a good card game, and find him a hot-loving hussy to get his cowpoke on with.

However, Sly might have met his match when a visit to bathroom leads to terror and death. Can Sly and his poker buddies solve the mystery before more of the townsfolk are murdered? Find out in this exciting premier issue of *The Tailsman*!

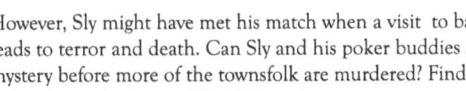

WWW.BURNINGBULBCOMICS.COM

THE HAGS OF BLACK COUNTY

by Michelle Bowser

Ruled by a committee of Hags, and fueled by toothless rivalries, Black County lurks just far enough out of the way to be completely unnoticed by the rest of civilization. Its inhabitants have been mentally warped for generations and the land itself seems to have the power to drive anyone unlucky enough to visit into ridiculous hillbilly madness. When a construction Company needs to bury a pipeline through its ludicrous hills and valleys, a twisted charm goes to work and every aspect of already bizarre Black County life takes a gory turn for the hysterical. Take a preposterous trip along with its citizens, both native and new, through escapades such as the Hag parade, the grand opening of Madame Skunk's House of Ill Repute, the demolition derby riot and the rabid, zombie clown apocalypse.

THE ABANDONED SOUL

by Daniel Sellers

After spending most of his 20s in a drug and alcohol fueled daze, a young man finally hits rock bottom. Having used up his friends and their good graces, he ends up squatting in an abandoned house. Forcibly sobering he begins to realize that he is not alone in this abandoned house. Left with one last friend and a mountain of regrets, he must decide if this presence is a guilty conscience, or a malicious hunter.

WE WISH YOU A HAPPY KILLDAY

by Jason Heroux

"We Wish You a Happy Killday" is the story of an international b eloved holiday called "Killday" where one day a year everyone over the age of fifteen is permitted to register for a license allowing them to kill one other person. But this year Chad Ovenstock doesn't feel like killing anyone. His friends and family urge him to participate in the festivities, but he can't seem to get into the holiday spirit. On the day before Killday Chad comes in contact with Ambrose, an old friend who suffered a nervous breakdown and is now part of The One Ant Army, a mysterious cult dedicated to making the future disappear. When the holiday finally arrives Chad refuses to participate and tries to survive on his own, surrounded by constant gunfire, countless corpses, and the nagging suspicion that Ambrose may have secretly brainwashed him into becoming a member of The One Ant Army cult.

Burning Bulb
PUBLISHING

www.ingramcontent.com/pod-product-compliance
Lightning Source LLC
Chambersburg PA
CBHW071144170626
46809CB00002B/765